Pr

'Price develops her plot and characters with tight, punchy writing and a sure, confident touch. There must be a movie in this . . .' *Daily Mail*

'Pure, adrenaline-fueled plot' *Booklist*

'The only thing better than a terrific concept is one that is as well executed as **STARTERS**. Readers who have been waiting for a worthy successor to Suzanne Collins' *The Hunger Games* will find it here.' *Los Angeles Times*

'**STARTERS** is a smart, swift, inventive, altogether gripping story' Dean Koontz

'Price is a gifted writer.' Lionel Shriver, bestselling author of *We Need to Talk About Kevin*

'**STARTERS** is a dystopian read you'll want to snatch up for yourself . . . With its intriguing plot-twists and dash of romance, Lissa's novel is a bona fide page-turner that proves you can't take anything – or anyone – at face value.' *MTV.com*

www.**totallyrandombooks**.co.uk

Also by Lissa Price

STARTERS

Digital Short Stories

PORTRAIT OF A STARTER
PORTRAIT OF A MARSHAL
PORTRAIT OF A DONOR

LISSA PRICE

ENDERS

CORGI BOOKS

ENDERS
A CORGI BOOK 978 0 552 56560 8

First published in Great Britain by Doubleday,
an imprint of Random House Children's Publishers UK
A Penguin Random House Company

Doubleday edition published 2013
Corgi edition published 2015

1 3 5 7 9 10 8 6 4 2

Set in Parango

Corgi Books are published by Random House Children's Publishers UK
61–63 Uxbridge Road, London W5 5SA

www.**randomhousechildrens**.co.uk
www.**totallyrandombooks**.co.uk
www.**randomhouse**.co.uk

Addresses for companies within The Random House Group Limited can be found at:
www.randomhouse.co.uk/offices.htm

THE RANDOM HOUSE GROUP Limited Reg. No. 954009

A CIP catalogue record for this book is available from the British Library.

Printed and bound by CPI Group (UK) Ltd, Croydon, CR0 4YY

To Gene, my favorite Ender

ENDERS

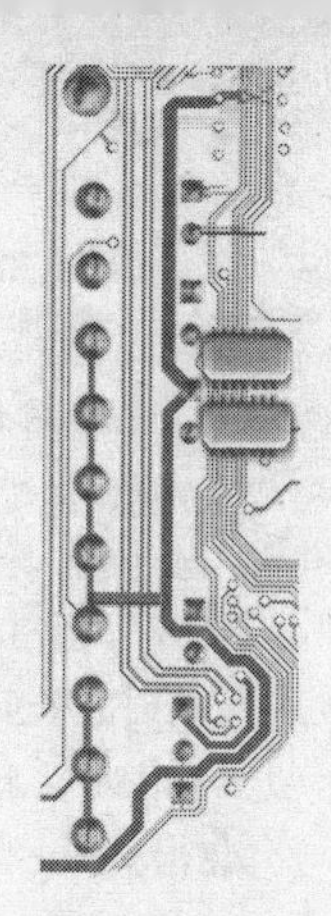

CHAPTER ONE

My hand went to the back of my head and I swore I could feel the chip underneath my skin. But I couldn't, of course; it was buried deeply under the metal blocking plate. It was just the surrounding scar tissue I felt, hard and unforgiving.

I tried not to touch it. But it had become an obsession to finger it like a splinter in a palm, or a hangnail on a thumb. It haunted me all the time, even here, making sandwiches in the kitchen. Helena's kitchen.

Even though she was dead and had left the mansion to me, I couldn't help but be reminded daily that it had been hers. Every choice, from the sea-green tiles to the elaborate island in the center of this gourmet kitchen, was hers. Even her housekeeper, Eugenia, remained.

Yes, it had been Helena's crazy plan to stop the Old Man by using my body to assassinate Senator Harrison. But it was my fault that I had volunteered to be a body donor in the first place. I had been desperate to save my little brother, Tyler, then. Now I couldn't take it back, any more than I could get rid of this horrible chip stuck in my head. I hated the thing. It was like a phone the Old Man could call anytime, a phone I had to answer and could never disconnect. It was the Old Man's direct line to me, Callie Woodland.

The last time I had heard from him was two days ago, while I was watching his precious Prime Destinations being demolished. He had sounded like my dead father, even used his code words: *When hawks cry, time to fly*. I'd been thinking about that ever since. But as I stood at the kitchen counter spreading the last of the peanut butter on whole wheat, I decided that it had been the Old Man playing tricks on me. Cruel, but no surprise coming from that monster.

"Finished?" Eugenia asked.

Her crackly Ender voice cut through me. I hadn't heard her come in. How long had she been watching? I turned to meet the scowl on her wrinkled face. If this was my fairy-tale life, living in this castle, she would be the ugly stepmother.

"That's enough. You're emptying my entire pantry," she said.

That wasn't true. I'd made several dozen sandwiches, but our pantry could feed us for a month. I placed the last one in the insta-wrap machine, and the thin veg-wrap encased the bread instantly with a high-pitched zip.

"Done." I tossed the sandwiches into a duffel bag.

Eugenia didn't even wait for me to leave before she began wiping the counter. I'd obviously ruined her day.

"We can't feed the whole world," she said, scrubbing invisible stains.

"Course not." I closed the duffel bag and slung it over my shoulder. "Just a few hungry Starters."

⊗ ⊗ ⊗

As I put the bag in the trunk of the blue sports car, I couldn't get Eugenia's disapproving glare out of my mind. You'd think maybe she'd be nicer, knowing my mother and father were dead. But somehow she resented me for Helena's death. It wasn't my fault. In fact, Helena had almost gotten *me* killed. I slammed the trunk. Eugenia only stayed because she adored Tyler. That was okay; I didn't have to answer to her. She wasn't my guardian.

My hand went to the back of my head, and I absentmindedly scratched at my chip wound before I caught myself and stopped. When I looked at my fingers, my nails were dirty with blood. I winced.

I pulled a tissue out of my purse and wiped them as best I could. Then I walked out the door of the garage that led to the garden. Mossy stones, wet from the morning dew, led to the rose-covered cottage guesthouse. The place was quiet, no movement behind the windows. I knocked on the rough-hewn door, to see if he was back, but no answer.

The handle turned with a squeak. I poked my head inside.

"Michael?"

I hadn't been inside his cottage since we'd all moved into the mansion. The place had taken on Michael's scent, a mix of artist's paints and freshly cut wood. Even when we had been squatters, he had always managed to smell good.

But what really marked the place as his was his amazing drawings, which covered the walls. The first one showed thin Starters with hungry, haunted eyes. They wore ragged layers of clothing, water bottles draped across their bodies, hand-lites banded around their wrists.

In the next image, three Starters fought over an apple. One lay on the ground, hurt. My life just a few months ago. But the next drawing was even tougher to look at.

My friend Sara. A Starter I had hoped to rescue. I'd told Michael about her and our time together at Institution 37, the nightmarish place where marshals had locked me up with other unclaimed Starters. The sketch showed Sara after she had diverted the guards' attention away from me and ended up ZipTasered, clinging to barbed wire as she was dying. Michael had never met her, but like most street Starters, he was familiar with desperation and bravery. He portrayed the willing sacrifice in her eyes.

The drawing blurred in my vision. I'd never find a friend that loyal if I lived a million years. She'd given me everything and I'd let her down.

That was my fault.

Someone entered the cottage. I turned to see Tyler coming in.

"Monkey-Face!" he shouted.

I quickly wiped my eyes. He ran up and wrapped his arms around my legs. Michael was behind him, standing in the doorway, smiling. Then he closed the door and put down his travel bag.

"You're back." I looked at Michael.

He shook his shaggy blond hair out of his face and looked surprised at the concern in my voice.

Tyler pulled away. "Michael brought me this."

He waved a small toy truck and ran it over the top of the couch.

"Where've you been?" I asked. Michael had been out of my sight since Prime was demolished.

He shrugged. "Just needed some space."

I knew that he wouldn't say anything with Tyler there. I knew he had seen me holding hands with Blake, Senator Harrison's grandson. Two puppets of the Old Man.

"Look, what you saw, that didn't mean anything," I said in a lowered voice. "And you, you and Florina—"

"That's over."

We stared at each other. Tyler was still playing, making car sounds, but of course he could hear us. I tried to think of what to say to explain my feelings, but I honestly didn't know what my feelings were. The Old Man, Blake, Michael—it was all so jumbled.

My phone beeped a reminder: three unread Zings.

"Someone dying to reach you?" Michael asked.

The Zings were all from Blake. He'd been trying to contact me since the day I saw him at Prime's destruction.

"It's him, right?" Michael said.

I shoved the phone into my pocket, cocked my head, and gave him a look that said "don't push me."

Tyler glanced anxiously from Michael to me.

"We're going to the mall," Tyler said. "To get me shoes."

"Without asking me first?" I clung to my shoulder bag and stared at Michael.

"He begged me," Michael said. "And his favorites are too small now."

"He's growing so fast, better buy two sizes."

We were all glad to see Tyler healthy after a year squatting in cold buildings. "Come with us," Tyler said.

"I'd love to, but I'm off."

"Where to?" Michael asked.

"Our old neighborhood. To feed the Starters."

"Want help?" Michael asked.

"Why? You think I can't do this alone?" I said.

As soon as I snapped, I wished I could suck the words back in. Michael looked so hurt. Tyler's mouth fell open in an "uh-oh" moment.

"I'm sorry," I said to Michael. "Thanks for offering. Really. But I think I can handle it. You guys should go to the mall."

"You could meet us for lunch," Tyler said. "After we get my shoes."

He took Michael's hand and gave me his best "please please" face. We were the closest thing he had to parents, and he was doing everything he could to pull us together. What I really wanted was to make our parents magically reappear; to have our family back again. But I would have to settle for just fulfilling my brother's small request.

⊗ ⊗ ⊗

I balanced the duffel bag on my shoulder as I pushed open the side door of the abandoned office building that had been home for Michael and Tyler—and Florina—when I was being rented out. I stepped into the lobby and saw the reception desk, vacant as usual. I would never have admitted it to Michael, but my heart was beating harder. Faster. I held my breath to listen for any signs of danger. I was familiar with the place, but things change. Who knew which Starters lived here now?

I walked over to the reception desk to make sure no one was hiding, ready to attack. It was clear. I set my duffel bag on the counter, unzipped it, and pulled out a towel. As I was wiping the counter, I heard footsteps behind me. Before I realized what was happening, someone darted by and grabbed the whole bag.

"Hey!" I shouted.

A chubby little Starter ran to the exit, clutching my bag. Several sandwiches spilled out and dropped to the floor.

"That's supposed to be for everyone, you little jerk!" I yelled.

He burst through the door. I'd never catch up.

I ran around from behind the desk and bent down to pick up the food that had fallen. I had my hand on a wrapped sandwich when someone stepped on me.

"Back off." It was a Starter girl, maybe a year older than I was.

She held a plank of wood like a bat, ready to strike. The rusty nails at the end of the plank convinced me not to fight. I nodded. She eased her foot off my hand and I pulled it away.

"Take it," I said, nodding to the smashed sandwich.

She grabbed it and the other two on the floor. She bit right through the wrapper and started eating, making feral sounds. Thin, with short, dirty hair, she had probably once been just a middle-class girl. Like me.

I'd been that hungry before, but no one had ever come to my building to feed me. And now I knew why.

She swallowed. "You." She stepped closer and touched my hair. "So clean." Then she examined my face. "Perfect. You're a Metal, aren't you?"

"A what?"

"You know, Metal. One of those body bank people. You've got that chip in your head." She took another bite of the sandwich, peeling back the wrapper this time. "How does it feel?" She circled me to stare at the back of my head.

I wore the plainest clothes I had been able to find in Helena's granddaughter's closet. But I couldn't disguise my now-flawless skin, shiny hair, and perfect features. It was too obvious to the world that I had become a kind of chip slave.

"Like someone owns me."

⊗ ⊗ ⊗

The glittery mall was completely different from the harsh, lawless squatter life. Ender guards stood watch outside the shops, examining each passing Starter with steely stares. One guard spied some scruffy boys advertising their unclaimed status with dirty faces and stained jeans. He signaled mall security, and they roughly escorted the boys to the exit.

This had been a high-end mall even before the Spore Wars widened the gap between the rich and poor. Though not all Enders were rich and not all Starters were poor, it often seemed that way. But here, I passed plenty of hot Starters, shimmering in their illusion tops and jeans, which changed color and texture as they moved. They were like exotic birds, even the guys, wearing airscreen glasses, layers of scarves, hats with slim solar panels to charge batteries. Those who had temperature-control chips in their glistening metallic jackets kept them on. Others used insta-fold to compress their outerwear so it could be tucked into a wallet. People said they dressed this way to distinguish themselves from the street Starters. I had a closetful of clothes just like theirs, inherited from Helena's granddaughter. But that wasn't my style.

These were the claimed Starters living in mansions like mine. I couldn't always tell them apart from people like me who had received makeovers from the body bank. "Metals," that girl had said. These mall Starters were beautiful because they could afford to be. They had the best Ender dermatologists, dentists, and hairstylists and all the creams and beauty supplies their grandparents could buy. The Spore Wars had barely put a dent in their spending habits.

I stopped myself. There I was, judging them, but they'd lost their parents too. Maybe their grandparents weren't nice to them, but cold and resentful, having to see faces every day that reminded them of their lost sons and daughters.

The Spore Wars had changed us all.

I scratched the back of my head and looked around, hoping to see a shoe store. I was supposed to meet Michael and Tyler at the food court, but since my mission to feed the homeless had been a failure, I was early. I swallowed hard, thinking about it. Michael was right—I shouldn't have gone alone. I should have remembered my street smarts: Never take your hand off your bag. Never stand with your back to an entrance. Always be ready to fight. All that work and I'd only fed two Starters, who had run off without even thanking me.

I directed my attention to the airscreen display directory in the middle of the mall.

"Shoes," I said to the invisible microphone.

The display pulled the shoe store out of the map and projected a holo into the air. It was the only athletic shoe store in the mall. Knowing Tyler, he was trying on every pair there. I needed to go rescue Michael.

I headed toward the store, passing an Ender grandmother leaning on the arm of a pretty Starter, probably her granddaughter.

She's easy on the eyes.

I stopped.

It was that artificial, electronic voice in my head, and it set my teeth on edge.

The Old Man.

Hello, Callie. Did you miss me?

"No. Not a bit." I struggled to make my voice sound even. "Out of sight, out of mind."

Clever.

I then remembered he could see through my eyes. I put my hands behind my back so he couldn't see that they were shaking.

I don't buy that at all. I'm sure you thought about me every day. Every hour. Every minute.

"It's all about you, is it?" I really wanted to scream at him, but the guards would think I was crazy.

I eyed the guards. Were they staring at me because I was talking to myself? No, I could be talking into an earpiece. Maybe they had picked up on my nervousness. Not that they could do anything to help me.

"What do you want?"

I want your full attention. And you will want to give it to me.

A chill ran through my body.

Look to your left and tell me what you see.

"Shops."

Keep looking.

I turned to my left. "Just . . . a chocolate shop, a jeweler, a shop that's closed."

You're not looking hard enough. What else?

I took a few steps. "Shoppers. Enders, some with grandchildren, some Starters . . ."

Yes. Starters. Keep looking.

My eyes scanned the area. He wants me to find some Starter?

"Is this a game of hot and cold?"

More like hot and hot. Only you'll soon see it is no game.

I stood in the middle of the mall as Starters and Enders had to move around me. He wanted me to see a Starter. There were plenty of them . . . but which one? Then I saw a girl with long red hair. I knew her.

Reece.

She was the donor my guardian, Lauren, had rented to search for her grandson. I remembered Reece as a friend, but of course that was actually Lauren. The real Reece wouldn't know me. But there was so much I could tell her.

"Reece," I called out.

She looked as pretty as ever, in a short print dress and silver pumps with little heels. I dodged the shoppers to get closer to her. She was about ten feet ahead of me when she stopped and turned.

"I'm Callie," I said as shoppers weaved between us. "You don't know me. But I know you."

She gave me the strangest look, an expression I'd never seen on her. The corner of her mouth turned up in a half smile, but it wasn't a fluid move. It was more—mechanical.

Something was wrong.

She quickly turned and walked off.

"Wait," I called out.

But she kept going. An Ender walked behind her. I wouldn't have noticed him, but he had a large silvery tattoo on the side of his neck. The head of some animal. I could barely make it out. A leopard, maybe.

"It was Reece, wasn't it? You wanted me to see her?"

I can always count on you, Callie.

Did Reece know the leopard-tattooed Ender was following her? I wasn't sure. She darted into a shop. He moved to the next one and pretended to be interested in the pearl chokers in the window.

I took a step toward the shop.

No. Leave her alone.

She came out moments later and the leopard-tattooed man resumed following her. I kept walking, staying behind, watching them both.

"She's in danger," I said to the Old Man.

You'll see.

A horrible sense of dread washed over me. "Is somebody inside her?"

The body bank had been destroyed. But the Old Man was accessing me. He could have someone inside Reece's body as well. The idea was putting my stomach in knots. His electronic voice. The leopard tattoo. Reece's body being used.

I saw the shoe store ahead, past Reece. Tyler and Michael were just entering it.

"Michael!" I shouted across the mall, hoping he could hear me over the shoppers and the music. He was maybe six or seven shops away. He stopped and looked around but didn't see me. He went inside.

Reece must have heard, though, because she turned and stared at me. I didn't mean for that to happen. That gave the tattooed man a chance to catch up to her. He said something in her ear, and she shook her head with an unnatural movement. He touched her arm and she—or whoever was inside her—pulled it away.

"What's going on?" I was frozen there, struggling to solve this dark puzzle. "Tell me."

Just because you destroyed Prime doesn't mean you destroyed me. It wasn't my only facility. I can still access any chip.

Reece backed away from the man and ran toward the shoe store.

And I can turn it into a weapon.

"No," I said to him, to myself, to anyone around.

Time stopped as I held my breath. It all happened so fast. The crowd around me became a frozen blur as I started to run toward the shop. It felt like running through water—I couldn't move fast enough.

I was two doors away when, like a bullet, a dark-haired Starter wearing a puffy metallic airjacket came at me. I just got a flash of his face—strong jaw, piercing eyes. He threw himself against me, wrapped his arms around my body, and dragged me backward as fast as he could.

Before I could react, there was a horrible, heart-splitting explosion. It came from where Reece had been standing. As we went sailing through the air, I could only see a blinding white flash.

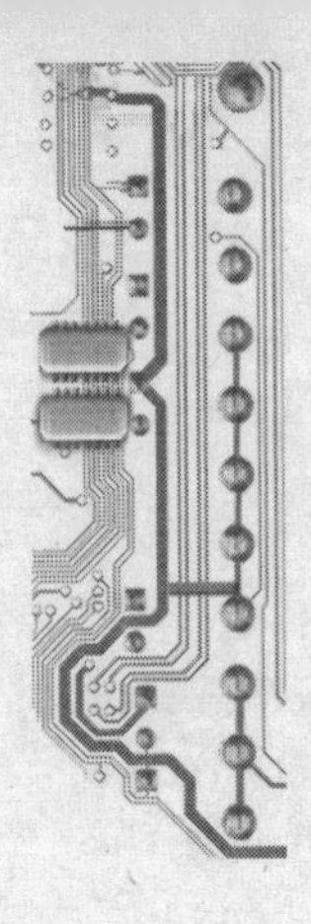

CHAPTER TWO

Pieces of glass and metal rained down from above, bounced up from below. I was on my back with the Starter squatting over me, acting as a shield, protecting me. I closed my eyes and crossed my arms to cover my face. Some Ender cried out that she'd been hit.

Screams of pain and fear came from all directions, and I couldn't say for sure that one didn't come from me. It felt like it lasted forever, but it was probably only seconds.

Finally, the horrible crashing and clanging from the explosion ended. The mall went silent for a moment, as if everyone was still holding their breath. Then, in a group exhale, the noise began again, somewhat muffled. It came to me in ghostly echoes. Enders moaned from their injuries; Starters sobbed. Some called out hopelessly for their mothers and fathers, who, of course, were long gone, from the spores.

I opened my eyes. The Starter who'd been protecting me leaned in, examining my face.

"You're all right," he said. He turned his head to look at

something else. "The marshals are coming." He was on his feet.

"Wait." I started to sit up.

"You'll see me again."

By the time I got to my feet, he was already gone. I shook pieces of glass from my clothes.

Blood marked the backs of my hands. How could this happen? How did the Old Man turn the chip into a bomb?

Tyler. Michael.

No! Please.

I oriented myself and spotted the shoe store right by the worst of the wreckage. I began to run but stumbled on the debris. I worked my way to the front of the store, where a guard had just finished covering what was left of Reece's body with his coat. One of her shoes—those heels I had just admired—lay on the floor, bits of glass littered across it, as if Cinderella's slipper had shattered.

My own shoes crunched as I made my way inside the store. People sat on the benches meant for trying on shoes. The injured held handkerchiefs, paper towels, and even store socks—tags still on—pressed to their heads, faces, and arms.

Then I spotted Michael behind a display counter in the rear of the store, looking down, his head hanging low. I ran through the store to get to him.

"Michael!"

He looked up at me with an expression of relief. "Callie."

"Where's Tyler?" I screamed.

Tyler stood, revealing himself from behind the counter. A few scratches, but fine. I came around and hugged him to me.

"What happened?" he asked.

"It was an explosion," I said quietly.

"But why?" Tyler asked.

I could see the confusion in his eyes. He might be all right physically, but this would leave another scar inside.

"I wish I knew," I said.

⊗ ⊗ ⊗

Hours later, marshals had blocked off the shoe store and turned the space outside it into an interrogation area. Marshal detectives, wearing suits instead of uniforms, borrowed tables and chairs from the fancy shops and created stations set far enough apart that witnesses couldn't hear each other. Tyler and I stood in line waiting our turn. I had my hands on his shoulders, keeping him close to me. We were up next. Should I reveal what I knew? What would they do with me if I told them I could hear voices in my head? Would they believe me? Or think I was crazy?

A Starter finished her interrogation and left one of the tables. A marshal nodded to us and motioned for Tyler to take her place. He walked to that table while I went to the next empty station and sat in the chair, facing a detective. Even sitting, he towered over me. He was a muscled Ender maybe a hundred years old, with a tan and a full head of white hair. I noticed his gun, but it was the sight of his ZipTaser that made me tense.

"Name?" he asked.

"Callie Woodland."

His palm-sized airscreen recorded my voice as I spoke. I could see the words in reverse, spelled out in the display.

"Age?"

"Sixteen."

"Grandparents?"

I shook my head. I explained that Lauren had recently become my legal guardian so I wouldn't be considered an unclaimed, and gave him my address and phone number.

"What were you doing in the mall?" he asked.

"Going to meet my brother, Tyler, to get shoes."

"Is he here?"

I nodded. He pointed at the airscreen display.

"Please state it verbally," he said.

"Yes, he's being questioned at that other table."

I scratched the back of my head and then realized what I was doing. I stopped. The detective looked at me—had he noticed? I tucked my hand under my leg.

"Tell me what you saw," he asked.

I inhaled. I had practiced this while in line. But would I get it straight?

"I saw a girl walking in the mall."

"Can you describe her?"

"She had long red hair, was about five four, beautiful. . . ."

My eyes filled with tears. I tried to fight them. I didn't want him to guess I'd known her.

He squinted at me. "It's all right. Tell me when you're ready to go on."

I nodded. "I'm okay."

"What was she wearing?"

"Um, a green print dress. And silver shoes." My voice cracked.

Our eyes met. I hesitated.

"And . . . ?"

"She was acting strange."

"How?"

Don't say anything.

I became alert. The detective looked up from the airscreen.

"Are you all right?" he asked.

You know what I can do now, Callie. Understand?

I nodded.

"Can you continue?" the detective asked.

"The girl seemed nervous. She was looking around."

His eyes narrowed. "Go on."

"She stood in front of the shoe store. All of a sudden, there was an explosion. I closed my eyes. And—and then I saw she was dead. She must have had the bomb on her." My voice broke as the pain of the awful memory returned.

He looked at me. His expression softened and he seemed sympathetic. I almost wanted to tell him the truth. But I didn't dare.

"That's all I know," I said.

He detained me a while longer. I saw Tyler stand. Michael escorted him in the direction of the long walk to the mall exit.

⊗ ⊗ ⊗

By the time I left the interrogation, the Old Man had left me. I knew because I heard the vacuum, the total silence whenever he disconnected. I guessed he had to talk to his minions, maybe whoever had controlled poor Reece. I was thankful he had any reason at all not to be with me.

I walked like a ghost through the empty mall. I remembered what my Ender friend Redmond, Helena's tech guy, had told me. He'd predicted that the chips in our heads might act like bombs and explode.

Poor Reece. How had the Old Man done it? Why? To prove that we could demolish Prime but not him? Or just to terrorize me?

My stomach tightened. I really hated this chip—this

thing—in my head. I was not going to let one creepy Ender control me for the rest of my life.

Big words, trembling hands.

I felt unsteady. I stepped into an alcove near a service door and took a few deep breaths. I couldn't get the image of Reece and her shoe out of my mind. Was there anything I could have done to save her? I wrapped my arms around my belly to calm myself down, hold it in, pull myself together.

I looked back. I was far enough from the disaster site that no one would notice me. I pulled out my phone and called Senator Bohn. I made an effort to sound calm and rational. I was pretty sure I succeeded at rational.

The senator had helped me take down Prime Destinations. He was one of the few people who knew the whole story and had the connections to do something about it. I explained what had happened. He had been trying to locate the Old Man, without any success. I explained that the bombing was his doing.

"I have an idea how we might track him down," I said, describing my plan.

Senator Bohn listened. After a moment he said, "Callie, let me see what I can do. We're going to need a special search warrant. If I pull favors, I might have it in a couple of hours."

After we hung up, I called my guardian, Lauren, and filled her in. And then there was something else I had to do. I was going to have to break a promise.

Michael and Tyler were waiting for me at the mall exit. I saw through the glass doors that marshals were stationed outside to bar anyone from entering. We paused there, still inside, all of us looking a mess.

"How did it go?" I asked them.

Michael threw his hands up in the air. "We told them what little we knew."

"A big explosion." Tyler followed by putting his arms up too, and spreading them to shape a huge ball.

I couldn't help but hug him. "You're squishing my nose," he said with a muffled voice.

He was handling it much better than I'd expected. Maybe living on the streets had actually toughened him. I let go and turned to Michael.

"Can you take Tyler home and help him clean up?" I asked.

Michael cocked his head. "Where are you going?"

"I'm going to wash up in the restroom. Then I have something to do."

Michael didn't look happy. "Come on, Tyler, let's go. She'll catch up to us later."

I took both of them into my arms in a group hug. Michael felt warm. "I don't know what I'd do without you guys."

"You won't have to worry about that," he said close to my ear.

I turned to look at him. "Thank you." I rubbed his back, gave Tyler a kiss on the cheek, and then let them go.

As they left, I sighed, grateful to have Michael to watch over my brother. Then I took out my phone and stared at the Zings from Blake.

⊗ ⊗ ⊗

As I drove over to meet Blake, my vision started to get hazy. I knew what was next because this had happened before, recently. I pulled over to the curb.

I was reliving a memory of Helena's, as if it were my own.

This was some aftereffect of the transposition—the mind-body transfer process.

It played in my mind the way one of my own memories would. I could see it happening, and I could feel Helena's feelings. She walks into Prime for the first time. Everyone smiles at her: the receptionists, Mr. Tinnenbaum, and then the Old Man. Her thoughts become mine, but it is not like I hear her voice; no, I actually feel her desperation. *How these people stole Emma from me, ripped her away and lasered her and cut into her flesh and changed her. How, because of them, she's lost. Gone. Disappeared. And probably dead.*

I felt Helena's emptiness. How deeply lonely she was. Like most memories, it was short and then it was gone. But it passed through me like an emotional wave, and the sadness lasted for most of the drive. Why was this happening? And was I the only donor experiencing these strange souvenirs of our mind-body transfers?

I'd picked Beverly Glen Park to meet Blake. When I saw him waiting for me, sitting on top of a picnic table, my heart skipped a beat.

Seeing him with the setting sun backlighting his hair, I couldn't help but be reminded of the time we had met there before. Only then, it was really the Old Man inside Blake's body. I'd picked this place because it was close by and there was a private guard to protect us. But maybe there was another, subconscious reason I'd picked the same park.

I continued walking, watching him all the way. He leaned his elbows on his thighs, his hands clasped, just like I remembered. But I had to remind myself this wasn't the person I'd been with then. This was the real Blake, Senator Harrison's grandson, who thought he had been sick, who knew nothing of the body bank, whose only clue that we once had a relationship was a photo on his phone of us together.

He held out his hand to help me onto the tabletop.

"Glad you came," he said.

"I'm really sorry, but I don't have long."

"Why not?"

"I'm waiting for an important Zing." I knew that sounded lame. "But I came because there's something I have to tell you."

"There's something I've been wanting to ask you. You know everything about us. I know zip."

"That's not important now."

"It's important to me." He pulled out his phone. "So what about this picture of us?"

He showed me the happy image of the two of us, arms around each other. But it was a lie. It was really the Old Man.

It hurt to look at it.

"What were we doing?" he asked. "I mean, that day?"

"Riding horses."

"At my grandfather's ranch?"

"Yes." I hated thinking back on that day. At the time, I'd thought it was one of the best days of my life.

"Looks like we had a pretty good time."

I sighed. "We did."

His eyes met mine. "What else did we do?"

"We went to the music center and to a drive-in restaurant. We watched the sunset."

I didn't fill in the details that I saw in my mind's eye: How we'd watched the sun set over the mountains, our horses side by side, shuffling their hooves. How he'd handed me that spotted orchid, the first flower any boy had ever given me. Reliving those memories hurt. Not because they were gone, but because they never really existed. Not with him, anyway.

"No, I mean, did we do anything else?" He stretched his neck as if his collar was too tight. "Anything . . . more?"

"No. We just kissed."

At the time, it wasn't "just" a kiss to me. But he didn't need to know that.

"I wish I could remember that," he said.

"I wish you could too."

He hesitated for a moment, as if he was trying to see if I meant what I'd said. Then he leaned forward, tentatively, his eyes searching for clues every step of the way.

I leaned closer until our faces were almost touching. He smelled wonderfully woodsy and grassy, same as before.

We kissed. It was . . . not like before.

It started out the same, the smoothness of his lips, the smell of his skin. But the spark I had once felt, that sweet electricity, was gone. It was only in my memory. I tried again. Maybe it was there, and I just wasn't being sensitive enough. Maybe it was me. Maybe I was nervous.

Relax. Find it.

But I stopped. Pulled back.

No.

It wasn't.

He pulled away too and looked off in the distance. We sat back, side by side, not touching each other. He ran his hand through his hair. I looked at my phone. No Zing yet.

"You seem eager to go," he said, looking resigned.

"No, sorry, it's really important." I put the phone down.

"So what did you want to tell me?" he asked.

I turned to him. Finally, I could do what I came to do. "You're in danger. We both are."

"What?" He looked at me as if I'd said the world was flat.

I needed to start with something he already knew. "You've heard the news about the bombing at the mall?"

He frowned. "Bombing? They just said it was an explosion on the news. A gas leak."

"It was a bombing. And it could have been you or me who got killed."

He leaned away from me. It wasn't going to be easy to convince him.

"I made a promise to your grandfather that I wouldn't tell you," I said. "He wants to protect you, but you have to know now. That building that we watched being destroyed in Beverly Hills, Prime Destinations?"

He nodded slowly.

"You were kidnapped and brought there. They implanted a chip in your head. Your body was used—inhabited—by the head of Prime. It's called transposition. That's why you have no memory of that picture. It wasn't you then."

"Where was I?"

"It's like your brain was asleep." I waved my hand as if to dismiss that. "The important thing is, you want to keep away from him—he's called the Old Man. You'll know him because he has an electronic mask for a face and he's got this creepy artificial voice. He had a plan to make thousands of Starters permanents—so we'd never wake up. But we stopped it."

Blake let out a sound that was half laugh, half huff. "This is crazy."

"I know it sounds crazy, but it's real. I have the chip too." I touched the back of my head.

He rubbed his temples, as if it hurt to think about all this craziness. My phone flashed a Zing from Senator Bohn's office.

Obtained the search warrant. Call me.

"That's him. I have to go," I said.

"Already?" He slumped. "But I've got a million questions."

"I'm sorry, but we have to stop him. Ask your grandfather. Just do me a favor and don't say I told you."

I hated leaving him there after giving him the mind-boggling news. But they were waiting for me.

"Don't talk to anybody until you talk to your grand-father," I said.

As I rushed off, I felt an aching pain in my chest, as if my heart had been ripped out. I couldn't lie to myself—I missed Blake.

Just not this Blake.

But that meant I missed . . . No. What that meant, I didn't want to think about. It was too horrible. Disgusting. I needed to push that out of my mind and focus on how we were going to stop him.

⊗ ⊗ ⊗

I sat in the back of the limo with the senator's chief of staff and Lauren. Before the bombing, Senator Bohn had been heading up a Congressional investigation of Prime Destinations, but it had run dry. The computers that had been confiscated from Prime had been wiped clean, so there was nothing to learn from them. The team was hitting dead ends.

But the bombing had reenergized our drive to find the

Old Man. With the search warrant the senator obtained for us, we headed off to the one place we knew had done business with him. The only snag was that because this was done so quickly, our search warrant was conditional: for inspection only. When we reached our destination, we could only examine their files and computers, not copy anything. That made my role all the more essential, as I was the only one of the three of us who had spent time there.

"Horrid about Reece," Lauren said. "I feel terribly responsible."

"It's not your fault," I said. "Reece chose to be a donor before you came to rent her." Then I wondered, why did the Old Man do this? Was it a coincidence that he picked my guardian's donor body to sacrifice? I kept this to myself, not wanting to make Lauren feel any worse.

"You said she was acting strangely?" Lauren asked.

"I think she was being controlled. But they weren't doing a very good job. Her expressions and movements were jerky. She looked unnatural."

Lauren shivered.

"And then there was this Ender," I continued, "this man she spoke to, right before the explosion."

"What man?" the chief of staff asked.

"A tall Ender, fit, maybe a hundred," I said. "With a leopard tattoo on his neck. He was following her through the mall right before it happened."

"How long did they talk?" he asked.

"A few seconds." I swallowed. "It happened in a mall, of all places," I said. "With little kids."

"He wanted to show that we could shut down Prime," the chief of staff said, "but we couldn't stop *him*."

So it wasn't Lauren's fault, it was mine. The Old Man targeted the mall I would be going to, used my guardian's donor body, the Starter I knew, and showed me he was still capable of hurting us. It was my fault those people were injured and Reece was killed.

I closed my eyes a moment.

The driver pulled over. We'd arrived. I didn't move.

"You don't have to come in," Lauren said.

"I do. It's why I'm here," I said. "I know him better than any of you. There might be a clue, something that relates to something he said to me. You can't copy anything, so you need my eyes."

I didn't really want to go inside, but I had to. I got out of the car and looked up at Institution 37. The massive gray walls made my heart feel heavy. The complex looked like the prison that it really was, with heavy iron gates and a security booth. The walls mocked and challenged, daring me to return. Was I an idiot to come back? The last time I had, I'd lost my best friend on those walls.

Lauren stood beside me. She smiled, and gentle wrinkles formed around her eyes.

"It's okay, Callie. We'll be right beside you."

The driver stayed with the car while the three of us walked toward the gate. I was safe, wasn't I? We had the power and the money, much more than these horrible people in this place. Much more than that vile head of security, my old prison guard—Beatty.

So why were my hands shaking?

Lauren noticed and touched my shoulder.

"Don't worry. You're not going to see her. We're only going to speak to the headmaster."

I nodded. Even though Beatty haunted my memories, odds were we wouldn't run into her there. She was probably off in that dungeon of a confinement cell, torturing some poor Starter.

The gates opened with their awful grinding noise that made my jaw clench. I looked down and noticed that my hands had stopped shaking.

Soon we were in the main office, waiting for the headmaster's arrival. The chief of staff and Lauren sat in old leather chairs. I was too fidgety to sit. I paced the room. There wasn't a bit of color in it. On the wall hung a faded painting of an English hunting scene. One hunter proudly held up a dead fox. Fitting, I thought.

On the desk, a glint drew my attention. It came from a stiletto letter opener with a handle shaped like a snake and emerald-green stones for eyes. Next to it, the airscreen's screensaver was not the usual waterfalls and wildlife but a screenshot from *Huntdown,* a first-person shooter game where unclaimed Starters were hunted. I knew better than anyone how brutal this place could be, but that shocked even me.

I felt sick to my stomach. I hated being there. I just wanted to get our answer and go. All we really needed was an address, a contact number, maybe even a bank account. Some sure way to find the Old Man.

"Callie? Don't you want to sit down?" Lauren asked.

The door opened and I tensed. Instead of the headmaster, I found myself face to face with none other than Beatty.

"Callie," Beatty said in her raspy voice. "So nice to see you again."

She extended her gnarled hand to me. The moles on her face had grown bigger, it seemed. I folded my arms. If the hate in my eyes could have started a fire, she'd have been burned to a crisp.

The chief of staff stood and came to my side. "We're expecting the headmaster."

A small smile crept across one side of Beatty's face. "Yes. You're looking at her."

"You?" I blurted out.

"Yes. I've been promoted."

I took a step back. I think I gasped, because the chief of staff put his hand on my shoulder. How could that be? She should have been arrested for ordering the marshals to shoot Sara with Tasers. She knew about Sara's heart.

"You're the headmaster?" I said.

"That's correct, Callie." She emphasized my name as if I had just been called for execution.

Her white hair was cut close at the sides, and the rest reached for the ceiling. She no longer wore her severe gray uniform or badge. Instead, she had on an expensive-looking wool suit with an orange scarf tucked in at the neck.

I wanted to take that scarf and pull it until her face turned blue.

"We're here to discuss the CEO of Prime Destinations," the chief of staff said.

"What about him?" Beatty asked.

Lauren joined us as the chief of staff continued. "We have a subpoena for the Senate investigation," he said, taking out an envelope. "To examine any records that have to do with Prime Destinations and the institution."

"What are you looking for?" Beatty asked as she opened the envelope. "Specifically?"

"We need to find where he's hiding," I said.

"The institution must know how to get in touch with him," Lauren said. "Since they were doing business with him."

Beatty shook her head as if we'd asked for a million dollars. "He always initiated contact with us. The previous headmaster had no way of getting in touch with him."

"Perhaps there's someone here—the assistant to the past headmaster—who might know more?" Lauren asked.

"She is gone as well." Beatty's lips formed a smug little smile as she handed the envelope back to the chief of staff.

"People just disappear right and left around here." I couldn't help myself.

"You would know," Beatty said, leaning in much too close to my face.

I wanted to slap her.

Three tall Ender marshals entered the room. Each one positioned himself behind one of us. One of them passed Beatty a piece of paper, which she handed to the chief of staff.

"What's this?" the chief of staff asked.

"A writ of prohibition," Beatty said smoothly.

"What does it mean?" I asked Lauren.

"It means this case will be tied up in court before we'll ever get any answers," the chief said. Then he looked up from the paper to Beatty. "You must have friends in high places."

A smile crept across her face. "You have no idea." She turned to the guards. "Get everyone out of here."

The chief and Lauren were escorted out first. My marshal took me by the elbow and followed them to the door. But Beatty whispered to him. At the last moment, he let go of me and exited alone, shutting the door behind him and leaving me inside.

I stood there alone with Beatty. My heart raced. She pulled me by the wrist away from the door, over toward her desk.

"How dare you come back here and think you can peer into my private files?" she said. "You should have left well enough alone, you with the mansion in Bel Air."

She knew where I lived. It wasn't a surprise, but it was a threat. She gripped my wrist harder.

"Let me go!" I shouted. The door was too far and too thick for anyone to hear.

"You have so much to lose now, Callie." She stared at me with her mole-ridden face. "And you will. It won't be long before you slip. And I'll see you're locked up in here again, where you belong."

My hand was turning white. I tried to pry off her fingers, but she dug her fingernails into me. I could have bitten her arm to get loose, but that was what she wanted. She'd have them throw me in the cell again, and Lauren would have to use more than one lawyer to get me out. With Beatty's connections, I might never get out.

I looked at the snake-handled stiletto letter opener on her desk. I knew I couldn't use it. But I kept looking, to draw her attention away, a trick I learned on the streets. She fell for it and took her eyes off me.

In that moment, I was able to get free.

I ran to the door and tried to open it, but it was locked. I banged on it. "Let me out!"

The door opened and Lauren and the chief of staff stood beside the marshal putting away his key. Lauren put her arm around my shoulder.

"Are you all right, Headmaster?" the marshal asked.

Beatty smoothed her suit as she walked up to us. "Escort them to the exit."

As the marshals led us away, I turned my head to get one last look at Beatty. I wished I hadn't. She leaned in her doorway, a vicious and victorious smile spread across her face.

There was no way I could beat that look. Score one for Beatty.

⊗ ⊗ ⊗

We all huddled in the back of the limo as the driver took off—Lauren and I and the chief of staff.

"How can she be the headmaster? After what she did?" I asked. The car was silent. "So now we give up? Can't we get a judge to reverse this?"

The chief of staff shifted in his seat. "It's possible they didn't even have his information. The Old Man might have insisted on face-to-face contact—using secondaries. No digital footprints that way."

I sank back in my seat, defeated. "But how are we going to find him, then?"

No one had an answer.

When they let me off at the house, I knew that was as far as they were going to take it. Lauren got out of the limo to hug me.

She held me tightly, then pulled away.

"Now what?" I asked.

She shook her head. "Just stay safe."

"I have a potential bomb in my head. I'll never be safe now, and neither will any of the other Metals, including your grandson, Kevin. You can't give up."

She stared into my eyes.

"Callie, I'm a hundred and sixty-one years old. I've been

searching every day for seven months. I managed to resurrect some hope for today, but now . . ." Her voice cracked. "I'm not saying I'm giving up, but you can't imagine how empty I am inside. There's nothing left." She paused. "You're young. You have the fire in your belly. Use it for me."

Her eyes pleaded with me. Then she turned and got back into the limo.

I watched as it pulled out of Helena's curved driveway, the iron gates automatically closing behind it.

They aren't going to help you. They can't help you. You are alone.

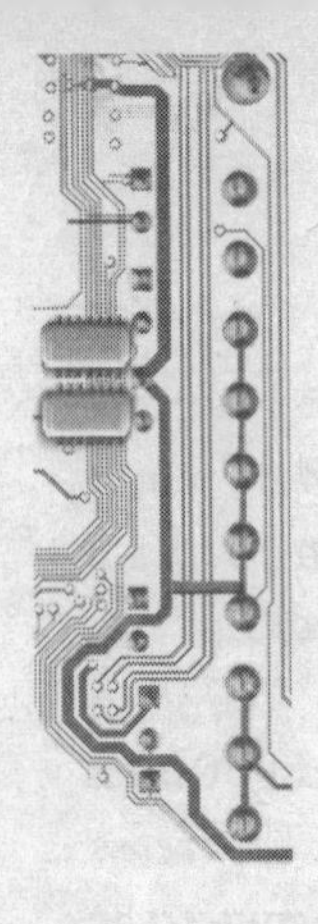

CHAPTER THREE

He was in my head again, the Old Man. Here, at my home. I didn't want him to see anything through my eyes. It was too creepy.

Callie?

I hurried into the garage and closed the door. I turned the lights off and stood near the wall in the darkness.

"So who's next? Who are you blowing up today?"

No need to be in the dark. I don't have to see where you are. I can send a signal to your chip. I thought I demonstrated this quite well at the mall.

"So you can blow up anyone's chip by sending a certain signal to it?"

Something like that. I'm not going to give up my secrets.

"You wouldn't blow up my chip."

So you understand that your chip is special. And so are you.

"What I understand is that you are a monster and a killer. And I can't trust anything you say."

I will tell you one thing that is true. And will be true for all time. Are you listening?

I wanted to kill him and his metallic voice. "Yes."

His words came out slowly. *Trust no one but yourself.* After a long pause, he added, *And then question that.*

"That makes no sense."

And remember, I may not want to blow up your chip, but there's nothing special about Michael's chip. Or Michael, for that matter.

I clenched my fists.

Or Tyler's chip.

What was he talking about? "Tyler doesn't have a chip."

Yes, he does.

"You're lying. I checked him."

Sweat formed on my neck. I thought back. We were so glad to find Tyler, so grateful to see he was in good condition, better than before the Old Man kidnapped him. He was healthier. In the excitement and relief, I hadn't checked him right away, but I did later.

How did you check him?

"The back of his head. There was no scar."

We're always making improvements in our technology. We lasered his incision point. Good job, don't you think?

Could it be true? I slid down the wall I was leaning against until I rested on my haunches. My head fell forward. I hoped this was a trick. Otherwise, it would be the worst news ever and, like me, Tyler was tethered to the Old Man.

"You killed Reece, you chipped my brother," I said, gritting my teeth. "Stay away from him," I said to the floor.

That's up to you.

I lifted my head.

You are going to meet me at a location I choose.

My mouth went dry. I licked my lips. "Where?"

You are not to tell anyone, alert anyone, Zing anyone. If you do, I will do to Michael what we did to Reece. And then Tyler. Do you understand?

What could I say? "Yes, it's clear."

You're in the garage already. Get in your car.

I didn't see any way out. I wasn't dealing with some enemy I could fight—he was inside my head. I walked over to the blue car and got in. He gave me a street number I didn't recognize.

I started the car and the garage door opened. I pulled out of the garage, went down the curved driveway. The gate opened automatically and I turned onto the street.

I gripped the wheel and drove in silence, my heart pounding.

You don't have to be afraid, Callie. I'm not going to hurt you. I need you.

I wasn't sure what that meant, but it made the hairs stand up on the backs of my arms. How could I get out of this? I couldn't go to a marshal, couldn't call Lauren or the senator. Anything I did, he would see. Anything I said, he could hear.

I couldn't even warn Michael. Not that he could hide anywhere.

The freeway on-ramp came into my view. I passed it by, thinking that the longer I was in the car, the more chance I had to somehow avoid the unavoidable. I hated being the Old Man's puppet from a distance, but I was terrified of being under his control in person. The times I had been close to him at the institution, he had scared me more than anyone I'd ever known. That mask with the electronic buzz that crackled—I often had nightmares where I was alone with him in the dark and all I could hear was that sound.

And yet he was also capable of being inside Blake and acting smooth and charming. How was that even possible? How do you disguise that much evil? He has no soul, no heart. I should have been able to tell when he was in Blake. How did I miss it?

I see where you are, you know. You should have taken the freeway.

"You're getting what you want. I'm coming to you," I said. "And you want to tell me how to drive?"

It was all put on so he wouldn't see how afraid I was. Inside, my stomach ached.

"So how do you access our chips anyway?"

You'll see soon enough.

I thought back on all his cruel acts. "Did you kill Helena yourself? Or just watch?"

Someone else killed her.

"Who?"

It doesn't matter. They work for me.

"You killed Reece." My mind flashed back on the bombing. "You hurt a lot of people in the mall. Grandmothers. Children. Some were injured badly. They were in pain."

I had to demonstrate my power to you. They were just casualties of war.

"Whose war? You against everyone? Starters, Enders, everyone?"

Now you finally understand me.

I drove in silence. I couldn't take him anymore. I didn't want to hear his creepy voice in my head. After a while, I approached the cross streets he had given me. I was already there, in Hollywood, near the hills. My heart started beating faster. No, it couldn't be. I thought somehow I'd find a way out of this.

Do I cause an accident? Run away?

Don't try anything. Remember why you are doing this. For Michael and Tyler.

It was like he could read my mind—which of course he couldn't. But he knew what he held over me.

"Which way?"

Up the hill.

I turned around the curve of the road and had to slam on my brakes.

A strange vehicle blocked my way. It looked like a cross between an SUV and a tank, and it was stopped in the middle of the narrow street, facing me. I couldn't see the driver: the windows were tinted. The whole thing was steel gray.

"What is that?" I asked.

But before I could hear an answer, or do anything, the SUV door opened and a guy ran out. He wore black clothing, gloves, and a ski mask that covered his face.

I jammed my finger on the button and locked my doors. He held something shiny in his fist and aimed it at my car. *CLICK*. My doors unlocked.

What happened next came in flashes. Black clothing against my window—my door yanked open—a black bag thrown over my head.

Before I knew it, my hands were cuffed behind my back. I resisted as best I could, kicking and screaming, but the bag muffled my voice. It was hot and so heavy it had to be made of metal.

The man pulled me out of the car and carried me to what

I figured was his SUV. I was tossed onto the seat. I heard the door slam, then footsteps, then him getting into the driver's seat and shutting that door.

As the car started to move, I soon heard scraping. He must have been forcing his SUV past my car. It didn't really matter anymore.

"Please take this bag off," I said. "I can't breathe."

"Just hold on."

I was surprised to discover his voice sounded really young, like my age. Like a Starter. It seemed strange the Old Man would send a Starter to get me.

We drove in silence. Of course the Old Man wouldn't give me his address. He just wanted to get me close enough so he could be in charge. Take me someplace where I wouldn't know the address—or maybe even the city.

I felt the driver reach over and tug at the Velcro at the base of the bag. He pulled the bag off my head. The tinted windows kept the car dark, but I saw that he had removed his ski mask. I could make out the outline of his face, his cheekbone, jawline. And those piercing eyes.

It was the Starter who had protected me from the explosion.

I'd never forget those eyes. He was good-looking in such an intense way, it almost scared me.

"Can you remove the cuffs now?" I asked.

"Not until I'm sure you understand."

"Understand what?"

"That I'm not going to hurt you."

"You pushed me out of the way just before the explosion."

He didn't deny it. It made no sense. First he saves my life;

then he kidnaps me? Was he sent by the Old Man to retrieve me or not?

"My name's Hyden."

"Like the composer."

"Just spelled differently."

I noticed weapons of all types hugging the walls and ceiling. They fit into special slots, cut to accommodate them perfectly. A shiver ran up my back.

He pulled over to the curb but left the car running. "Lean forward."

I hesitated, then cooperated.

"Don't move." He pulled out a knife.

He used it to cut through my plexi-cuffs. Managed to do it without even touching me.

While he was busy putting his knife away, I went right to my door handle to make my escape. But it was locked.

"Hey, you said you trusted me," he said.

"I never said that. I said I understood you weren't going to hurt me. Now open the door."

"You really don't want to go out there."

"I have to go. If I don't, my brother and a friend will be killed."

"By the Old Man? He said that?"

"So you know who he is."

I wondered if he was a Metal. I scanned his face. He looked perfect. Well, maybe not exactly. He had a few flaws, some tiny scars.

"I know who he is, how he thinks. I know exactly what he's capable of. I know him better than anyone else."

What he was saying was outrageous. How could he know the Old Man so well?

"Better than anyone else?" I asked. "A man who always wears a mask? How?" I stayed close to my door.

He leaned forward and said words that seemed painful to get out, as if he'd never said them before.

"Because I'm his son."

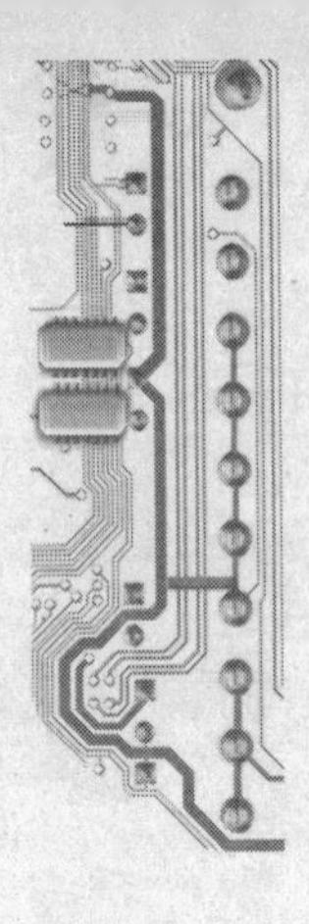

CHAPTER FOUR

My eyes locked on Hyden's as we sat there in his SUV. Was he going to break into a grin and say he was joking? Was he lying? Or crazy?

His expression never wavered. I sucked in a breath of air.

He was serious.

"I know him better than anybody," he said. "And I hate him."

He stared at me with those eyes. I saw a flash of pain behind them. But was that real or faked?

"He's your father?" I struggled to make my voice sound even. If he was crazy, I didn't want to anger him.

He took a deep breath, then exhaled. "Yes."

"He can't be." My mind whirled. "He's an Ender. More like your grandfather."

"He wore a disguise."

"His white hair—"

"Wig. Didn't you wonder why he always wore all that clothing, even indoors?"

"We were told he had a condition. That he was always cold."

"More like coldhearted. Condition?" He shook his head. "That lie was just his cover."

This was too much for me to accept. "So you're saying he's your father and he's actually a *Middle*?"

"That's right."

"Then how come he's alive?"

"Black market vaccine."

I'd heard of Middles doing that. You didn't see them very often because they weren't welcome on the street unless they were part of the privileged class that was allowed the vaccine—politicians, generals, scientists. Then there were the well-connected Middles with clout—holo stars and the über-rich. Stars were forgiven, but the others were so resented that if they were caught in the wrong place without their bodyguards, they had a habit of turning up dead.

"Must have been really expensive," I said.

"Cost him half his fortune."

That was hard to believe. We were talking about a cruel, hard man. I doubted he'd given up so much. "What about your mother?"

"Gone."

"Spores?"

"Something else." He looked so pained.

I didn't want to push and make him feel worse. I thought back on how my parents had argued over the vaccine. My mother wanted my father to use his connections to get the vaccine for them, so they could survive to take care of us. But he refused on principle, because he didn't feel he should push ahead of Starters and Enders who were more vulnerable and should have the vaccine first. I admired that, but I also resented it.

Hyden's eyes glazed over. "My father's evil. There's no other way to say it."

I glanced out the window. Was he lying to me? It didn't seem like it. "I don't know what to believe. But the Old Man threatened my brother, Tyler, and my friend Michael. Said he'd blow them up. So you have to let me go."

An SUV pulled up and parked behind us.

"I think that's my father's men now." Hyden peeled off his gloves.

"What're you doing?"

"Getting ready." He dropped his left hand to the side of his seat.

I hoped he wasn't reaching for a gun.

Two men cautiously emerged from their SUV and walked toward our car. They were Enders, their short white hair made whiter by the contrast with their black suits.

"Callie Woodland?" one of them shouted. "It's all right now. We're here to help you."

"Let her go!" the other Ender shouted at Hyden.

"Unlock my door," I begged Hyden. "Let me go, please."

The Enders were almost at our windows. Hyden moved and I thought he was going to press the unlock button. But instead, he grabbed the steering wheel and pulled away from the curb.

"No!" I screamed.

I reached for the wheel but he yanked hard to the left, blocking it with his elbow. I turned and saw one of the Enders take a gun out of his jacket. He aimed it at my head. Everything stopped, my breath, my heart. The other Ender reached out and pushed his gun away. Then they bolted back to their car.

"You want to turn yourself over to those guys?" Hyden said.

I gulped a breath of air and watched as they pursued us in their car. "They're coming."

Hyden made a sharp left turn.

"Hold on," he said. "I'll make sure they can't follow us."

He drove with purpose, making sudden sharp turns. He was an expert driver, and soon he lost them. Moments later, he pulled into an underground garage.

"Where're you taking me?"

"Down where it's safe." He held his phone up to the entry gate to pay to admit us.

The gate opened and we started our descent. We curved down, level after level. Once we had made it to the lowest level, he parked the SUV in a spot in the corner. This far down, we were the only vehicle.

He turned off the engine.

"I'm going to let you out, but you've got to listen to me. You can't run away. There's nowhere to run. Give me a chance to explain everything and you'll see why the safest place to be is with me."

I was trapped down there in a garage with a Starter who said he was the son of the Old Man. Great.

"Okay?" he asked.

I nodded. He unlocked the doors and we got out. I looked for the exit. There was one door that led to the stairway, one that was a service door. And an elevator. Otherwise, there was the ramp we came down on.

"Hey," he said, leaning his back against the side of the

SUV. "Remember our deal? You're going to listen and give me a chance to explain."

I stood several feet away from him and also leaned against the SUV. One of the many things I learned from my year living on the streets was that mirroring a pose put a person at ease.

What he was claiming, could it be? Why would anyone claim he was a blood relation to a monster unless it was true?

To gain my trust.

"So you ready to trust me? Enough to listen?" he said.

"I don't know who to believe anymore. I've been told not to trust anyone."

"Let me guess. My father told you that, right? I know. I know that he can communicate with you in your head."

Hair rose on the back of my neck.

"So he said, 'Trust no one but yourself, and then question that,' right?" He folded his arms.

The eerie feeling of having someone repeat words you heard inside your head . . . there was nothing quite like it. It was worse than if he had seen me naked. "How did you know?"

"That's exactly what he used to say to me," he said. "He messed with my mind my whole life. He's good at messing with heads."

"In more ways than one," I said.

So Hyden *was* the Old Man's son.

"We have to protect you from him. This is the safest thing for you." He knocked on the side of his SUV.

I looked it over. It was painted a matte gunmetal gray and was built low and heavy, like a squashed tank. I guessed that it was bulletproof. Maybe even bombproof.

"Your car?" I asked.

"My protection," he said. "And now yours."

I was about to protest when we heard the hum of an engine. A car was coming down the ramp. I got closer to him and accidentally brushed his hand with mine.

He sucked in air as if I'd burned him.

"Sorry, did I . . . *hurt* you . . . ?" I asked.

He pulled his arm close to his body, as if he was wounded. "No, it's all right."

It was clear it wasn't from the visible pain in his eyes. Even the edge in his voice betrayed him—he was lying. But there wasn't time to pursue it because a vehicle entered our level, drawing our attention. It was a beat-up truck. As it passed us, I saw that the driver was an Ender wearing a scruffy green uniform. Maintenance man, maybe. He stared hard at us and parked his truck at the other end of the level.

Hyden watched the maintenance man get out of his truck and walk toward the service door before he unlocked the van doors.

"See this?" Hyden pointed to the thick walls of the vehicle. "It's a blocker." He knocked on the side of his door. "Lined with ti-steel."

"This must have cost a fortune," I said.

"How much is your life worth?" He looked directly at me.

"I don't know."

"You're priceless to some people," he said, looking away. He patted the side of the car. "When you're in here, my father can't access your chip."

Just hearing those words made me shiver. I was there, talking with the *Old Man's son*. I never could have predicted this.

"What does he want with me?" I asked.

"You're one of a kind. The only Metal whose chip has been altered so you can kill when someone's occupying you. And you retain your consciousness. I'm sure he wants to study your chip."

"I'm happy to give it to him. I'd like nothing more than to get it out of my head."

Hyden looked at me with serious eyes. "If only it were that easy."

My stomach tightened.

"There's so much I have to explain," Hyden said, "and it's all going to sound weird."

"What's not weird? Voices in my head, a chip that could explode, now you telling me the only way to be safe is to be in a tank lined with ti-steel for the rest of my life."

"Or very high up. Or deep enough underground, like here. That way my father's scanning technology can't access your signal."

"He accessed me when I was in my renter's mountain cabin."

"I know. I've been able to follow him in the chiptalk air-space."

"What?"

"It's like this: sometimes I look for his signal trying to access Metals—I call it chipspace. And I work to block him."

"How do you know how to do that?"

"Before I was born, my father—his name is Brockman—was working on developing a chip for mind-body transfers. Lots of other scientists were trying. My mother told me that when I was young, I'd wander into his lab and stare at the whiteboard. She said I was listening, absorbing. I don't remember it. My father didn't believe her. Then, as she told it, one summer day, before I could speak, I picked up a pen and figured out an equation that had been eluding him for days."

"Really?"

"Maybe she was exaggerating." He smiled. It was the first time I'd seen that.

"From then on, he observed me, treating me like another research project. Eventually, I figured out how to make it all work. We developed it together but argued about how it should be used. I saw medical uses, but he of course chose to go for the money."

"Why didn't he just sell it off, then, instead of building Prime?"

"He needed Prime to raise capital to perfect it. Prime also publicized the tech to the top-level buyers."

"Like who?"

"Foreign governments, terrorists."

"He'd be selling out his country."

"That's the kind of man he is. He only cares about himself. That's why you have to be in a safe location."

Something about the way Hyden said those words made me wonder. "You mean I can't go back to my home?"

"There's no choice."

"But my brother, what about him? And Michael?"

"First of all, they'll be safer if they're not with you. You're the prize, the one he must have."

I squared my jaw. "I'm not going to leave them."

"Your mountain cabin would be safe for them," he said.

He reached in his pocket and pulled out a package of mint strips. He popped one in his mouth and then looked embarrassed. "Sorry, would you like one?"

I took the mint strip and it melted quickly on my tongue.

"But he accessed me there, at the cabin."

Hyden squinted. "He knew your chip identification number, which makes it easier to access you. It's a unique number. But he lost the other chip numbers when Prime was shut down."

"So how did he hijack Reece?"

"He found her on a scan."

"Just a random scan?" I said.

"He's looking for Metal. I can do that, but it takes time."

"A Metal detector?" I pictured something I'd seen in an old movie.

"A very sophisticated one," he said. "So now that you believe what I'm saying, that the Old Man is really my father, and you understand more about how this all works, you're ready to hear the next part."

I waited to see what could possibly be next. "Tell me."

"I've already arranged for Michael and Tyler to be delivered to the mountain chalet."

"You what?"

"And Eugenia." He looked at his watch. "They should be there now."

I was about to ask him more, when I started to feel sleepy. I leaned against his SUV.

"You okay?"

I nodded. "I'm fine. Just really tired."

He opened the passenger door and I climbed in. I settled back in the seat and felt like I could sleep for a . . . hundred . . . years. . . .

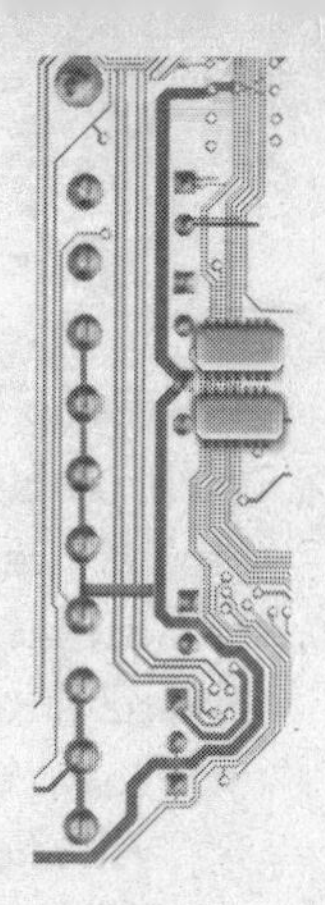

CHAPTER FIVE

I was having a dream: I was in our house. It was before Tyler was born. My dad and I were huddling on the couch with a blanket over our legs. I could smell the buttery popcorn my mom was making in the kitchen. We'd ordered up a vintage movie on the airscreen, an old Western.

My dad laughed his warm laugh at how the gunslingers were mishandling their guns.

"That's all wrong," he said.

All of a sudden, a gun appeared in his hand. He wrapped my hands around the gun and pointed it at the airscreen.

"Hold it like that, see?" he said.

I wrapped my tiny fingers around the big, heavy gun. When I pulled on the trigger, the airscreen actor fell back, shot.

"I killed him, Daddy!" I cried. "I killed him."

My father laughed.

I woke up with a dry mouth, in the SUV, rocking to the movement as Hyden drove the freeway. Below us, in the distance, the city lights sparkled.

"Hey, have a good nap?" Hyden asked, taking his eyes off the road for only a second.

"I was so sleepy," I murmured, stretching my arms.

"All the excitement must've gotten to you."

He exited the freeway. I didn't recognize the area. Industrial. Seas of empty asphalt surrounded silent warehouse buildings. We entered the driveway of one of them.

"Where are we?" I asked, still groggy.

"My lab."

I felt so tired. What had we been talking about before I dozed off?

Hyden drove behind a boxlike, windowless building, then pulled up close to a metal panel. A red laser beam scanned his license plate. Then the panel rose, revealing an orderly garage. No bikes or toys stored there, just some strange tools and a few metal containers. He drove in, and the panel shut behind us.

Hyden turned off the engine and I reached for my door handle.

"Wait," he said. "Don't move."

"Why?"

"Let me check it out first."

"But this is your lab, your home, right?" I asked.

"My safe house."

Hyden got out and examined every corner of the garage, holding a device and running it over the walls and behind each container. I figured he was looking for electronic bugs. I noticed a heat sensor panel on the wall showing Hyden's body as a moving red blotch. His was the only one, but still he checked everywhere, looking up, down. He couldn't have been more thorough.

He went to an old-fashioned communication system on the wall and pressed a button. After talking into the speaker, he came back.

"Okay," Hyden said. "You can get out now."

He watched over me as I exited the SUV, then led me to a thick metal door and pressed some numbers on a pad on the wall. An elevator door slid open with a heavy grinding sound, like a sliding stone revealing a portal to a magic lair.

As we rode down, the air grew colder, making me more alert. I wasn't particularly claustrophobic, but the idea of going so far below ground level seemed wrong. Unnatural.

Hyden must have read my face, because he gave me a small reassuring smile.

The elevator door opened up to a corridor. From there, Hyden opened a metal door that led to a large, darkened tech lab. Small lights illuminated various spots, giving the space the effect of a museum exhibit. Airscreens dominated every corner, and strange components filled the room, some hanging from the ceiling—twisted bits of metal, thin, glistening strands of poly-tubing with colored specks moving through them. When I examined them more closely, I saw that the specks were tiny geometric shapes with moving parts. It was geek heaven.

Across the room, hunched over a desk, a man with long, wild white hair kept his back to us as we approached. Could it . . . ? Could it be him?

"I brought someone," Hyden said to him.

The Ender turned around. Even in the darkened space, I recognized him.

"Redmond!" I shouted.

I rushed up and hugged him. No sooner had I done it than I felt the awkwardness of it. He was an Ender who wasn't even related to me, and I felt more for him than I was sure he felt for me. Embracing him just made me ache for my father. I pulled away.

"Callie," he said with his clipped British accent. "That's a much better greeting than the last time, when you held a gun to my head."

I felt my cheeks redden.

"No hard feelings," he said.

"I thought the Old Man had you captive," I said.

Redmond looked at Hyden. "Hyden came to me, explained what he was doing, and I signed up. The paycheck is rather good, and I can't say I mind working for a genius."

Hyden shrugged in a halfhearted attempt at humility.

"But if the Old Man didn't take you, who burned down your lab?" I asked Redmond.

"I did," Redmond said. "We didn't want to leave anything behind."

I thought about the safe where he had indeed left something for me—the special key drive that detailed how he had adapted my chip. I didn't know if he'd ever told Hyden about it, but there was no reason to bring it up. It was more of a backup in case anything happened to Redmond. And he was fine.

"So you've been working together. What can you do now?" I asked. "You can't remove the chip?" Even though Hyden had already told me, I had to ask.

He shook his head. "No. I haven't made much progress there."

I knew he was going to say that. But the chance that we could get it out of me and Michael and my brother . . .

Suddenly I remembered Hyden saying something about the chip and my brother before I fell asleep. I turned to face him.

"What was that you said about everyone going to the cabin? My brother, Michael, Eugenia?"

"Ernie, my bodyguard, made sure they got there safely," Hyden said.

"They're safer there, at that altitude," Redmond said. "He can't access a chip there that he can't identify."

Redmond's level of comfort with this plan reassured me . . . somewhat.

"Like the way they say phone reception used to be?" I asked.

"Very much so," Redmond said.

"There was no time to discuss it with you," Hyden said. "Once I saw that my father could blow up the chips, I had to move to protect your family."

My brother. So far away in the mountains. "I didn't even get to say goodbye."

"I know. I'm really sorry about that. But I've rigged up something for you." Hyden brought me over to an airscreen. "We can't risk this again—the fewer signal links, the better. But I knew you'd want to see for yourself. So we're doing this once."

He pulled up a chair in front of the screen and I sat. He touched an icon and Tyler's face appeared.

"Tyler!" I leaned in closer to the screen.

"Monkey-Face!" Tyler grinned.

I recognized the weavings behind him from the family room of the chalet. "You look so good. Everything okay?"

"We had ice cream sundaes for dessert tonight."

"It's really late. You should be in bed."

Michael joined him on the screen. "I let him stay up to see you."

"So everyone's all right there? Eugenia too?"

"We're all fine," Michael said. "Now."

"What do you mean, 'now'?"

"Well, it was weird," Michael said. "One minute we were at home, and the next moment we woke up at the cabin. None of us can remember coming here. This guy, Ernie, shows up—"

"You tackled him," Tyler said.

"What would you do when a strange guy shows up—"

"A Middle!" Tyler bounced up and down.

"Don't interrupt," I said softly

Michael continued, "He explained to us why we're safer, but never how we got here."

"We were kidnapped," Tyler said in that half-joking, half-truthful way that only kids can pull off.

I glared at Hyden standing beside me. He shrugged as if to say it had been the only way. Then he motioned to his watch to remind me to wrap it up.

"I have to go. But you do what Michael tells you, okay?"

"Okay, Callie. You come join us soon," Tyler said.

Michael looked serious. "Be good."

"Be careful," I said.

The screen went blank as their images faded into pixels.

"Sorry it couldn't be longer," Hyden said, nodding to the airscreen. "But we can't risk any interceptions."

I stood and faced him. He stepped back.

"So you drugged my family?" I said.

"Ernie probably gave them a light sedative so they wouldn't panic. He had to get them out of the house fast, don't forget."

I felt my face get hot. "That's what you did to me. That mint strip. I never fall asleep in cars."

"Today was a rough day," he said. "We had to get you all to places of safety. And we did that. Tyler is safe there. You're safe here."

"Don't ever do that to me again." I clenched my fists at my sides. "Or to my family. Just try talking to me next time."

"Okay," he said. "I'm sorry."

His shoulders lowered. If he wasn't truly sorry, then he was a pretty good actor. I focused on the blank screen. I wanted to go back to that good feeling of seeing Tyler's face again, smiling. I had hated the chips for a million reasons before, but now it was worse. Now they were responsible for keeping us apart.

"Why can't you take me there?" I asked.

"They're safer without you," Hyden said. "You're the one he wants."

"How many times do I have to say goodbye?" I stared at the airscreen, willing it to come on again.

Hyden was silent for a moment. "It's late. You must be tired."

I rubbed my face. "Where do I sleep?"

He showed me the section with the living quarters, which were surprisingly modest. My room, like the others, looked like a dorm room. Really small, with just the basics. A tiny desk and bathroom.

"It's not fancy," Hyden said. "I put all the money into the technology. And I try to keep moving for security reasons."

"That's got to be hard."

"You know what it's like," he said. "Running from place to place."

Images from the past year flashed through my mind—sleeping bags on floors, overturned desks, running from marshals.

"How many Metals do you think there are?" I asked.

"I'm guessing my father has close to fifty. So there's about another fifty out there somewhere."

"Have you heard of a Starter named Emma?"

He shook his head. "I don't think so. No. She someone you're looking for? Or avoiding?"

"She's Helena's granddaughter. I promised I'd find her."

"I understand," he said, hands in pockets. "You just have to realize, not everyone wants to be found."

⊗ ⊗ ⊗

That night I dreamt I was standing in a field alone at night, with tall grass up to my waist. One tree stood in front of me. A red tree.

The Old Man walked out from behind the tree. The pixels on his mask danced and chased each other, glowing blue and giving off that slight buzzing sound.

"Callie. Where have you been?" he said in his raspy electronic voice. "I've missed you."

"I thought you were gone," I said.

"I'm right here, Callie. You know that. I'll never leave."

He approached. I backed up. Hyden rose from the tall grass underneath the tree. I thought he was going to help me. But he stood beside his father, walking toward me.

"We'll never leave," Hyden said.

As they got closer, all I could see were the blue pixels.

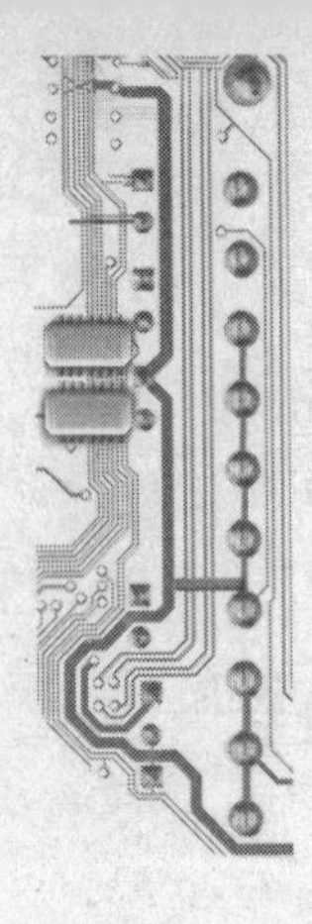

CHAPTER SIX

When I woke up, it took a moment to remember that I was at Hyden's place. My head hurt. It could have been whatever Hyden used to sedate me. Or it might have been my chip. I blamed a lot of things on my chip these days. Anything that messed with your head that much had to have side effects.

I went into the cramped bathroom, showering quickly because I wanted to go find Redmond. Alone.

But when I went into the main lab, Redmond wasn't there. Hyden stood at an airscreen, his sleeves rolled up, punching in codes. Before I could duck back out, he spotted me and waved me over. Surrounding him was a magical clutter of weird plasmas, elements that looked like bundles of tiny threads, the ends floating in the air. Liquids moved through invisible tubes.

"What are you doing?" I asked.

"I'm working on a blocker for you," he said.

"So my chip can't be tracked?"

"Don't get too excited. It could take a while." He stepped away from the airscreen.

"Redmond made a temporary one for me." I felt the back of my head. "It's still there, it just doesn't work."

I thought about my dream last night. How could I trust the son of the Old Man? My mom used to quote an expression, "The apple doesn't fall far from the tree." Hyden clearly had the technical genius of his father. But what else did he have?

He gave me a curious look. "Do I make you nervous?"

I shrugged. Was I that easy to read?

"I know," he said. "You woke up thinking, what am I doing with the Old Man's son?" He wiggled his fingers in a spooky motion. "Just because my father is a monster doesn't mean I am. In fact, I know exactly what I don't want to be, because of him."

"And sons never turn out to be a lot like their dads?"

"Well, you'll just have to watch me to make sure I don't go to the dark side." He ran his hand through his hair and stared at his airscreen. "I've been working twenty-four-seven to try and stop him."

Hyden had to feel responsible. Because he was. He was the one who'd come up with the technology.

"And now we're running out of time," he said. "He escalated everything with that bombing."

I stared at one of the tubes near him. A rainbow of colors flowed through it.

"Wasn't it a waste for him to destroy a Metal?" I asked. "He can't make any more."

"It was worth it to him to get you. Which he almost did."

I turned at the same time he did and accidentally brushed his bare arm with my hand. Hyden recoiled, held his arm, and squeezed his eyes shut as if to will away the pain.

"Are you okay?" I remembered the way he'd reacted at the parking garage.

He sucked in a breath. "It's nothing."

But it obviously was something. He opened his eyes. A flush of embarrassment came over his cheeks.

"Don't worry about it," he said, not making eye contact.

"I didn't mean to," I said. "What's wrong, Hyden? What happened to you?"

He looked at me as if he wanted to explain but couldn't find the words.

"I have to go. Sorry," Hyden said over his shoulder as he left.

⊗ ⊗ ⊗

The sterile lab was empty. I went into the hall, wondering where else a scientist would be. Then I smelled coffee. I followed the smell, and it led me to the kitchen.

It was a utilitarian, almost industrial kitchen, very basic, but large. Redmond stood with his back to me, brewing coffee. "Hello, Callie," he said without turning.

"How did you know it was me?"

"Your footsteps are much lighter than Hyden's or Ernie's. And I knew you'd come looking for me." He turned and smiled. "Want some?" He raised the coffee carafe.

"Sure." I looked at the counter and saw various cereals in glass jars. "I thought you Brits only drank tea."

I took a cup and stirred in some milk.

He put his finger to his lips. "Shh. Don't tell the queen," he said with a twinkle in his eye. "So I hear you're living in Helena's house?"

"She left it to me. Half of it. The other half goes to Helena's granddaughter. Once I find her."

"I know Emma. Met her several times. And her mother." He looked down.

"I'm sorry." I sipped my coffee.

Emma's mother—Helena's daughter—would have been a Middle, of course. Whenever anyone spoke of Middles, it brought up the sadness. I didn't know her. Whether Redmond had known her well or not, anytime the conversation went to losing a Middle, it brought on the memories of all the Middles you'd lost. It would just make both of us sad. I wasn't going to let him go down that path.

"What's Emma like?" I asked.

"All the ladies in that family are stubborn and opinionated. Must be in their genes. Especially Emma. Thought she knew how to fix the world. Typical Starter, as you call them."

"If you see her, will you tell her about her grandmother? And her inheritance."

"If I do, I'll tell her." He stared at his coffee. "What's it like living in Helena's house?"

"Beautiful. Feels like she's still there."

"She was quite a gal," he said. "She wanted to save the Starters. If only she had known that the man she hated the most had a son, a Starter who shared her goal."

I thought about Hyden. He was so complicated.

"What's wrong with his arm?" I asked. "Do you know?"

"His arm? You mean his whole body, don't you?"

I was totally confused.

"I should let him explain it to you," he said.

"Was he injured?"

"Just don't touch him and you'll be all right. Once I accidentally brushed his hand. It took a week before he relaxed around me again."

"And he trusts you?"

"As much as he trusts anyone."

That reminded me of his father's warning.

"Do you know his father?" I asked.

"I know of him. And what he wants to do. If he can get ahold of the full technology, he'll have no qualms about selling it to the highest bidder—a terrorist regime or worse. And that's why I'll put up with living like a gopher."

"Can't we just reclaim it? Get the rest of the Metals and find a way to eventually remove or nullify the chips?"

"We can't take it back. We need to work on countermeasures."

"Why not just give it to the government and let them work on it?"

"Hyden doesn't trust them. I'm not sure I do either. It's an outrage, locking up homeless Starters in institutions."

I saw his point.

"Redmond, for someone to connect to my chip, they'd have to have access to the technology. But only Hyden and his father have it, right?"

"Far as I know."

I thought about the voice that had sounded like my father. Where would he have gotten access to the technology to get in my head anyway? One more reason it couldn't have been my father.

⊗ ⊗ ⊗

When I found Hyden later, studying a pad in his tech lab, I asked if we could talk. He was working with equations I couldn't decipher. Redmond was on the other side of the lab.

Hyden got up and walked me to a conference room. We

sat at chairs around a table. A fat, leafy plant decorated the middle of the table, with a grow light aimed on it.

"This space is perfect for thinking. And private conversations," he said. He opened a drawer under the table and pulled out two Supertruffles. "You look like you could use one of these."

He tossed me one, making sure we didn't touch.

"What did you want to talk about?" he asked as he unwrapped his Supertruffle.

"Don't worry, it's not about you." I fiddled with my Supertruffle. "Your father pretended to be my father."

"He did? When?"

"The day of Prime's demolition. He sounded just like him. Even knew our personal code phrase."

"I wouldn't put anything past him. It's not hard to create a voice. He just needed to find a sample on the Pages and then extrapolate from that. I'm sure your father had a voice sample on his Page, right? Everyone does."

Images of my dad fishing, talking to the camera, flashed through my memory. Only the oldest Enders didn't believe in documenting some part of their lives for everyone to access.

"Of course," I said.

"He used his voice to get to you." Hyden thought for a moment. "What did your father do?"

"Inventor. He was part of the team that invented the handlite." I unwrapped my Supertruffle.

Hyden leaned forward in his chair. "The handlite? That's huge. What else did he work on?"

"I don't know. He didn't talk about his work much. If we asked, he would joke, say it was too boring to be of any interest. And then he'd talk about holos or old films. He loved those." I took a deep breath. "He never knew his parents," I said. "And my mother lost hers to a car accident. Then she had me in her thirties. But the spores took her."

"I'm sorry."

I shrugged. "You just never know, do you?"

An image of my mother rose in my mind, and I suddenly felt exhausted and on the verge of tears. The chocolate tasted bitter in my mouth.

"I saw the spore fall on her arm," I said softly. "My world stopped that day."

"I know," he said.

For a moment, his eyes locked onto mine. I knew he wanted to comfort me. This was the kind of moment where any normal person would touch your shoulder or offer a hug. But not Hyden. I swallowed hard and tried to change the subject.

"Do you hate Enders?" I asked. "Except for Redmond, of course."

"I don't hate all of them, just the ones who make the rules, who set the laws that say Starters can't work and have to be locked up in institutions. Didn't they see they were giving Starters no way out?" He shook his head. "You must hate them too. Look at what they've done to you. Killed your parents, forced you out on the streets."

"I don't hate all of them." I rolled the wrapper in my hands into a ball. "Some of them . . . I know they were scared too. They saw themselves getting older with no income to support themselves. They needed those jobs."

He finished his Supertruffle and rubbed his hands to wipe off the crumbs. "What do you want, Callie Woodland?"

"I want my family back."

"Can't have it, sorry. You have to make a new family out of what you have left," he said. "We all do. You're lucky you've got your brother."

Tyler. He was the one person who could make me stop obsessing over the voice.

"I want him to have real peace," I said. "A safe home where he won't have to worry about being kidnapped by your father, by anybody. I want the chip out of his head. That would be a start."

"I don't know if we'll ever be able to do that." He looked down. "Maybe you'll settle for just feeling safe a day at a time?"

"No. I won't be happy until I know he and I are no longer Metals."

Hyden's eyes told me he didn't think that was possible.

"What, you think we can't have that?" I asked.

"I didn't say anything," he said.

"You don't know what it's like, to feel this foreign object in your head that someone as vile as your father can invade. It's something I live with every minute of the day. Sometimes I want it out so bad I think I'll do it myself."

"Callie," he said, "you don't mean that."

"I want to have someone try to remove it."

Hyden shook his head. "We've never been able to successfully remove a chip. Not that Redmond's tried with humans, but he did with lab animals. And we lost every one."

"Don't tell me that." I took the chocolate wrapper I'd been holding and flung it into a trash can. "I need to believe that someday this will be out of Tyler and me. That we'll be free from him. I'm sure I'm not the only Metal who feels this way."

I looked at the green plant on the table and realized my vision was going blurry again.

"Callie?" Hyden said.

His voice seemed very far away.

Helena's memory this time was in Prime Destinations. Images of donor girls, with words—"skier," "snowboarder," "ballet dancer"—flashing around them. The voice of Tinnenbaum, the master salesman, selling her on their skills. A rush of feeling from Helena.

Those happy faces—No idea what they're getting into—Save them!

"Callie?"

The memory faded. But Helena's sense of purpose lingered. I knew what we had to do.

"We should go find the other Metals," I said.

Hyden stared at me like I was speaking a foreign language. I looked back at the plant on the conference table. Everything was now crystal clear.

"We need to find the other Metals, the donors that your father created," I said. "And keep them safe."

"Where?" He looked around the room. "Here?"

"Where else? It's big, it's underground. These will be Metals that your father can't get, can't blow up or use in other ways. Until you and Redmond can develop a way to block your father completely, this makes the most sense."

Hyden folded his hands behind his head and gazed at the ceiling. "I guess we have the space. We could get more furniture."

"You said you could scan for them. Show me how."

We entered the lab. Redmond was still working on the other side. Hyden went right to his airscreen, and began plucking the icons. A grid appeared over a map of greater Los Angeles.

He squinted at the image and changed the view, looking at different sections. Finally, he stopped and locked on the grid. A red dot pulsed.

"What's that?" I asked.

"That could be a Metal."

"It's not very far away," I said. "We could go find out in person."

"Wait, we're going to jump in without a plan? How can I trust this random Metal?" he asked. "Bringing them in here, with all my research?"

"Any Metal out there is like me, right? They don't know what to do with your research and they don't care. But if you're worried, there's a lock on your lab. Use it."

I could see he still had his doubts.

"What if you had found Reece before your father did?" I asked. "She'd still be alive. I think that's worth any imagined risk."

Hyden rubbed the back of his neck. "I don't know, Callie. We'd need help."

"You said your father was doing this, collecting the Metals," I pressed. "Don't you want to beat him at his own game?"

I saw his eyes narrow. That got him. He pulled out his cell phone and sent a Zing to someone. In less than a minute, a man appeared in the doorway of the lab.

"Callie, this is Ernie," Hyden said.

Ernie commanded attention, with his smooth, dark skin and muscles that threatened to burst out of his expensive suit. But his most unusual feature was the thick black hair that covered his head. It was a rare sight on an adult.

He was a *Middle*.

He extended his hand. I was still staring at that hair. I caught myself and shook his hand.

"You're the one who took Tyler to the cabin?" I asked.

"And the other two, yes."

"So you live here too?" I asked, thinking of his quick appearance after Hyden's Zing.

"He does. He's my full-time bodyguard and an all-around good guy." He turned to Ernie. "Callie wants to find more Metals. So we're going to try."

"I'll go prepare the car," Ernie said.

He gave me a polite nod and left.

"He's a Middle," I whispered.

"Yeah, very valuable," Hyden said softly.

I wondered how a Middle bodyguard could have afforded the vaccine.

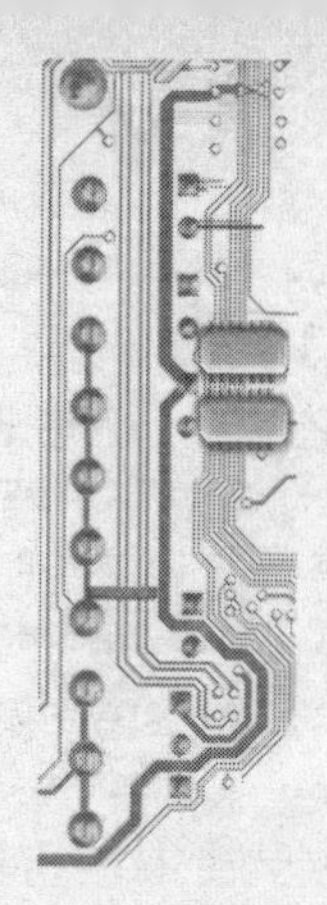

CHAPTER SEVEN

I sat in the passenger seat of Hyden's special SUV, and Ernie rode in back. Hyden pressed a button, and a massive airscreen came up between him and the dash. A grid of the area filled the space.

I looked around. "Where's the computer for that?"

Ernie popped the console between us. It looked like he'd opened up a service bot, there were so many parts inside.

"I have another one in the back," Hyden said. "You can never have too many computers."

The airscreen had everything: depth, dimensionality, and animation. Hyden reached in, plucked out a hidden page, and pulled it to the front.

"How can you scan when we're in here?" I asked. "Isn't it blocked?"

"Blocked from incoming signals. I raised the antennae to extend our reach."

"Where's the red dot now?" I asked.

"Long gone," Hyden said. "But there's got to be another one nearby."

I saw a black dot pulsing on the grid. It moved as we did, so I figured that was the marker for us. I watched the screen for any sign of a red dot.

"How long will it take?" I asked.

"I'm guessing it could be a lot like fishing," Ernie said. "Ever been fishing?"

"Yeah, I have." I thought about those times with my dad.

"Then you know. It could take all day." He stretched out the "all" to make it sound like an eternity.

⊗ ⊗ ⊗

We drove on the freeways for half an hour with no sighting on the grid. Ernie saw a city sign and suggested we exit. He said this zone had a reputation for being a little wilder, and he just had a feeling about it. Not long after we got off the freeway, a blinking red dot appeared.

Ernie pointed to the grid. "Chip alert."

Hyden zoomed in on the screen. "Okay, Metal, just stay there until we can get to you."

"How far away are we?" I asked.

"About fifteen minutes—if that dot stays in one place."

I kept my eye on the screen. The red dot held steady. We drove a couple of miles on city streets. A group of protesters was holding signs near a government building. There were Enders and Starters, waving signs at cars. One read *Bring Back the Red Cross,* referring to one of the many charities that had lost its funding in hard times. Charities that would have helped unclaimed Starters.

I agreed with them, but they didn't know that. They just

saw a big, expensive SUV, and they shouted at us as we drove past.

Hyden looked at the grid. "We're almost there."

He drove a few more blocks, and I watched our black dot get closer to the red dot.

"Look around, the Metal could be here," Hyden said as he turned the corner.

The two dots overlapped. Ernie spotted her first. A Starter sitting on a bus bench. Asian, with short hair.

"That's her," I said. "The pretty one with black hair."

"The *perfectly* pretty one with zero physical imperfections," Hyden said.

She stood, as if tired of waiting for the bus, and started walking.

"You're sure she's the one?" I asked.

"Only one way to find out," Ernie said.

Hyden pulled over to park ahead of the girl as she walked toward us.

Several blue lights flashed on the computer. It reminded me of Redmond's monitor back at his old lab, the one that showed my chip.

"Go, Ernie," Hyden said. "Cover her eyes!"

"Wasn't I supposed to persuade her?" I said.

Ernie had his hand on the door. "You want to talk to her?"

"No," Hyden said. "We don't want to lose her."

As the petite girl passed our car, Ernie jumped out and lunged for her. But she spotted him. Her face registered alarm but she wasn't intimidated. She leapt straight up into the air to get away from him, then did a somersault midair and landed on a thick wall. She ran along it until she came to the end; then she leapt off and reached for a tree branch. She swung out and landed on a table at an outdoor café, sending cups flying and patrons scattering.

Ernie tried to chase her, but she was outsmarting him. He couldn't seem to anticipate her next move. She went right, he went left.

I watched it all from the car window. "This is not how I thought it would go."

"At least we know her body's not being hijacked. She's too good, too smooth," Hyden said. "That's all her."

"What do you mean?"

"You saw—Reece had the jerky movements."

"The Old Man used to be able to hijack people perfectly."

"Under perfect circumstances. Here, he has no cooperation of the donor body. It's not like he's in the Prime lab, setting up both donor and renter. His first-access signal from a distance has far less control."

I nodded, even though I wasn't positive I understood. I turned my attention back to Ernie. Finally, he anticipated the girl's move correctly. As she leapt out, hoping to catch a store's awning to get away, he caught her in his arms on the upswing instead.

"He's got her," I said.

Hyden unlocked the back panel door and raised it with a button so all Ernie had to do was throw the kicking, biting, screaming Metal in the back. He kept one hand over her eyes, then climbed in after her. She stopped screaming, but I was afraid she would tear his eyes out, because she reached for him as he slammed the back door. But in one quick move, he put his hand to her neck and she froze. Her eyes became glassy; then she slumped down as if she'd suddenly fallen asleep.

"She okay?" Hyden yelled back to Ernie.

"Out like a baby," he said.

I saw Ernie held a tiny disc in his palm. He slipped it into a pocket as Hyden drove us away.

"Why cover her eyes?" I asked.

"In case she was being hijacked," Hyden said. "But she wasn't."

"If I'd had time, I would've blindfolded her," Ernie said. "But she was hopping around like a bunny rabbit with its tail on fire."

Ernie sat beside her body in the back cargo area.

"Is she going to be all right?" I asked, staring at her shiny black hair.

"Sleeping Beauty will wake up," Ernie said. "Eventually."

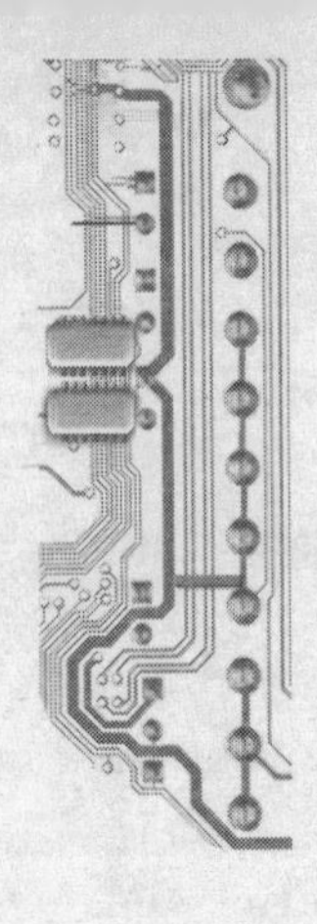

CHAPTER EIGHT

By the time we got to Hyden's place, the Metal Ernie had captured lay in the back, gently rocking to the car's movement. It was hard to believe this was the same girl who just an hour ago had been leaping through the air and clawing at Ernie like a wildcat. I wondered what she'd be like when she woke up.

"Wouldn't it have been better if she came of her own free will?" I asked. "Now she's going to be angry."

"You wanted her, we got her," Ernie said.

Hyden gave me an apologetic look as he pulled into the garage. Ernie got out, holding his gun close to his chest. He checked the place over just as Hyden had before. Then he pressed the button on the wall.

"He's talking to Redmond?" I asked.

"To make sure everything is okay," Hyden said.

When Ernie returned to the car to get the Metal, he slung her over his shoulder as if she were a duffel bag, her weight barely affecting his confident stride. He put her on a bed in one of the empty rooms not far from mine while we watched from just outside the door.

"It'll be best if you're here when she comes to," he told me, handing me the wallet he'd fished from her purse. "Her name is Lily."

I sat on the bed. I wondered how I'd feel, waking up in a strange place, having some girl I didn't know staring at me. But better she see me than Ernie.

After a few minutes, Ernie brought in a tray holding a turkey and cheese sandwich and a glass of apple juice.

Soon, Lily started twitching and mumbling. Then she opened her eyes with a start.

"What?" she said, disoriented. "Who are you?"

"I'm Callie. And you're okay. It's safe here."

She struggled to sit up.

"Just rest," I said. "Are you hungry?" Food could turn an enemy into a friend . . . or at least buy a little trust.

I brought the tray over. She picked up the sandwich and sniffed. Then she bit into it.

"Have you got more?" she asked.

I knew then we were going to be okay.

Over the next couple of weeks, we brought many more Starters to the lab. We were able to convince most of them by talking instead of using force. But no matter how we brought them in, they all wanted to stay. We had a real dorm going, full of Metals with various skill sets. Some of those skills had been exploited when the Starters were rented, like wrestling or martial arts, and they continued to practice them if it was possible. But other skills, like cooking or making repairs, became useful in our community.

Meals were taken in shifts to accommodate everyone in the dining room. It was just off the kitchen, a large, white-walled, bare-floored space with worktables, and dinner was the happiest time of the day. Breakfast and lunch were grab-and-run, but I wanted everyone to eat dinner together, partly because it made sense to share the cooking duties, but also because it made the Starters a community.

I missed Tyler. Hyden convinced me that the risk of doing another airscreen-talk session was too great. And I wasn't sure that it wouldn't just make it harder on both of us in the end. It was easier not to hear my little brother's voice. It kept me focused on what I had to do.

Rescue Metals.

Hyden and I got so good at it that sometimes we even did it without Ernie. If Hyden had to touch someone, he used a towel or a jacket as a barrier. We were both more relaxed around each other, but he still hadn't told me what was behind his inability to touch.

"Hyden, what happened to you?" I asked one day when we were driving on a stretch of highway, alone on a Metal hunt. "Why can't you be touched?"

He was silent for a long moment, then inhaled deeply. He held his breath as if considering whether to answer me. Then he let it out with a sound that I hoped was relief—but maybe was a huff.

"I was working in the lab, with my father. This was back before we split. My mother was there; she'd just brought us cocoa with marshmallows." He smiled. "I don't remember most of that day, but I remember the marshmallows. Weird, right?"

I shook my head. I knew what that was like, remembering

some bizarre detail about my life before the spores. Before I became a Starter.

Hyden cleared his throat. "There was an accident, an explosion. We never figured out why, but it happened. My dad was all right, but my mother and I were burnt." His voice cracked on the word "burnt." "We had treatments, surgeries, but there was pain for months."

"That's awful."

"Once we were healed to the point where we could handle cloth on our skin, we still couldn't handle touch. They tried skin desensitization therapy, where a therapist touches you skin on skin, but neither of us could take it. It was excruciating."

"When was this?"

He gripped the wheel more tightly. "Two years ago. They said I was lucky to be alive, that in the past they wouldn't have been able to fix me. Look at me—you can't really tell."

He pushed back his shirt and held up his arm. The skin was perfect.

"So if your skin has been repaired—"

"And my nerves."

"And your nerves, then why—"

"There's a disconnect in my brain. My brain perceives pain when I'm touched."

I thought about that. "And when you touch someone else?"

"I can only do it with some barrier, like gloves or my jacket."

"Like when you pushed me away at the bombing."

He nodded.

"So it could get better someday?" I'd been feeling sorry for myself, missing my parents' warm hugs. But Hyden couldn't be touched by anyone.

"If it's determined to be a phobia, then yes. They're not sure."

I stared out at the torn billboards by the highway that no one could afford to rent anymore. Then something occurred to me.

"You wanted the mind-body transfer for you and your mother, didn't you? That's why you invented this."

He breathed in again. Only I didn't hear the exhale.

"I hoped it would have many medical applications." He sounded so weary.

"But what happened?"

"She died of complications before I could get it going."

"And then your father had his own ideas?"

"He lied to me about what Prime would be," he said slowly. "And then it was too late."

We continued driving for another half mile before the scanner picked up a signal.

"It's south. Get off the freeway," I said.

He took the next exit and turned right. We drove about a mile. The scanner showed we were close.

I pointed across the street. "It's coming from that direction."

We looked and didn't see any Starters. Just Enders.

He turned right. "It's from down this street."

We saw a dark-haired Starter, average height, good-looking, wearing an unbuttoned plaid shirt over a T-shirt. He leaned against a concrete planter and drank from his water bottle.

Hyden slowed down and pulled over while we looked at the Starter.

"His clothes look shabby," I said.

"What are you, the fashion police?"

"You know what I mean. He doesn't look like an ex-donor, a Metal."

"Most of them went back to the streets," he said. "Not like you. They didn't even get paid when Prime came down."

He was right. I felt so stupid. I wasn't judging him, just looking for clues. But only their appearance could really tell us, and now that I had a better look, this one was close to perfection. He closed his water bottle and slung it over his shoulder.

Hyden parked the car. "Stay here. Don't get out."

Before I could say something, he was out and walking toward the Starter.

Hyden tried to be casual, but the guy wasn't returning Hyden's smile. Instead, he looked nervous, shaking his head at Hyden's questions.

Suddenly the Starter pushed him and ran down the street. Hyden flinched in pain but took off running after him. I climbed over the console to get to the driver's seat and followed them.

I didn't know what Hyden was going to do when he caught the guy—he obviously couldn't touch him. The Starter ran into a dead-end alley and saw that he was cornered. I pulled the SUV in right behind Hyden. The Starter turned his back to climb a wall, but Hyden reached up and held something small to the back of the guy's neck so that only the item made contact. The Starter fainted.

Hyden wrapped his jacket around his hands, and together we picked the guy up and put him in the SUV. An Ender at the end of the alley yelled at us, but we ignored him. Hyden climbed into the back with the Metal while I got in the driver's seat.

"Go," he said.

I started driving. "Where?"

"Head to the freeway."

I set the navigator and concentrated on the road.

After some rustling around from the back, somebody climbed up to sit in the passenger seat next to me. Only it wasn't Hyden. It was the guy with the plaid shirt.

Panicked, I accidentally swung the car into the next lane. "What happened to Hyden?"

I turned around and saw Hyden's body sprawled out in the back of the car.

Plaid Shirt guided the wheel with his left hand. "Careful with my car."

I looked at him. He smiled, and something about him seemed familiar.

"Hyden?" I asked.

"Yes," Plaid Shirt said.

It was so weird. "Is that really you?"

"In the flesh. Well, actually, in the borrowed flesh."

"What do you think you're doing? You jacked that guy."

"It's for his own good. He would have fought us." He took his hand off the wheel but nodded toward the road. "Focus."

I climbed the freeway on-ramp. Hyden put his hand on my right arm. But it wasn't his hand—it was the plaid-shirted guy's. The whole thing was so weird. I wasn't even sure I trusted Hyden. How well could you know someone who could be anyone they wanted to be?

"Are you really okay back there?" I craned around to get another look at Hyden's body in the back.

"Don't worry."

"What's his name?" I asked.

"Who?"

"The guy you're in."

Hyden started patting his pockets. He pulled out a wallet and looked at a photo ID of himself.

"Jeremy Stone." He looked through the wallet. "Not much cash. Either he was one of the donors at the end who didn't get paid, or he ran through the money."

"How did you get in Jeremy so fast like that?" I asked.

"Guess."

I thought it over. "You have a chip in your head."

"I was the first one. To test my invention."

His hand remained on my arm, sending its warmth through me. I didn't want to like it. I refused to like it. But the warmth was undeniable.

"This isn't so different from your father," I said. "He wears a mask, and you're wearing a whole-body mask."

He stared out the windshield. I suspect he was a bit ashamed. If he wasn't, he should have been.

"You wouldn't want to be me, Callie. Can you imagine hating your own body? I'm a prisoner inside it."

I'd been a real prisoner, inside Institution 37, and it had been the worst time of my life. Much worse than being a squatter. But I had been able to escape.

Could Hyden?

"All the Metals are prisoners," I said. "Until we can defeat your father."

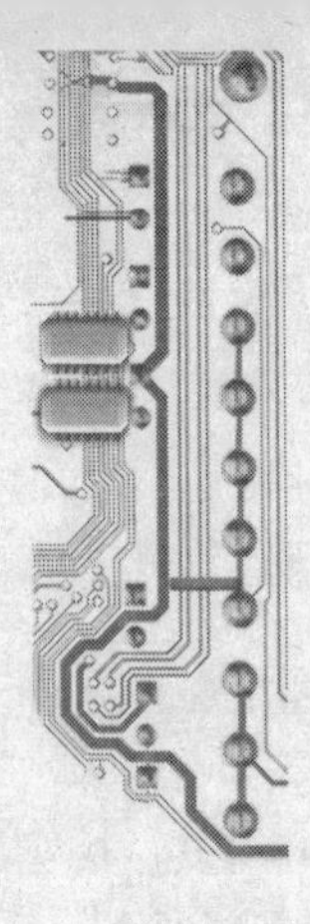

CHAPTER NINE

Hyden guessed that Jeremy had not eaten for a while because he soon got very hungry and wanted flash food from a drive-thru. He started to order for just us.

"No!" I shouted at the order machine. "Make that thirty of everything—burgers, fries, and chocolate shakes." I turned to Hyden. "We can't just bring back food for ourselves. Food will make them trust us."

When we drove back to his place, he hesitated before getting out of the SUV. "Listen, I don't want the Metals to see me in a borrowed body. Too weird." Then he told me about a private room where I could meet him. We went up separately, me carrying the large bags of food. The Metals were so thrilled to see the food that they didn't bother to ask why I wasn't sitting and eating with them.

Hyden's secret room was about the size of two of our dorm-type rooms, with a bed and a desk.

"So this is where you hide out sometimes," I said, admiring the decor. "Nice of you to share it with me."

He pulled a sheet from a shelf and spread it on the floor.

"Picnic?" I asked.

"Why not?"

One wall was covered with an image of a cliff overlooking the ocean, and I could practically feel the brisk spray on my face.

"That's beautiful," I said.

"It helps." He shrugged. "But it's not the real thing."

I put the food on the cloth on the floor. He remained standing, so I did too. He moved closer to me than ever before, about a foot away. He put his hands out toward me, palms to the ceiling, in an invitation to touch.

"Callie."

I placed my hands over his. He closed his eyes, as if he was savoring the sensation.

Finally, he opened his eyes. He gently held my hands, caressing them, then turning his palm until ours matched, in front of us. He slid his fingers down to meet the crooks of mine, and we were grasping each other's hands.

My heart was beating faster. I unclasped my hands and pulled back.

"What's wrong?" he asked.

Jeremy's face looked puzzled. I had to get used to a whole new set of expressions now that it wasn't Hyden's eyes, brows, and mouth.

"It's too weird," I said, motioning to his body.

He moved closer to me. "Please." He touched the back of my hand lightly with his fingers. "Come on. This is the only way I can touch you."

I didn't move. I wanted to see what he'd do next.

"Let's check out his body." Hyden lifted his shirt. "Hey, abs!"

He pretended to be surprised at Jeremy's toned physique. He grinned and then let his shirt fall, covering it again.

He took my hand and gently placed it over his shirt, over his abs.

I let it rest there a moment. Then my mouth went dry and I pulled away.

"What?" he asked.

"It's not you," I said. "I don't want to be part of this." I shook my head. "You stole his body."

He hung his head. I couldn't see his face, but his hesitation suggested he was conflicted. "This is the best I can do. I'm the same inside. It's me in here. You know that."

I knew it, but I didn't know how I felt about it.

"The me inside this shell is still me. What defines me? Skin? You know you can change that with the wave of a laser. Muscle? EMS can build that. Fat? It can fade away with freezing. I hope I'm more than that. Than this." He swept a hand in front of Jeremy Stone's body. "That I am what I think, what I believe. What I feel."

He brought his hand to my face. Slowly, he traced his finger along my temple, to the side of my cheek.

"I miss touching," he whispered.

He ran his finger down my jawline. I closed my eyes and felt the caress.

"Nice." It was so faint, it was like a breath.

I moved closer. Our lips inched toward each other, pulling together in a kiss. My head spun, feeling the electricity.

We kissed until our lips burned. I traveled to another place, a place that would never have anything as mundane as a name. And then I remembered. . . .

"Your body."

He pulled back to look at me with sleepy eyes. "What about it?"

"We left it in the car."

⊗ ⊗ ⊗

I'd heard of people leaving babies or dogs in cars by accident, before the war, but this was a first. We rushed to the garage.

Hyden unlocked the car and opened the back door hatch. We looked at his body lying there.

"You're still breathing," I said.

"Of course I am."

It felt so bizarre to see it lying there. Hyden cradled his body with a blanket.

"I look so sweet," Hyden said.

"That's not funny."

"I'll take the top part if you can handle the feet," he said.

We carried the body, me behind Hyden. It wasn't hard at first, but after a minute he became ten times heavier. Hyden leaned against the wall so he could press the code to open the door in the garage.

As we entered the elevator, Hyden bumped his real body, the one we were carrying, against the wall.

"Careful," I said. "It's still your body, remember?"

"I know."

"No matter how many people you jack, you can't change who you are," I said.

He had no answer for that.

My arms began to burn from holding him, but I couldn't bring myself to put him down.

Finally, the elevator doors opened to the lab level.

"No one's here," I whispered.

"They must still be in the dining room," he said quietly.

We took his body to his private room and rested it on the couch. Hyden put the blanket over the legs.

"How long will you be asleep?" I asked.

"Hours." He pointed to a disc patch on the neck. "Or longer."

"You're not thinking of keeping that body?" I asked, gesturing to Jeremy's torso.

He stared back at me. I didn't know if I was giving him a new idea or whether he'd been considering it all along.

"It would solve a lot of problems, wouldn't it?"

"You can't." I said this with the firmness I remember my mother using with me at crucial times.

He rubbed his forehead and looked down. "No," he said finally. "I'd never do that to Jeremy."

My shoulders relaxed. "Good."

It was so weird, talking to him in Jeremy's form but staring at Hyden's real body, resting there on the couch.

"We're going to have to explain this to the group," I said.

"You tell them."

"Why not you?" I asked.

"You'll do it so much better. They like you more than me." He forced a smile with Jeremy's lips.

"That's because I listen to them," I said.

My phone rang. I looked at it and saw it was Michael. Michael?

The rule was not to call each other so that the calls couldn't be traced.

"Don't answer," Hyden said.

"It's got to be important." I pressed the talk button. "Michael?" I said into the phone. "Where are you?"

"I'm in Flintridge," Michael said. "Outside the old library."

"Where's Tyler?"

"With Eugenia, at the cabin. He's okay."

Hyden came closer to follow the conversation.

"Why did you leave the mountain?" I said. "It was safe. No one could scan your chip."

At that Hyden shook his head. "Why'd he leave?" he muttered.

"I remembered something," Michael said. "Something that didn't happen to me, but to my renter. I needed to get away from the house so my call wouldn't be traced to it."

"What did you remember?" I asked.

Hyden took the phone from me. "Don't say any more," he said to Michael. "We'll come get you."

He pressed the off button and grabbed his jacket off the back of a chair. "Let's bring him in."

⊗ ⊗ ⊗

When we got to what used to be the Flintridge library, we parked across the street. Sometime during the Spore Wars, the library had been closed and barricaded. A chain-link fence surrounded it.

"I'll go alone," I said. "You stay."

"Callie." Hyden put his hand on his door handle.

"He knows me. He's never even met you. And you aren't even you right now," I said, looking at Jeremy's face. "I'll just go get him and we'll be right back."

I got out and climbed under a hole in the fence. A sea of encampments covered the parking lot. Tents filled with unclaimed Starters, some with down-and-out Enders who'd run out of their money decades ago.

Living longer isn't always the greatest thing.

Some of the Starters stared at me. I didn't look like them

anymore. My clothes weren't in tatters, and my face and hands were clean. I had no water bottle over my shoulder, no handlite. And I was no longer emaciated like them.

I tried not to look scared, tried not to draw any more attention to myself as I scanned the crowd.

Michael, where are you? Why aren't you out front?

I made one whole sweep of the parking lot and came back again. Someone touched my arm, asking for money. I started to open my purse and a swarm of people surrounded me. I felt clammy. This was not a smart decision.

I was having trouble breathing. People grabbed at my arms, pulling me in different directions.

"Please, stop," I said.

I threw down some bills. They scattered off in the wind and the crowd chased after, leaving me free to get away.

As I made my way toward the car, I heard a familiar voice in my head.

Cal Girl? Can you hear me? It's Dad.

I gasped. Don't get excited, this could be the Old Man. "Yes, I hear you." I stopped walking and concentrated.

I'm alive. Don't worry.

It sounded just like him. But it had before too.

Callie?

"How do I know it's really you?" My heart was pounding. "How can I tell?"

Remember what I gave you for your tenth birthday? A red bicycle?

I gasped. The bicycle with the big ribbon. "Where did you hide it?"

In the laundry room. Behind the door.

My heart leapt. It was him. "Where are you? I want to see you."

I know. I want to see you too. How's Tyler?

Tears formed in my eyes. "He's fine. He misses you so much. He used to look at your holo every night, but then we lost it. . . ."

It's okay, Cal Girl.

"Dad? How are you doing this? Reaching me this way?"

Suddenly it was very quiet. I sensed the vacuum, the lack of any sound, emptiness. That awful disconnect that happened sometimes. He was gone. I was hollow inside, worse than when I was hungry and starving on the streets.

I became aware of my surroundings again. Several people were standing in a semicircle behind me. They were sizing me up, this rich girl who talked to herself. Was I crazy and dangerous? Or someone they could attack?

Now that I'd made eye contact, they moved in.

I had to sprint to the car. Hyden saw me and opened the door. He reached out to hoist me up with Jeremy's strong hand. I jumped in, and he screeched away before I could even close the door.

"Where's Michael?" he asked.

"I don't know, couldn't find him."

I pulled the door shut. The people chasing us were a mix of Starters and Enders, all in tatters. They looked like monsters chasing our car, their faces contorted with anger.

It didn't take long to lose them. I wanted to tell Hyden about my father, but this was not the time.

"Use your phone. Call him," Hyden said. "It's worth the risk, just do it!"

I pulled out my phone and called his number. It rang and rang.

"He's not picking up."

The airscreen started to beep. We had a signal on the chip scanner.

"Could that be him?" I asked, looking at the screen.

"It's toward the mountains," he said.

We drove a short distance, tracking the signal. Flintridge was in the foothills, so the terrain became mountainous quickly. The homes thinned out, giving way to stretches of land where some houses had been burned down due to fear of spore contamination.

I prayed the signal was Michael's. It got louder, brighter, and faster.

"We're close," I said. "Here."

"Where?"

"There." I pointed to a body lying on one of the scorched lots.

He slammed his foot on the brake, and I jumped out of the car. Michael's body lay facedown.

"Michael!" I shouted.

I knelt beside his body. Hyden came and stood behind me.

"Michael!" I said, but no response.

I eased him over onto his back and put my ear to his chest. It was warm.

"He's breathing," I said to Hyden. A sense of desperate helplessness filled me. I didn't know what to do. It was awful seeing him like this, unconscious and limp.

I cradled Michael's head on my lap. "What happened?"

"My guess, he was jacked. Then they lost the connection. It's like a dropped call." He looked around. "We can't stay out here in the open. Between us, we've got three chips here. Might as well hang up a sign."

I glanced down the street. I saw some people coming our way. Friendlies? Or not?

"We have to move him," I said.

I was so glad Hyden was in Jeremy's body; his being able to touch people without some barrier made all this a lot easier. He bent down to pick up Michael.

"You know the drill," he said.

I wrapped my arms around his legs. Hyden did most of the lifting.

⊗ ⊗ ⊗

Once we got back to the lab, Ernie took over, carrying Michael's body. Hyden had sent him a Zing explaining everything.

"So this is the body you're borrowing," Ernie said, nodding. "I've been waiting for you to do this."

Ernie put Michael in one of the unused bedrooms. One of the Metals, Avery, checked him over, taking his vitals. Avery was petite and gentle. Her mother had been a nurse.

"All his numbers are pretty normal. Blood pressure, temperature," she said. "Sometimes, all you can do with a patient is wait." She eyed Hyden in Jeremy's body.

"That's actually Hyden," I said to her.

"I know. Ernie told us," she said.

I sensed some disapproval there. But she was too polite to say anything outright.

"I'll stay here with him. You guys can go," I said.

After they'd gone, I looked at Michael lying there. It was good to see him again, but not like this. He looked so vulnerable.

Would he come back to us? What happened?

"Michael." I took his hand in mine. "Michael," I whispered,

as if that would somehow reach his subconscious.

It didn't.

If someone had jacked his body, they would have given it up by now. So why wasn't he coming to?

I sat on his bed for a while, thinking about how fragile life was. Thinking about what Hyden had said about how we're more than just our flesh. I sponged Michael's forehead and spoke softly to him, trying my best not to think negative thoughts. I grew more fearful, wondering if he was ever going to be revived.

His eyelids fluttered.

"Michael?"

He started kicking and tossing from side to side.

"Michael, it's me, Callie."

He stopped thrashing. His eyes opened. He stared at the ceiling.

"Michael?" I whispered.

I wondered if it really was Michael in there. He patted the bed as if trying to find his bearings. Then he looked at me.

"Callie?"

It was him. "It's me, Michael. How are you?"

He sat up. He was covered in sweat.

"Easy," I said.

Michael swung his legs over the side of the bed and sat there a moment, looking down. "My head hurts."

"How do you feel? Other than the head?"

"Foggy. Like I slept for a thousand years."

"What do you remember?"

He rubbed his forehead. "We talked on the phone. . . ." He seemed uncertain, as if fishing for confirmation.

"Yes," I said. "You called me."

"After that, I walked around looking for someplace to wait for you. There were so many people outside the library: Starters, Enders. I headed for the street. Then—then . . ."

"What?"

"Everything went black.

Hyden was right; he was probably hijacked outside the library. Why? Were none of us safe?

"What about Tyler?" I asked. "Is he okay?"

Michael nodded. "He loves Eugenia. Don't worry. He's good, Callie."

Someone knocked at the door. I opened it and saw Hyden and Avery standing there.

"We heard you talking," Hyden said.

"Is he okay?" Avery asked.

They stepped into the room, their voices hushed, as if they were visiting a patient in the hospital.

"He looks pretty good," Hyden said.

"Very good." Avery nodded.

"This is Avery," I said to Michael.

"And who's he?" Michael asked, staring at Hyden inside Jeremy's body.

"His name is Hyden," I said. I decided it was easier not to explain that he was not in his own body.

Avery took Michael's temperature with a forehead monitor. He looked at me with raised brows and a smile.

"How do you feel?" she asked Michael.

Michael rubbed his head. "This is a killer headache."

"I'll get some ibuprofen. And something to eat." Avery hurried off.

"Callie said you had something important to tell us. Something about a memory?" Hyden prompted.

Michael stared off, not looking at any of us. "The strangest thing happened to me at the mountain house. I was outside, watching Tyler fishing in the lake, when I got this flash in front of my face like an Xperience. Like I was right there in the theater. It was like I was watching a movie where I was the star—no, the camera, really. It was my point of view as I walked through the body bank. I had just come out of the restroom and couldn't remember my way out. I went down the wrong hallway and turned a corner and saw a thin body on a gurney, completely covered with a sheet. It looked like a woman, a dead woman. The gurney was being backed out an exit door and the person pulling it was outside already. The sheet slipped, revealing the face. It was an Ender. Now here's the weird part. In the memory, I didn't recognize her. But as me, watching this memory, I knew who it was."

He looked at me. "It was Helena."

I think I had guessed it, but it was hard to hear. "Helena," I repeated.

Michael nodded. "I recognized her from all the pictures in the mansion. But anyway, in the memory, I looked up and saw that it was Trax pulling the gurney."

"Trax? Glasses Trax?" I pictured his thick black rims. "The Ender geek who handled my rentals at Prime?"

"Transpositions. Call them transpositions," Hyden said in a monotone. He seemed a bit shaken.

Michael looked from him to me, as confused as I was over Hyden's reaction. "Yeah, that guy with the glasses. Anyway, I pulled back before he could see me. That was it."

Hyden now looked pale. Sick, even. He stood and walked slowly out of the room.

"What's it mean?" Michael asked.

"The memory belongs to your renter." I rubbed my arms. "So this must be what he saw."

"But why would I remember it?"

"It's been happening to all of us. Your renter must have just gotten your body. Then he stumbled onto this." I paced the room. "I heard Helena die in my head. Trax killed her."

"You don't know. I mean, it could have been someone else. He could have just been doing the cleanup."

"He was hiding the body," I said. "At minimum, he's involved."

Michael looked at me with pleading eyes, as if I had all the answers. I wish.

"Why do we have their memories?" he asked. "Isn't it enough that we gave them our bodies to use?"

I could only close my eyes and nod.

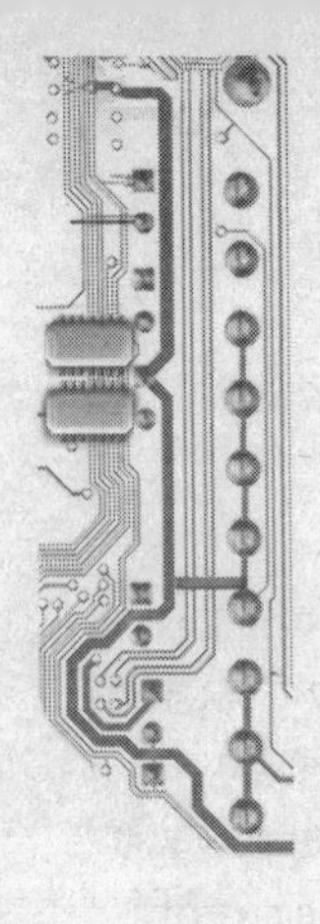

CHAPTER TEN

Hyden drove me to downtown L.A., still in Jeremy's body. Michael wanted to come, but Hyden insisted only the minimum number of Metals could risk getting scanned by being outside. I stared out the window at the grayness and graffiti.

"You sure you want to do this?" Hyden asked.

"I have to try," I said.

"My father has the technology to re-create anyone's voice," he said. "He can access old phone records, any recordings left on the Pages, and extrapolate to create new sentences. You can't trust what you hear, you've seen that now."

I'd told him about my dad accessing me. How he knew about the birthday present. Hyden told me that it was just wishful thinking—that it was his father, not mine, in my head. I leaned my forehead against my hands, searching myself for some way to make him see. Feeling empty was worse when no one understood.

"I can't help it." I pulled my hands away. "If you were me and you loved your father and heard his voice in your head, alive, you'd want to investigate, wouldn't you?"

"You lost me at the 'loved your father' part."

A sigh escaped my lips. "He asked about Tyler."

"It's easy to find that information, even for a normal person. This is my father you're dealing with." He said "father" as if the man were a demon.

"But it sounded so much like him . . . the way he spoke . . ." I stretched my mind for any bit of hope. "And he was cut off." I was grasping at straws, but I kept going. "If it had been your father, he would have gone on longer. Messed with my head more."

Hyden looked at me the way you'd look at a child trying to revive a dead goldfish. "I wish I could convince you how dangerous it is for you to be out there"—he pointed out the window—"with your chip signal just blowing in the wind for my father to access."

He pulled up to a block of government buildings decorated with once-noble statues, now chipped and crumbling. Bored marshals ensured that the line of protestors stayed behind ropes. Hyden paid to park in an underground lot. We climbed the stairs to ground level and looked up at the building with the large engraved letters reading *Hall of Records*.

"You sure you want to do this?" Hyden asked.

I gave him my best "don't ask" look and climbed the stairs.

Inside the lobby, we passed through a body scanner. It went off as I stepped through. Did my chip set it off? I started to perspire. What would I say?

A guard motioned for me to step aside. She waved a wand over me and stopped on my pocket. I pulled out some dollar coins.

We continued walking and passed a Starter leaning against

a wall, at the end of a long line. She had the typical Starter gear: layers, tatters, handlite, and a water bottle slung across her shoulder. But she also had a perfect shape, a model's face, and no visible flaws.

Metal? Maybe if examined under a magnifying glass, she'd display signs of a normal Starter—a few acne scars, some freckles.

Hyden glanced in her direction, then quickly looked away. I smiled at him.

"Bet you'd like to scan her," I said.

His lips barely hinted at a smile. "I think we need to go to the second floor," he said as he pointed to the stairs.

The building was ancient, and neither of us would have trusted the z-lift. Some of the newer buildings were zaprophyte-powered, a complex system of energy created by plants feeding on fungi. The spore dust was a temporary resource for that, and some enterprising people were turning lemons into lemonade that way. But it was controversial, as some felt it released dangerous spore contamination into the air. And it wouldn't last.

On the second floor, after waiting in line, we finally spoke to an Ender at a counter. She had an old airscreen in between us. The images it produced were faded, scratchy, and broken, a lot like the Ender herself.

"Ray Woodland, did you say?" she asked in a croaky voice.

"Yes, he's my father."

"But he's a Middle, right?" she said.

I nodded.

"Then, honey, he's gone," she said in a tired voice, as if this wasn't the first time she'd had to tell a teenager that a parent was dead. "They're all gone."

"Not all of them," I said. "I personally know one. And what about the holo-stars and politicians?"

"They're in a special category," she said, as if I were a child. "But everyone else . . ." She shook her head.

"Can you just look him up, please?" Hyden said.

Her lips pressed together and she started moving her fingers across the airscreen. It was slow to respond and she had to retry several times.

Finally, she came up with a result. She pushed an icon that then reversed the text so I could read it.

RAY WOODLAND, *age 55, deceased.*

It had his address and occupation, "inventor."

"I don't . . . Couldn't there be some mistake?" I said. "There were so many Middles at the same time, there were bound to be some errors."

Hyden looked at me. His expression—on Jeremy's face—was so sad.

The Ender tilted her head. "I feel for you, honey. I really do. You Starters need closure. I'm going to show you something I really shouldn't. But—"

She made a motion like she was zipping her lips shut.

"Okay?" she asked.

"Sure," I said.

I looked at Hyden. We were both confused.

"Just wait over by that door," she said.

She motioned to a door a few feet away. We did as we were told, and a moment later, she opened the door and let us in.

She put her finger to her lips. We nodded and followed her

silently to a back room that was filled with Enders sitting at desks. It was an eerie sight, with no light other than what was emitted from their airscreens. All the screens showed corpses.

"This is where they do all the data entry for the deceased, mostly from treatment facilities," the clerk said.

She leaned over the shoulder of one of the workers and whispered to her.

The worker typed in the air my father's name, birthdate, and address, and an image came up. A man, lying on a cot. A tented sign balanced on his chest showed his name and a long number. His face was white and frozen.

"Ray Woodland," the clerk read from the screen.

My father. Dead. The hope I'd felt spring inside me vanished. It was as if he'd died all over again.

I put my hand to my mouth. Tears flowed down my cheeks. Hyden put his arm around my shoulders. The Ender clerk looked at me and nodded.

"It's better to have closure, dear," she said. "Now you know."

The words stung like acid.

"Let's go," Hyden said quietly.

⊗ ⊗ ⊗

As we made our way to the stairs, Hyden kept his arm around me.

Inside the stairwell, he stopped and faced me. "You okay?"

"It's my fault."

He handed me a tissue. "No, it's not."

"I wanted to find out." I wiped my eyes and struggled to get the words out. "I just didn't think this would be the answer."

"I know." He wrapped me in a gentle hug.

I rested my head on his shoulder and let the tears fall. He held me tighter, as if he could squeeze away the pain.

He couldn't.

And he couldn't squeeze away the creepy feeling I had when the voice came into my head.

Hello, Callie. Sorry to interrupt.

I pulled away from Hyden.

"Who is this?" I said.

A friend.

It was a male voice; sounded like a Middle. I had a guess who it was. Hyden looked at me questioningly.

I put my finger to my lips. Hyden was disguised in Jeremy's body. My jacker could see out of my eyes, but all he would see was Jeremy, a stranger.

And I see you have a friend with you. I'm guessing that's my son in there.

I sighed. It was too late and he was too smart. Jeremy stood back, watching, his expression suggesting he knew what was going on.

"Why aren't you using your electronic voice this time?" I asked Brockman.

It's so pretentious. I decided to just be me.

"So was that also you doing my father's voice?"

He was silent a moment. *What do you mean?*

The stairwell began to feel hot. Stuffy. I tugged at my top, airing it out. Maybe it wasn't him pretending to be my father.

Hot in there? Why don't you leave?

"Why?" I asked. "Do you want me to leave?"

Hyden was fuming. I shaded my eyes so they wouldn't provide a view for his father.

Tell my son to stop fooling around in other bodies, will you?

"Tell him yourself," I said.

I have another idea.

I looked at Hyden and pantomimed something was up. We heard footsteps at the bottom of the stairs. They continued, echoing in the hollow space. Whoever it was, they were coming up to where we were.

Ready?

The hair on the back of my neck rose. It was a girl on the stairs. We'd seen her before. It was the stunning Starter we had seen standing in line. But her eyes had a glazed, dead look. Something was wrong.

"She's jacked!" I shouted to Hyden.

Smart girl.

"Look out!"

The girl—probably an Ender inside—rushed toward Hyden, her arms bent at the elbows in some martial arts stance.

Black belt expert.

"She's a black belt," I said to Hyden.

Hyden—in Jeremy's body—stepped aside quickly, expertly. The girl ran up against the wall.

"So's Jeremy," he said.

The Starter turned and went after Hyden again. They locked arms and struggled, a battle of strength and wills.

She slammed Hyden against the wall, banging his head.

As they continued to fight, I felt something strange. I looked down at my hand. My right pinky moved up and down. Which would not have been so scary except . . .

I wasn't doing it.

Did you see? That's me, making you move. Like a puppet.

My heartbeat raced. At least that was my doing. I threw my hand down to my side. I focused my concentration as hard as I could to make my fingers like steel.

The Metal had a hold on Hyden's neck. She was choking him. I ran over and came from behind, grabbing her around the waist with both arms. I pulled her off Hyden.

"Grab her feet!" I shouted.

She thrashed and kicked, but Hyden managed to get her ankles. She didn't weigh a lot, so we carried her down the stairs.

"What should we do with her?" I asked.

"Take her underground."

As we passed the first floor, we continued down the stairs that led to the underground parking structure. She stopped kicking and screaming.

"Is this low enough?" I asked.

"Go one more," he said.

We climbed down to the lower level. We'd cut off the signal and she became limp. She felt much heavier.

"He's gone," Hyden said, nodding to the girl's body.

"Who?" I asked.

"Whoever was jacking her. One of my father's men."

We pushed the door open with our feet and came out into the underground parking area. Not seeing any guard on this level, we put her down on the ground.

"I'll go get the SUV," he said.

I looked down at her. She was suddenly so harmless, so peaceful, her brown hair flowing around her shoulders. I held out my hand and stared at my pinky.

It was still. Motionless. The way it should be.

Before long, Hyden drove up in the SUV. He leaned out the window.

"How should we do this?" I asked.

He looked past me. "Hey there," he said.

I turned around and saw that she was awake and sitting up.

I walked toward her. "Hi. I'm Callie."

She put her hands on the ground as if she was going to bolt like a feral cat. I came a little closer.

"It's okay, I'm like you." I turned and lifted my hair to expose the scar. "See?"

"You're a Metal," she said with a Southern accent.

"Yes. And I can help you."

She relaxed. "Do you get strange dreams? Not just at night?" Her lip trembled. "They're so weird."

"Yeah, I get them," I said. "Come with me. We've got food, and you'll be safe."

"Y'all have food?"

"Supertruffles in the car," I said.

She gestured at the SUV. "Are there Enders in there?"

"No," I said. "Just us Starters."

She approached cautiously. Hyden stayed in the driver's seat and unlocked the passenger's-side back door. She hesitated, looking at me with a question in her eye.

"He's okay. He's with me," I said.

Hyden's eyes connected with mine, and the Starter climbed inside.

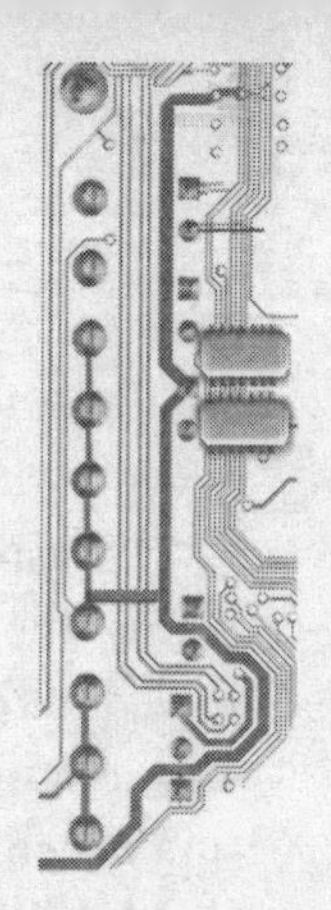

CHAPTER ELEVEN

The girl's name was Savannah. She ate three Supertruffles while we sat in the car. We had to stop her before she ended up emptier than when she started.

"You're right. I should know better," she said as she wiped her mouth with the back of her hand. "My father was a nutritionist."

"So do you know anything about medicine?" I asked. We could always use more medical help.

"A lot. My mother was a surgeon," she said. "I wanted to be premed, but then everything changed with the war."

"What made you go to Prime Destinations?"

She stiffened. She looked at me out of the side of her eyes. I could see she was trying to decide whether she should reveal her story.

"It's okay. We understand better than anyone," I said. "I went there to get money for a home for my sick brother. He had this respiratory condition, and living in abandoned office buildings was just making it worse. I saw it as our only way out."

"I wasn't going to let the marshals take me. I saw them taking the other kids on our block," she said. "I could have stayed in the house, but the government condemned it, said it was contaminated. So I did the body bank."

"When?" Hyden asked.

"A few months ago," she said. "But then some renegades stole all my money. The first day back."

I nodded. I'd heard that story before.

"Guess that didn't happen to you," she said, looking at the SUV.

"We've got plenty of time to tell our stories," I said. "The main thing is, you can trust us."

She hugged her knees to her chest and rested her head against the window. "That sure sounds good to me."

⊗ ⊗ ⊗

When we brought Savannah into our place, I tugged on Hyden's shirt. I mouthed, *What about . . . ?* and gestured to Jeremy's body.

He shrugged.

"Wow, this is nice," Savannah said as she walked into the main room. "Thanks so much for bringing me here, y'all," she said, turning to us. "So this is your place, Hyden?"

"Yeah. By the way, this isn't my body. I'm just borrowing this one," Hyden said.

"Really? I thought only Enders wanted to rent out our bodies," she said, squinting.

"Usually, that's true," Hyden said.

"Where is your body?" she asked.

"In another room," I said. "Why?"

"Can I see?" she asked.

Hyden started to shake his head, but I stepped forward. "Sure. You might as well meet the real Hyden."

Hyden shot me a look. I knew he wasn't crazy about this, but I thought it was important not to make any of the Metals feel excluded.

We went to the room where his body was. There he was, the real Hyden, sleeping on the bed. His breathing was shallow. He looked pale.

"How long has the body been like this?" Savannah asked.

"Not long," Hyden said.

"Because if it goes too long, he needs fluids," Savannah said.

"I know," he said. "I'll take care of it."

"Good," she said. "It's a very nice body, by the way."

"Thanks," Hyden said.

His surprised expression almost made me laugh.

"Come on." I motioned to Savannah. "Let's go find you a room."

⊗ ⊗ ⊗

Savannah wasn't picky. In fact, she was so exhausted, she fell asleep on top of her small bed while I gathered towels and toiletries for her.

I went back out to the main room and found Hyden standing there.

He was in his own body.

His back was to me, but I easily recognized his muscular shoulders, his tousled hair that was neither curly nor straight. My legs weakened. Everything was upside down. He was there, but he was gone. It was the way it should be; he was back where he belonged. In his own body.

But it meant no more touching.

"Hyden?" I whispered.

He turned. I looked at his real body, with that face that I was getting to know, that handsome face with the pain in the eyes.

"What?"

"You didn't wait for me? You just did it?"

He cocked his head. "You wanted me to," he said. "Didn't you?"

I did, of course. But this seemed so sudden. I realized I was secretly expecting something—some last kiss or touch goodbye. Some small moment before it was back to "don't-touch-me" Hyden.

But that was selfish.

"I thought maybe—" I said.

"I know," he said. "Me too."

An invisible wall seemed to stand between us. Finally, the words came out of my throat.

"I hoped . . . you'd wait for me."

"Couldn't. It was getting to be too long. Savannah was right—my body would need fluids."

He was acting like he didn't care, but his eyes met mine and they betrayed him. He looked away. Jeremy's body was lying on the couch next to the bed where Hyden's body had been. Near Jeremy lay a small airscreen unit.

"That's linked to the one in the car?" I asked.

"Shhh . . ." Hyden put a finger to his lips.

Jeremy's eyelids fluttered, and his lips twitched.

He was coming to.

"Aren't you going to do something to control him? He might just come out swinging," I said quietly.

"I'll call Ernie," he said. He pulled out his phone and sent a Zing.

But before Ernie could arrive, Jeremy opened his eyes. His face registered panic. He scrambled to a sitting position, his back pressed against the couch. His head jerked around as he fought to make sense of his location.

"It's all right, Jeremy," I said.

Hyden motioned for me to be silent, but it was too late. Jeremy had heard me.

"You? Who are you?" he asked, turning to look at me.

I could have said that was no way to talk to a girl he'd kissed, but that wouldn't have gone over well. He held his head, as if he had the world's worst headache.

"My name is Callie."

"I don't know any Callie," he said.

His voice was sharp. It made me feel like he was issuing orders every time he spoke.

"That's right, you don't know me," I said. "Can I get you anything? Do you want some water?"

He started to nod and then stopped, from the pain, no doubt. "Yeah."

Hyden motioned he would get the water. As he left the room, Jeremy noticed him for the first time.

"Who's that?" Jeremy pointed.

The guy who used to be you, I wanted to say. But I stopped myself.

"That's Hyden. He's a friend."

"I think I know that guy. . . ."

I didn't want him to think about the confrontation, when Hyden first captured him. "No, you're just a little disoriented. We're Metals, like you."

"Metals. Like me . . . ," Jeremy said to himself.

Hyden returned with the water. Jeremy took it and downed the glass.

"So, you two have the chip too?" he asked. "From Prime?"

We both nodded.

"That body bank," he said. "If I ever see that Old Man, I swear I'll break his wrinkled neck."

I looked at Hyden, but he never took his eyes off Jeremy.

"You look really fit," Hyden said. "What skills did you list at Prime?"

"Mixed martial arts," he said. "Tae Kwon Do, Kali, Gatka."

Hyden nodded slightly.

We'd seen Jeremy's skills in action. Deadly. We opted not to reveal very much to him right away but to let him get used to things gradually. Except for my adapted chip, the chips prevented a Metal from killing anyone while being rented. But we doubted that held true when we were just being ourselves. And this was no time to find out.

⊗ ⊗ ⊗

That night, as we all filled our plates in the kitchen, Hyden came up beside me—keeping his distance—and smiled.

"What?" I asked. "You're that happy over chili night?"

"I just wanted to tell you thanks."

"For what?"

"For this. For convincing me we should gather the Metals."

"It makes you feel good, doesn't it? See, I was right."

"Yeah. It's good to see all of these people protected from my father. To be part of our community." He grinned. "And now we have better cooks."

I rolled my eyes and went around the table to get the bread.

In the dining room, I sat by Redmond. Hyden was at the other end, sitting opposite Jeremy. Near them were Lily, the acrobat, and Derek, known for his climbing skills. He was trying to pass a salad bowl to Savannah, but she was busy laughing with Michael. He'd finished his food already and he was sketching her. The other tables were filled with more Metals.

Someone tapped their water glass and the conversation quieted down. It was Jeremy.

"I want to talk memories," Jeremy said to the group.

"You mean from our renters?" Savannah asked.

"I know I'm not the only one who has them. I hear things. So let's get it out in the open. Who'll start?"

Savannah raised her hand. "My renter wanted my black belt body to go beat up her old boyfriend—some old Ender guy. When I relived that memory, I was shocked. I don't know what he did to her, but she felt so satisfied."

Michael raised his hand. "My renter was a sleazy Ender."

"I know, I met him," I said under my breath.

"He wanted my artistic talents to impress Starter girls with. He offered to draw them," Michael said.

"In the buff?" Jeremy asked.

"Of course."

Everyone reacted with disgust.

"You must have some interesting memories," Jeremy said to him.

"No, they turned him—me—down," Michael said. "Guess they saw right through the jerk."

Lily raised her hand. "My renter was a hundred-year-old Ender dying of cancer. Her dream was to soar on the trapeze. I felt how thrilled she was, how light she felt. It was wonderful."

People murmured and then went back to their private conversations.

Redmond turned to me and spoke softly. "So that key I left in the safe for you?"

"The one that told how you altered my chip?" I said quietly. "What about it?"

"Do you still have it?"

I wondered why he was asking. "I put it in a safe place."

"Good." His eyes narrowed. "Keep it there. Don't give it to anyone."

I saw a sadness behind his eyes and wasn't sure why. I nodded.

"I have a favor to ask you," I said.

"I can't take that chip out of you, if that's what you're thinking."

"Not the chip. The plate in my head. The one you put in as a blocker."

"Why?"

"It doesn't work anymore."

"I told you it would only last a short time."

"So I want it gone. I think it's irritating me. I keep scratching at it."

He pushed his bowl away. "It's better to just leave it alone. Less trauma to your head. It's not causing you any harm, the way it is."

"It's my head. And I say the less metal, the better."

Redmond pursed his lips. I folded my arms. I wasn't going to back down, even though I knew he was right. It was just that somehow, I felt if we removed the plate that covered the site of the chip, then we were one step closer to removing the chip . . . someday.

⊗ ⊗ ⊗

Redmond got Hyden's approval to remove the plate. I made Michael come with me, for moral support. We followed Redmond to a small medical room with a sink, bottles of medicines, and drawers of instruments. As Redmond prepped the instruments, a sharp medicinal scent stung my nose. Michael stood close by.

"Ready?" Redmond asked.

I nodded. He had me lie facedown with my head resting in a hole in the operating table. It was anything but comfortable. The edges of my face stuck to a sanitary paper protector as Redmond put something cold on the back of my head.

"What are you doing?" I asked.

"Just placing waterproof strips around the plate to protect your hair."

"The plate's tiny. It feels like you're covering my whole head."

"The wider the protective barrier, the safer it is."

"Is this going to hurt her?" Michael asked.

"It shouldn't," Redmond said. "There's no cutting involved."

I wished he were cutting and removing my chip. But this was the next best thing. I heard the sound of a spray and felt my scalp go icy.

"This forms a final protective bond over your scalp so the solvent I'm about to use won't burn you."

"What's the solvent for?" Michael asked.

I imagined Michael's expression as he watched Redmond's

procedure, picturing him observing it with the fascination of a science experiment.

"I better not see a sketch of this, Michael," I said.

He touched my arm. "Hey, where's my drawing pad?"

"The adhesive used to attach this tiny metal plate to the back of her skull has to be dissolved in order to break down the compound. It was strong to begin with—which is why I didn't want to remove it"—he said this last part louder for my benefit—"so it needs an acidic solvent."

"Just do it," I said.

"All right now, don't move."

I could hear the solvent foaming, bubbling, near my ears. A pungent smell filled my nose.

"Whoa," Michael said. I imagined he was waving his hand over his face.

"Don't get too close," Redmond said to Michael. "These are just tweezers so I can get a grip on it and pry it off."

Then I felt Redmond tug on the plate.

"I have the left side loose . . . just need the right."

Redmond kept working, and this time I felt the plate release.

"There. It's off," he said. "Brilliant. Just let me clean up the area."

It was just my imagination of course, but I felt lighter. Michael patted my arm.

"Good job," he said.

As Redmond turned away to get the sterile solution, a high-pitched siren screamed in the hallway.

"What's that?" I shouted to Redmond over the noise.

"Security alarm. Stay here."

He rushed out of the room and closed the door.

I sat up.

"I don't think you should move, Cal," Michael said, looking nervous.

My throat felt scratchy, and another smell mingled with the medicinal scent in the room. I coughed. Michael and I exchanged worried glances. Then he coughed.

I looked up and saw a white smoky mist streaming in through the vent like dragon's breath.

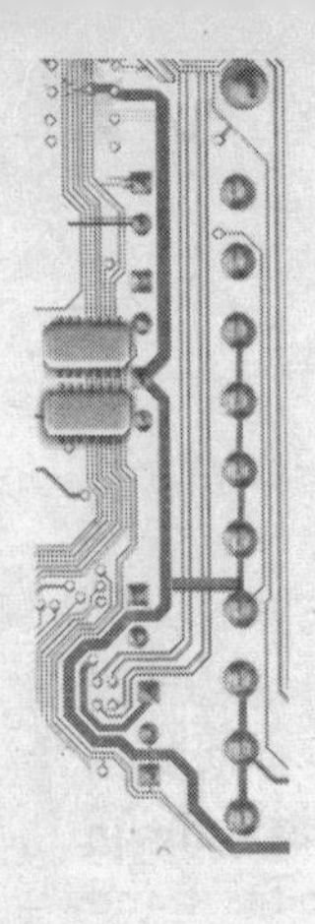

CHAPTER TWELVE

I scrambled off the operating table and grabbed a towel. I wet it quickly with cold water and handed it to Michael. "Put it over your mouth."

I wet another one for myself. The towel blocked the smoke but didn't make it any easier to breathe.

Outside, in the hall, smoke poured in from every vent, and the bitter odor overwhelmed us. Michael stayed close to me.

"Redmond?" I shouted, pulling the towel away from my mouth for a second. I heard nothing but the pulsating alarm ringing in my ears.

The hazy air stung my eyes. I was barely able to see more than a couple of feet. Movement was only possible by feeling my way along the hallway with my free hand.

"Redmond!" Michael shouted over the alarm. "Hyden!"

I looked back over my shoulder, but the smoke was so thick now I couldn't even see Michael following me. That, and the blasting alarm, were deadening my senses. Then someone gripped my arm. Hard.

It wasn't anyone I knew.

It was a beefy Ender wearing a gas mask that made him look like an overfed space alien. He had a ZipTaser in one hand and a slim, lightweight gun that Enders favored in his belt.

I brought my leg around the back of his and tried to push him off center, but it didn't faze him. Michael tried to help, but the Ender slapped him with the butt of the ZipTaser and he fell. I dropped the towel and used both hands to fight off the Ender, but he was strong and soon had my wrists in his grip.

And now that the towel was gone, the bitter gas was making my head swim.

The Ender aimed the ZipTaser at me. I pulled to the side just as the Taser shot out—and the dart of electrodes burned the wall.

He yanked me hard. I was inches from his masked face, weak from the gas. Suddenly, his eyes widened in surprise, and he dropped to the floor. Ernie stood behind him, gun in hand, gas mask on his face. The alarm must have covered the sound of Ernie's gun. He ripped off the Ender's mask and gave it to me. I only hesitated a second. Breathing trumped squeamishness.

"Okay?" Ernie asked, his voice muffled by the gas mask.

I pushed a stray lock of my hair out from under the mask and nodded. "Michael. He's hurt." I pointed back behind me.

"Anyone left here?" Ernie asked.

I shook my head. "Where's Hyden?"

"He's okay. But they took everyone else." Ernie pushed past me, looking for Michael in the smoke.

"Everyone?" I said to myself.

My skin felt clammy. I looked down at the Ender who'd been shot.

"Scum," I said to his body.

He opened his eyes and I gasped. He reached out and grabbed my ankle.

"Ernie!" I shouted. I tried yanking my legs free, but the Ender held on.

Our Middle bodyguard returned, gun extended, with Michael right behind him. Ernie bent and pointed the gun at the Ender's head.

"Release her now!"

The Ender let go of me and fell back, drained from his efforts.

"Callie, move." Ernie gestured with his head.

I stepped away and Michael put his arm around me. The smoke had cleared enough that Ernie and I could remove our masks.

"Who do you work for?" Ernie asked the Ender.

He kept silent, a bitter look of resignation on his face.

"Look, grandpa, you're bleeding to death every second that goes by. I'd say you only have sixty of those left," Ernie said. He reached into his pocket. "See this?" He pulled out a jet-syringe. "This will stop your bleeding."

The Ender perked up, his eyes wild, alert.

"It'll save your miserable life. Just talk. Who sent you?"

I looked at Michael. Would the Ender talk?

The Ender's lips began to move. "Brockman." He coughed.

"What's he going to do with our Metals?" Ernie asked. "Blow them up?"

He shook his head. "Sell them . . . big . . ." He reached for the syringe. "Gimme."

Ernie pulled his arm back, out of reach. "When?"

The Ender grimaced from his pain. "Ten . . . days."

"Who's he selling them to?"

"The richest . . . Enders . . . in the world."

"Where?"

"The shot . . ." The Ender reached out.

Ernie looked at his watch and injected the syringe with a touch of his thumb. The Ender didn't even flinch.

"Where?" Ernie asked, getting right in his face. "Where's the auction?"

The Ender's eyes went glassy and his head listed to the side.

"Where's Brockman's lab?" Ernie shook the Ender.

"Ernie." I touched his shoulder. "I think he's gone."

Ernie felt the Ender's pulse and then got up.

"The shot didn't work," Michael said.

"Yeah, I knew that," Ernie said. "But it made him talk."

He took the lead as Michael and I followed to the main lab. Hyden appeared with a thick black duffel bag over his shoulder. Redmond was behind him.

"They took all the Metals." My voice broke.

"Not all," Hyden said, a flash of sadness in his eyes. "Not you. Lucky you were in surgery."

We made it to the end of the main lab room. Just as I wondered why Ernie was leading us to a dead end, Hyden slapped the wall, and a panel slid open to a narrow hallway. We entered, and it closed behind us with a snap.

Hyden opened a door and we rushed up the stairs. I stopped counting the flights; I was gasping for breath. Ernie put his arm under mine and helped me the rest of the way. Redmond, being an Ender, was also panting. He was lagging a half flight behind us.

Finally, we reached the last landing. Hyden pressed another pad, and a steel panel opened to the garage. It closed behind us, totally masking this secret passageway.

We stepped out into the garage and were near the SUV when the elevator door opened. Two Enders with gas masks and guns poured out. One was very tall, with long white hair like a Viking.

Hyden motioned for Ernie to get Michael and me into the SUV. I climbed in the front, Michael in the back, and Hyden scrambled into the driver's seat. Redmond was coming, running as hard as he could, but he was grabbed from behind by the tall Ender.

Ernie lunged back to help him, but the shorter Ender took aim and shot Ernie.

"No!" I yelled.

Redmond turned on his long-haired captor and they struggled. The gun went off and Redmond slumped to the ground, shot in the heart.

I screamed Redmond's name. Hyden was shouting, but I couldn't make out his words.

Ernie grabbed the SUV door and put his feet on the step. Michael reached out and held on to his arm.

The men rushed us. Hyden sped in reverse out of the garage as Michael hoisted Ernie into the backseat. Hyden pressed the button for the garage panel and it started to lower.

The Enders raced toward us. They were almost to the garage door just as our SUV left.

Hyden pressed the button again, and the panel roared down at five times the normal speed. The Ender with the long hair was caught by the door, which dropped on him like a guillotine. I averted my eyes, focusing on his gun as it flew out of his hand and spun on the ground.

My stomach lurched.

"Don't look," Michael said.

Hyden sped away.

I glanced at Michael in the rearview mirror. His face was pale.

"Redmond . . ." My voice cracked. I put my hand over my mouth as tears rushed hard to my eyes.

"I know," Hyden said.

Everyone was quiet for a moment as I sobbed through my palm.

"He was gone fast," he continued softly.

I nodded. Ernie groaned from the backseat.

"Callie, I need you two to check on Ernie," Hyden said.

Michael was sitting right beside Ernie. I knew Hyden just wanted to take my mind off Redmond. I pulled myself together and turned around to see our bodyguard slumped in the backseat, his hand covering his heart. Blood stained his jacket.

I felt sick. But I leaned over the seat to get a better look.

"Can you see where the wound is?" I asked Michael.

Michael carefully opened Ernie's suit jacket to look. The hole was high on his chest, well above his heart.

"It's in his shoulder," I told Hyden, relieved. "Shouldn't we be putting pressure on it?"

Michael put his hands over the wound and pressed.

"He needs a doctor," Hyden said, keeping his eyes on the road.

Ernie shook his head, trying to be brave. But he couldn't hide a grimace from the pain.

"He doesn't want one," Michael said to Hyden.

"He's overruled. One of the perks of being boss," Hyden said.

Hyden drove fast. The navigation system directed us to the Sisters of Mercy Hospital in minutes. We pulled onto the property, passing plastic flowers in planters—another hospital barely holding it together, a victim of our times. We drove toward the emergency entrance. Ernie was perspiring, and his eyes appeared glassy. Michael was comforting him, his hand on the top of his shoulder.

"You're going to be okay," I said. "We're here."

Ernie pulled out his gun and pointed it at Hyden.

"Stop the car," Ernie said.

Hyden stopped it a little short of the patient unloading zone.

"I'm taking you in," Hyden said. "You're wounded."

"Bleeding is in my job description." Ernie waved his gun to punctuate his words.

"Cut the drama, Ernie," Hyden said. "We both know you're not going to shoot me."

"You Metals can't be sitting in a hospital. They could be after you." Ernie struggled to get the words out. "My way . . . or no way."

Hyden looked resigned. Michael and I exited, opened Ernie's door, and helped him out. He leaned against the wall near the emergency entrance and put his gun away.

"I'm sorry I couldn't save Redmond," Ernie said.

"Hey, man, you tried." Michael patted Ernie's forearm.

"You saved us, Ernie. Thank you." I hoped he was going to be all right. I squeezed his hand. "Get well."

"Get outta here," he said with a small smile.

He waved us off and we got back in the SUV. I watched as an orderly came out of the hospital with a wheelchair for Ernie.

"He's tough," Hyden said, pulling onto the freeway and heading east. "He'll contact me when he can."

I perceived a note of doubt in his voice. Hyden gripped the wheel as if it were grounding him. Maybe not being able to touch people also meant it was harder to let them touch your heart. I knew he cared about Ernie—and Redmond—but he sure wasn't letting himself show it.

I looked at back at Michael. He looked about as shell-shocked as I felt. My face felt itchy. I scratched my cheek.

"Don't," Hyden said. "Don't touch your face."

He opened a panel near the ceiling and pulled down a slim medical kit. He took out two white packets, each about the size of my palm. He tossed them to me. "Open them."

I handed one to Michael. The only thing printed on the packet was a long chemical name I didn't recognize. I tore mine open and pulled out a wet cloth.

"Wipe your face first. Be sure to get your nose. Then do your hands, legs, any exposed skin."

I pressed the cool cloth to my cheek. "Feels good."

"It neutralizes the residue from most gases."

Michael wiped himself with his cloth. "What would it do to us?"

Hyden shook his head. "You don't want to know, trust me."

"Poor Redmond." I wiped my face and the rest of my exposed skin.

"If it helps," Hyden said, "he would have taken himself out before he'd ever work for my father."

A hollow feeling ate away at my insides. It was like when our building was smoked and we lost everything, including the last pictures of our parents. A desperate feeling came over me to go to my little brother immediately, grab him, and hold him tightly.

"I need to be with my brother," I blurted out.

"You'll lead my father's men right to your cabin."

"He's right, Cal," Michael said.

Hyden opened the scanner.

"What're you doing?" I asked.

"Scanning." He said it like it was obvious.

He punched a button and the car went into autodrive, allowing him to let go of the wheel.

"Is it really the time for this?" Michael asked.

"I'm trying to see if we can grab their signals," Hyden said as the airscreen came on. "They've got all our Metals. This thing should light up like Christmas."

"You mean we might get them back?" I asked.

"That would be the idea," Hyden said.

I watched the screen as Hyden plucked it, widening the search area. Michael leaned forward from his backseat so he could also focus on the screen.

But the grid was quiet. After a bit, Hyden ran his hand through it, sending the display into disarray for a moment.

"They're too smart," Hyden said with an edge of cynicism in his voice. "They've got protection the way we have." He sighed. "They're gone." He slapped the steering wheel. "All those Metals, they depended on me."

"What're we going to do?" I asked.

"I don't know. We can't go back to the lab."

He took the autodrive off and we continued for a few miles. I turned and saw that Michael had fallen asleep.

"Can you raise the panel?" I whispered to Hyden.

Hyden glanced in the rearview mirror, then pressed a button. A plexi-panel slid up to meet the roof, making it impossible for Michael to hear us if he woke up.

"What's up?" Hyden asked me.

"Back at the Hall of Records, when your father got in my head, he did something new."

"What?"

"He was able to control me."

"How?"

"He moved my little finger. Against my will."

"Why didn't you tell me?"

"We haven't exactly had a quiet moment, you know."

"But it shows he's advanced. I need to know these things."

"Well, now you know." I touched the back of my head a moment and then stopped. "And there's something else I haven't had time to tell you."

"What?" He looked at me with narrowed eyes.

"He didn't claim to be doing my father's voice, when I confronted him."

"That's just him."

"No, he always takes credit for what he's done."

"He's messing with you. Forget about it."

Hyden got off the freeway. After a short time, we drove alongside the dry riverbed of the L.A. River. Hyden pulled his SUV over the curb and through a hole in the entrance. We drove down a steep embankment until we were on the cement of the riverbed.

"Hyden?" I asked, holding on to a hand grip.

Michael woke and banged on the panel between us. Hyden lowered it.

"What are you doing?" he shouted.

"The Department of Water and Power built us this nice little ramp years ago. We're going right down it."

He drove down an auxiliary shaft in front of us.

"But why? Where are we going?" I asked, holding on even tighter.

"Someplace low and safe," Hyden said as he wound his way down, level by level. "With a restroom."

When we got to the bottom, it was like another world. There was a large makeshift market with all kinds of Starters and Enders.

A scrappy Starter ran up to our car with a bottle and rags in his hands.

"Look out!" I said to Hyden so he wouldn't hit him.

"It's okay," Hyden said. "He's getting rid of any possible spore dust."

The Starter wiped down Hyden's car, wetting it with his spray while we were still moving into a parking space.

We got out and Hyden gave him a dollar.

"What is this?" I asked.

"The People's Flea Market. We're only going through it because of the restroom at the end," Hyden said.

"What are we waiting for?" Michael asked as he walked toward the entrance.

An Ender woman wearing a head scarf in a green flowery print sat at a table with a sign reading *Pay Here*. Hyden put three bills on the table and she held open the entrance gate, made from a No Right Turn sign.

"Enjoy," she said with a twinkle in her eye.

There was something familiar about her. But it wasn't the woman; it was the scarf. My mom used to have the same one.

I followed Hyden, as did Michael, dazed, numb, and no doubt in shock from the shootout. We sleepwalked past the sellers sitting on blankets or folding chairs behind tables displaying odd pieces of life, some from many years ago.

Michael noticed a large, flat piece of metal lying on a table. "What's that?"

The seller was an eccentric Ender with his long white hair in many tiny braids. He perked up at our interest.

"It's called a laptop," the seller said. "It's a computer."

"You mean that big thing is an airscreen?" I asked. "That's how they used to access the Pages?"

"They didn't call them Pages then," Hyden said. "Back then they didn't document every second of their lives the way we do."

"Not all of us," Michael said.

The seller smiled and touched the metal, popping it open. It was even bigger.

"Look at the keys," I said. "Like a typewriter." I gave the seller a nod. "Thanks for showing us." We moved on.

"What's a typewriter?" Michael asked.

"You haven't seen the old movies?" I thought of the ones my dad had shown me. The next time I saw one, he wouldn't be there.

"Why did they call it 'laptop'?" Michael asked.

"Because it was meant to be used on your lap," Hyden said. "But no one ever did."

"Why are they here and not outside?" I asked.

"They're part of the underground people," Hyden said.

"Starters and Enders afraid of another attack, or of spore residue."

"But aren't they vaccinated?" Michael asked.

"Not all. And the vaccine can't protect from a new bio-weapon attack," Hyden said.

Bio-weapon. Attack. Spore residue. I felt dizzy.

⊗ ⊗ ⊗

I washed my face in the restroom and wiped my hands with the paper napkins neatly stacked on the counter. The scarf woman must have swiped those from hot dog stands. As I stood there alone, the deaths at the lab finally hit me like a punch to the gut from an unfriendlie. It was surreal being here at the flea market after what we had just gone through.

Redmond. Ernie.

I joined the guys in the refreshment area. They had bottles of water and cheap chocolate patties trying to pass for Supertruffles. Minimal amount of vitamins just so they could say they had them.

Hyden tossed one to me. "Here."

I grabbed the chocolate. He threw the water bottle, but I missed and it thudded onto the ground. Michael picked it up and handed it to me. I stood there, not moving.

"What's wrong?" Hyden asked.

"What isn't wrong?" I said.

He came closer and carefully plucked the chocolate from my hand, opened it, and held it out for me to take. I took it without touching him, broke off a small piece, and chewed it slowly.

"Come on," he said.

The fake Supertruffle was dry in my throat.

"I want my life back, okay?" I said.

Hyden stared at me. So did Michael.

"I only had a couple of weeks with my brother as a normal family, living in a home, and now he's up there on that mountain, and I'm down here, underground, wondering if I'll ever get to see him again. I was supposed to give him a life, not a nanny. And the way things are going, we might not all live to see tomorrow anyway."

Hyden took a step closer. "I want the same thing you do—to be untethered. I want all of us to be free. But not now. We just have to take it one step at a time, okay?"

I looked away.

"It's not like we've lost everything," Hyden said.

I swallowed hard. How could he say that?

"We haven't, Callie. Redmond is gone and we've lost the Metals. Lily and Savannah and Jeremy and the rest."

I thought for a moment about the danger they were in—no matter what that dying Ender said, Hyden's father could always turn them into human bombs.

"But we're going to work to get them back. I have a bag packed with essentials. And cash." Hyden gestured toward the car, where he'd put the large black duffel bag. "Research I can re-create." He pointed to his head.

"But your lab, the computers," I said.

"They didn't get my computers," he said. "I had a panic button set up to destroy the computers."

"But then you lost them."

"Let me show you guys something," Hyden said.

We followed him out the flea-market exit and walked toward his SUV.

"I have the scanner. And I have backup." He pointed to his car. "This is a portable lab."

"Where?" I asked.

He opened the back. A black leather lounge-style seat was carved into the cargo panel, running across the width. It was shaped so a person would sit back in it with their legs bent. Hyden reached over that and lifted a panel, revealing a mega-computer.

Michael let out a low whistle. "Not just an old Metal detector."

Okay, it was something. But no cause for celebration.

Hyden cocked his head. "You're right, Callie, it's bad. For the Metals. And Redmond. But don't give up."

I looked from Hyden to Michael. Their strength grounded me. And gave me a little hope.

⊗ ⊗ ⊗

We slept in the SUV—Hyden in the front, Michael and I in back. I'd drifted off after what seemed like hours trying to get comfortable with no blanket and no pillow, only to wake up disoriented in the dark. I could hear Hyden's and Michael's rhythmic breathing. It was dim, with just some small lights on the dashboard and around the interior of the car, glowing like luminescent bugs in a cave. Through the smoked windows I could see the handwritten Closed sign the scarf lady had propped up at the entrance. This was a permanent market, and many of the vendors had draped towels and rags over their wares. Other spaces were now empty. Several of the sellers slept in their parked cars so they could monitor the market.

As I looked through the window, my eyes focused on the window itself, and my vision became blurry. When it refocused, it was like the window was a screen, and across it played a scene that soon enveloped me. I was in Club Rune, moving across the dance floor, past the glamorous "teens," mostly Ender renters in donor bodies, the way Helena had rented me. I glided up to the bar and showed the bartender a small holo of a girl. It was Emma, Helena's missing granddaughter—blond and regal, with Helena's noble nose and strong chin.

It was another memory of Helena's playing out before me, a little differently this time, more visually. When she was using my body, she must have gone to Club Rune to ask about Emma. But the bartender looked at the holo and shook his head. I felt this heavy sadness tear at my heart.

Helena's sadness, a moment preserved from the past, was frozen now in my memory banks. I was not only reliving the memory, I was also feeling it as if it were my own.

The vision ended and I was back in the car, staring at the window, a tear running down my cheek. Helena would have been there over two months ago; that was how old this memory was. And now it was resurfacing.

I had many sad memories of my own since the Spore Wars, but Helena's dug into me. She had this intense determination, this desperation, this passion to find Emma. To find her answers. She wasn't giving up. So how could I?

⊗ ⊗ ⊗

"I had another memory last night," I said the next morning.

We'd all woken up around the same time, with fuzzy mouths and wrinkled clothes. I was in the back with Michael, leaning on my elbow. Hyden brought his driver's seat up to its regular position and smoothed his rumpled hair with his hands.

"A memory hit?" Hyden asked.

"Yes. And it made me think about my father."

Michael put his hand on my shoulder. "It's hard, Cal," he

said. "We just went through so much loss. You know how it turns everything upside down."

"I know, but . . ."

"Callie, remember what we saw in that Hall of Records," Hyden said.

"It's just a feeling. I can't shake it."

"What do you want to do?" Hyden asked.

I looked at each of them. "I want to go home."

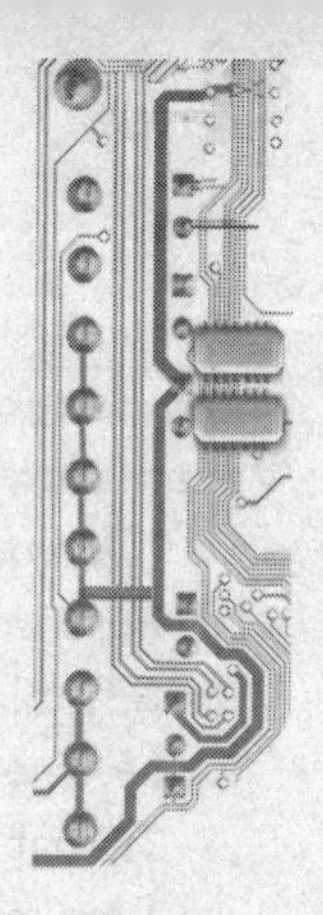

CHAPTER THIRTEEN

Hyden, Michael, and I drove through the neighborhood in the valley north of Los Angeles where Michael and I grew up. Now it was an abandoned suburb. We passed house after boarded-up house with markings on them in red paint. Some said Relocated but Condemned was the most common.

Being here reminded me of how awful it had been as all our parents came down with the disease inflicted by the spores. How the marshals came to take them away to treatment facilities where no treatment waited. They were places people went to wait to die. How the Starters were taken to institutions unless grandparents claimed them. These were the homes of my friends and neighbors, the Surratts and Perrys and Rogers. All empty now, with overgrown lawns of dead grass and Condemned notices stamped on every door. These were the houses where I had trick-or-treated, had barbecues, celebrated birthday parties.

Now it was as if zombies had taken it over.

I touched the back of my head. We passed Michael's house

and he turned around to look back at it. I couldn't read the expression on his face; I think that was the point.

"Do you want to stop?" I asked.

He shook his head. Hyden glanced at me.

"His old house," I said.

Hyden nodded. "You guys were neighbors."

"Yeah," I said. "But we didn't really spend time—"

"We didn't hang out together," Michael said.

Hyden nodded. "I get it."

We drove in silence for a few more blocks. I pointed to the right. "That's it."

He pulled up in front of my house. Strangling the barren rosebushes was a haphazard wire fence that wrapped around the perimeter.

My mother's prized roses were dead, the bushes just thorny skeletons reaching out for someone to save them, someone who never came.

I had to swallow what would have been too many tears. Michael reached forward from the backseat and squeezed my shoulder.

"Ready?" he said.

I took a deep breath. "Let's go." I put my hand on the car door handle.

"Wait," Hyden said.

"Why?"

He held up a gas mask for me. He tossed one back to Michael.

The idea of wearing a mask like that in my house made me sick. "I'm not wearing that. It's my home." This was the place where I'd had sleepovers with my best friends. Baked brownies. Had pizza night every Friday. Not a place for gas masks.

"It might be dangerous. If not the spore residue, the chemicals that were sprayed after," he said.

Michael fiddled with his mask strap. "He's right."

Hyden tossed him gloves.

"I don't care." I opened the door and got out while they were putting the gear on.

Hyden and Michael followed me out of the car. Hyden quickly got to work using a wire cutter to get through the fence. Michael looked up and down the street, always on the watch for unfriendlies. But there was no sign of life, not even a squirrel.

As we walked up the path, I felt my pace slow to a crawl. My home. We'd played in this yard, and it had been full of life and laughter. Now it was deadly quiet. The lush green lawn where my dad would play ball with Tyler was now brittle yellow weeds.

We stood at the front door. Planks of wood had been hammered across the middle of the door. *Condemned* was splashed across the planks in paint as red as blood. A cheerful tune broke the silence, startling the guys. It was my mother's small framed holo, activated by our presence. She used to change this with the seasons, and this one had a picture of us—Dad, her, Tyler, and me—smiling, holding a big cardboard heart. At the end of the short tune we all said, "Welcome."

A little of the red paint had splattered on the corner of the solar frame.

My legs felt weak.

Michael looked at me. "Want it?"

I nodded. He took a penknife from his pocket and pried off the frame. "Here."

I slipped it into my purse.

Hyden rolled down his sleeves to cover his arms all the way to his gloves.

"You should do the same," he said. "What's the best way in?"

I led them around to the back door. The backyard looked like a graveyard with brown grass and Tyler's toys lying on their sides—a small bike, a broken metal robot. We went to the back door and I waved my hand over the pad.

It didn't open.

"It won't work without electricity," Hyden said.

Michael used his knife to trip the lock. Hyden pried open the door with the help of the wire cutter. Together they got it open.

Inside, it was dark. It was as it was when we'd left it, the day Tyler and I had to run from the marshals. The sun fought to pierce the drawn curtains, casting a dark yellow light on our belongings. We needed handlites, but we didn't wear them anymore.

Michael pulled back one of the curtains in the kitchen. "Where do you want to start?"

"In my father's office," I said.

I pushed aside my temptation to grab every sentimental object in the house: the last sweater my mother was knitting, the last book my father was reading, a mold of Tyler's old baby shoes, and my last good report card stuck on the refrigerator. But we had to focus. We pored through my dad's papers, his file system. Hyden picked up my dad's airscreen.

"It's dead. I'll have to charge it," Hyden said.

I waved my hand. "Just take it."

We spent longer in his office than Hyden wanted us to, going through boxes and drawers. We didn't find anything that would give us any clues to where he might be—if he was still alive.

We were almost ready to leave. I had filled a box with a few mementos and was trying to decide whether I should also bring one of my dad's physical file folders. Hyden watched over my shoulder as I flipped through the small pieces of paper and business cards it held.

"Wait. Stop," he said.

He plucked a business card from the file.

The holo-mation set off, a thumping beat sounded, and Starters danced on top of the card.

"What is it?" Michael asked.

"That's Club Rune," Hyden said.

He was right; the words on the card said it all.

A Place to Be Somebody Else.

Where I first met Madison and Blake.

We all stared at it. "Club Rune?" I said. "My father?"

I couldn't imagine why my father would have a card from Club Rune. It was a hangout for renters and regular teens. What would a Middle—especially my father—be doing there?

Hyden picked up the box. "We should go."

"Just give me a minute," I asked. "Please."

"It's not safe for the three of us to be out here," Hyden said.

"Hey, give her minute, will you?" Michael shifted a box he was holding on his hip.

"You don't get it," Hyden said, putting down his box. "I do, because I know how the chipspace works."

"You're the one who doesn't get it." Michael practically threw his box down. "How about thinking about her? You, you can't even touch her unless you're in someone else's body."

I breathed in and stared wide-eyed at the two guys. "Michael!"

Hyden froze. I held my breath. They were like two animals, wound as tight as possible, ready to strike.

"No," Hyden said sadly. "He's right."

"Hyden . . . ," I said, wanting so much to reach out.

He picked up his box. "Go ahead, Callie. We'll wait for you outside."

He left. Michael looked at me. "Take your time," he said before he followed him.

I sighed as I stood in the middle of my father's office. What to do with my last precious minutes? I wanted something of his, but what?

One of his watches lay on a stack of papers on his desk. It was old-fashioned, like from his old movies that he loved. He had a couple of these; they were rare. Collector's items.

I put it on my wrist. It was too big. Heavy. I slipped it off and put it back. My eyes desperately scanned the room and stopped on his bookcase. At the top, hanging on the edge, was his old fedora. I used a fishing pole to get it down. I put it to my nose and breathed in. It still smelled like him, a tweedy, woodsy scent. I held it there, pretending he was with me.

Could I remember that scent? Memorize it so I could call it up when I ached for his arm around my shoulders?

I pulled my face away from the hat and stroked the felt. It still had his shape. But it wasn't him.

I left it by the watch so they could be together.

⊗ ⊗ ⊗

Downtown L.A. at night varied from street to street in terms of the crowds. Mostly it was quiet, but we made a point of avoiding the camping protestors around City Hall.

When we arrived at our destination, Hyden squeezed his vehicle past the line of empty parked cars and cruised to the valet pickup zone.

"That's it?" Michael asked.

I nodded and looked up at the club where so much had happened to me. I never imagined I'd see it again.

"Welcome to Club Rune," the cheerful Ender valet said.

"We don't need to valet it," I said to the Ender as I got out. "He's just letting us off."

I gestured toward Hyden as Michael and I got out.

"Have fun," Hyden said out the window and drove away.

I wondered what he was thinking. He—and Michael—had made zero reference to their argument at my house.

Guys.

We'd stopped to buy the latest tech clothing to be sure we would pass the rope test. Michael had on a great black shimmer jacket that changed color and texture when he moved. I wore a short 3-D illusion dress. When the light hit it a certain way, the design moved and transformed. Green leaves were falling right now, changing to fluttering red butterflies.

Even though Prime had closed and the rental business was gone, the look of the crowd hadn't changed. Two kinds of teens made up the clientele: those with bad skin and flyaway hair and those who looked laser-sculpted, lacking in imperfections. That could have been due to makeovers from their families or Prime. Or they could have been naturally beautiful.

An ultra-hip Ender with sculpted silver hair, wearing a

sleek black turtleneck and pants, spoke into his wire-thin earpiece as he stood at the velvet rope blocking the entrance. He stopped talking and looked us over.

"First time here?" he asked.

"Very funny," I said in such a dry, entitled way that the Ender had to let us in.

Two Ender doormen in uniforms opened the massive entrance doors for us. It always felt like you were entering some Egyptian temple. Until you got inside.

Lasers cut through the darkened room, jewel-colored slashes piercing the large dance hall. The newest hybrid fusion music throbbed, making it hard to think.

"Still the same," I said over the music.

"I can see why Hyden sat this one out," Michael said.

Hyden couldn't handle the crowd. But it wasn't for Michael either. He'd rather have been sketching this crowd than be part of it.

A server of indeterminate gender passed carrying a tray of drinks that glowed blue and left a trail of white smoke. Off to the side, a girl in a bathing suit crawled out of a fountain against the wall. The water looked like gold oil, and when she emerged, her skin was covered in it, making her look like a gilded statue.

We headed past the astrobar to the lounge. It wasn't as packed as the main hall, but it was still pretty active. The antigrav chairs were filled with gorgeous Starters. But they could have just been born that way.

"See anyone you recognize?" I asked Michael.

"No. And no one I want to know."

We'd decided that in addition to looking for clues as to why my father would have been there, we'd also pick up any good Metals that we found. Would we just be collecting them for Brockman again? We hoped not.

We walked around the lounge.

"What about her?" He nodded in the direction of a stunning, willowy girl with straight blond hair.

She leaned up against one of the mirrored columns. I remembered her face. She was one of the donors who had come in when we were shutting down the body bank. Of course, it was really her renter then.

"You talk to her," he said to me.

"Come with me."

"It'll be easier if it's just you. Less chance of scaring her."

He went over to the bar. I walked closer to the girl. I peeked at my phone in my purse. It identified her phone as belonging to Daphne. I moved closer and smiled.

"Hey, Daphne," I said.

She sized me up with a bored expression. "Am I supposed to know you?"

So she wasn't the nicest Starter in the club.

"Sort of. We're body bank sisters," I said.

"Oh." Her eyes widened. "There. Man, I don't want to think about that slimy place."

"I know." Then I decided to press a bit. "But I do think about it sometimes. I can't help it. I have memories. Do you?"

"Of my renter? Yeah," she said, and sipped her bottle of sparkling water. "I keep getting these flashbacks I'm walking a tightrope over a canyon. I'm a gymnast, not a tightrope walker. Can you imagine they let her do that? My renter obviously didn't have a fear of heights, but I sure do."

"Not good," I said. "Maybe someday we'll get the chips removed."

"I'd take a knife and do it myself if I thought I'd live through it."

A gymnast and gutsy.

"How are you doing since you finished Prime?" I asked. "Living okay?"

"I was smart. Saved my money."

Her clothes looked new, she looked healthy, and she managed to pass the inspection to get in the club. Whatever she was doing, she was all right.

"How long have you been coming here?" I asked.

"A few months. I learned about it after working for Prime."

She wasn't going to be much help to me in terms of finding out about my father, since she'd only started coming here recently. But she was one of the few remaining Metals we could maybe rescue.

"Let me introduce you to my friend," I said.

I brought her over to Michael and left the two of them to talk. I went to the one person who usually knew everyone in a club—the bartender. Like all the employees, he was a white-haired Ender. He was tall and slender, wearing an earring. His friendly face looked so familiar. Maybe from my first time at the club, when Helena was renting me? No, more recently. From Helena's memory. The memory she had of showing the bartender Emma's holo.

I ordered a soda and showed him the holo-frame of my family that we'd pried off my front door. "Do you recognize this Middle?"

"Hard to forget a Middle," he said as he wiped a glass. "We get so few."

My heart started racing, but I tried to keep calm. "You've seen him?"

He took the holo from me and stared at it a moment. Then looked at me. "You're his daughter?"

"Yes."

"What's your name, sweetheart?" he asked.

"Callie Woodland. His name is Ray."

The bartender leaned closer and examined my features. "I see it in your eyes." He put down the towel. "I've been waiting for someone to show up. Come with me."

I wasn't sure what was happening, but I waited while he came around from the back of the bar. I wasn't sure I should be following this Ender I didn't know.

"It's all right," he said quietly, as if he read my concern. "We're just going a few steps. I have something from your father."

What could he have from my dad? I followed him through the club to a side door. This was the backstage area of the club, with unpainted walls and concrete floors. We went into a small, plain office space, and he closed the door behind us.

I tensed.

He knelt down and pulled out a key attached to his belt. He unlocked a file cabinet and reached way in the back for something. He got it, relocked the cabinet, and stood.

"Take this," he said.

He handed me a small white object, about two inches long. It was made from a hard material with a glossy surface and was shaped like a flattened egg. A silver-colored design that looked like a feather decorated one side.

"What is it?"

"Don't know. But I'm mighty glad to get rid of it." He flopped into a chair. "You don't mind if I rest my feet, do you? When I'm standing all night, they swell up like baby pigs."

He sighed. "Your dad was a good tipper. I used to see him come in here a lot."

"Why?"

He shrugged. "He'd order a bourbon and just watch people."

I cradled the egg in my palm. "But how did you get this?"

"One night, about a year ago, your father was sitting at the bar when he turned and saw some men coming through the club."

"Enders?"

He nodded. "But they looked strong. Your father slipped that to me with some big bills and said three words—'Keep it safe.' I put it in my pocket and went about my business."

So this egg was that important. "And my father?"

"He got up to leave but the men surrounded him. They left together."

"What did they look like?"

"Like all us Enders—white hair. They were tall, beefy, and wore shades even though it was night." He grimaced a little.

I looked down at the egg. "I don't know if he's alive."

"I'm sorry, sweetheart. I wish I could tell you he was." He stood and patted my shoulder, but his eyes were on the egg. "Be careful. Those men who wanted it were nasty fellows. Maybe you should find someone else to keep it."

He gestured toward the door for me to go first. I slipped the egg into a zippered compartment inside my purse and left. As we made our way back to the main part of the club, I tried to make sense of all this.

It didn't prove anything. It didn't prove he was alive, didn't prove he was dead.

Guilt rose in my throat. Of course, if there was even the

slimmest chance that it really was my father in my head, I would be willing to live with the uncertainty for decades, until we found him. But that didn't mean it was easy.

I went back to the lounge and found Michael sitting alone.

"Find out anything?" he asked.

I was dying to tell him, but not inside the club. "Where's Daphne?"

"Gone."

"You lost her?"

"She got paranoid and took off. Maybe we should too."

I sent Hyden a Zing and he came to get us out front. Now I could show both of them what I'd found.

"My father left something at the club," I said as soon as I closed the passenger door.

Hyden drove away from the valet area. "What?"

I took the egg out of my purse. "This."

"What is that thing?" Michael leaned forward to see.

"I have no idea."

Hyden pulled over and stopped. We were still on the club property, at the end of the long, circular entrance.

"Let me see." He held out his hand.

I handed it to him. He examined it and then gripped the egg at both ends. He pulled but nothing happened.

"Don't break it," I said.

Hyden looked at me with a grin. "I think I can handle it."

He twisted it and I watched in horror as it came apart in his hands. Then he held up the main part of the egg, revealing a metal end. "It's a triple z-drive. Massive information storage."

"A drive?" I said. "Why?"

Hyden motioned for Michael to move aside and he climbed to the back of the vehicle.

"Can't you use the scanner airscreen?" I asked.

"Not powerful enough." He opened the back computer, the one that could be used for transpositions, and inserted the drive.

The airscreen popped up. A lot of junk came across it.

"It's encrypted," Hyden said. "I'm not surprised. Your father wasn't stupid."

"So can't you uncrypt it?" Michael asked.

"Decrypt. It's not a coffin," Hyden said as he plucked at the screen. "I'm setting it up now, but it could take a long time."

"How long?" I asked.

"Hours. Days." He shrugged. "We just have to wait."

The screen became a stream of numbers and letters flashing by at lightning speed.

I wondered what my father could have had on that drive that was so important. That those dangerous Enders wanted. The bartender was so relieved to hand it off—he was scared of them. What did they do to my father? Was he not taken to the treatment facility when we were told?

"Is it safe to be doing this here?" Michael asked.

"You're right," Hyden said, getting ready to move.

I looked back to see if the way was clear and saw the Starters waiting for their cars. One tall girl with blond hair to her shoulders got in her convertible and the valet shut her door. She looked like someone I recognized.

No. Really?

I pulled out my phone and aimed it at her. Across the top of the screen, it read: *EMMA*.

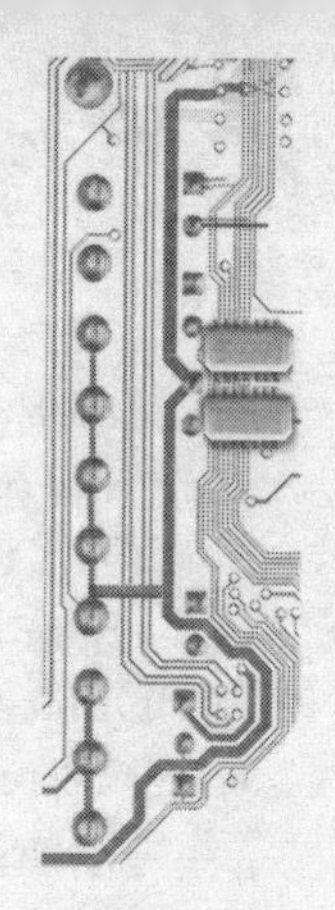

CHAPTER FOURTEEN

I kept my eyes on her as she started up her convertible. "That's Emma!"

"That blonde?" Hyden said.

"Yes."

He closed the airscreen and got out of the car.

"Emma!" he shouted as she drove right next to our car.

She turned, looked at Hyden, and sped away.

"Now you've scared her," I said, leaning out the window.

"Did she see you?" he asked me.

"I don't think so," Michael said.

"Don't lose her." I pointed in her direction.

Hyden jumped back into the driver's seat and followed. At that late hour, there weren't too many other cars, so it only took a moment until we saw her taillights glowing ahead.

"That's her," I said. Another car got between us, a mini-van. "Don't let her get away."

"Don't worry, we'll get her," Hyden said.

"It's not just that she's a Metal," I said. "I owe it to her grandmother. She doesn't know her grandmother's dead, and she's inherited half her estate."

"You'd think she'd want to know that," Michael said.

"I have her number, but . . . ," I said, holding my phone.

"Don't think she'd answer," Hyden said. "We have something better, anyway."

"The tracker," Michael said.

Hyden got the scanner going. Soon I could see her signal glowing on the airscreen.

"Got her," he said.

Hyden eased up on the pedal now that we had her signal. The few cars on the freeway helped keep us hidden, but also allowed us room to maneuver and keep sight of her, in case the airscreen lost her signal.

"How far can she be before she won't show on the screen?" I asked.

"About a quarter mile. Depends on whether there are buildings around."

She drove east for about twenty-five minutes. Then she changed lanes to the right.

"There she goes," I said.

"I see her."

She got in the far right lane. We waited a beat and then did the same. After a while, she exited the freeway.

"Stay back," Michael said.

"You want to drive?" Hyden looked over his shoulder. "I know how to follow someone."

"You think I can't drive this thing?" Michael asked. "It's got a steering wheel and pedals."

"Guys," I said. "Focus."

Emma turned left. We let two cars slip in front of us, and

then we followed. It was an iffy area of small stores with barred windows and signs in foreign languages and boarded-up auto shops.

"What's she doing here?" I asked.

Michael nodded. "Strange neighborhood for a rich girl."

"Did it occur to you she might be jacked?" Hyden asked.

"Could she be?" I touched the back of my head. "What makes you say that?"

"Only that it's possible. You always have to keep that in mind."

I thought how that would be. If she was jacked, it would have had to be by Hyden's father, or one of his people. Wouldn't they have used her better? Had her talk to me?

"I don't think she's jacked," I said.

She drove down a side street. We kept our distance.

"Dear Emma, where are you going?" Hyden asked.

"There." I pointed straight ahead.

In the middle of a row of barred stores was one place that was open. A small neon light flickered in the window. A café. A tiny place, kind of a dive.

"That café, see?"

"The princess goes slumming," he said.

We stayed back, double-parking in the street while Emma pulled into the small lot on the side of the café. It had a chain-link fence, but the gate was open for customers. She got out of her car and went inside.

"Callie, we'll get out here," Hyden said to me. "Michael, take the wheel. Park it a couple of blocks away and meet us inside."

We got out and walked to the café.

"Now, don't scare her," I said just before we entered.

"Don't worry, we'll play this low-key."

Inside, dusty maroon half curtains hung above windows thick with dust. Some blues played softly from cheap speakers that muddied the sound. The floors were unfinished concrete. It seemed like the kind of café you'd only go to if you needed to cry into your cappuccino.

One mopey, skinny Ender sat at one of the four tiny round tables, sipping his espresso. He looked like he would have been happier with a stiff drink.

Emma stood with her back to us, at the counter, staring at the airscreen menu. Little holo-mations popped out, illustrating the specials. A bacon sandwich spun around, emitting that bacon scent. A bored Ender barista waited with folded arms while Emma made up her mind.

A scraggly orange cat jumped up on one of the empty tables. I stroked his fur, trying to act casual, while Hyden put his hands in his pockets and glanced around. I'd shut off my illusion dress so it was just white. Hyden was dressed casually, but Emma and I were still in our fancy club wear, grossly overdressed for this place.

The cashier looked at Hyden and me and then looked away. He said something to Emma.

She mumbled something back to him, and then she walked to the back.

"Restroom?" I whispered to Hyden.

"I think she's slipping out," he said.

As the cashier turned his back, we followed Emma's path through a doorway curtain. Our eyes had to adjust in this darkened hallway, but we followed the sound of Emma's footsteps just ahead. When we passed the kitchen, something struck me as wrong. It was completely empty. No canisters of food or pickle jars or bread on cutting boards. Emma opened a door at the end of the hallway and exited. We followed, plunging into a pitch-black space.

The lights burst on, harsh white, blinding us. I blinked, and eventually the world came back into focus, but all through the prism of this disorienting light. We faced a huge warehouse-sized space, with various machines, computers, and equipment I couldn't identify lining the walls.

We'd happened upon the worst surprise party ever. Standing around us, guns drawn, were Emma and a few Enders, one with a splotch on his neck . . . a silver leopard tattoo. That was the man I'd seen talking to Reece just before she died. Several other Enders stood surrounding us, dressed in dark clothing. It looked like military gear, though like none I'd ever seen. They kept their rifles aimed at our legs.

My heart pounded in my chest.

One of the men ripped my purse out of my hands and pulled my arms behind my back. He cuffed my wrists just as another Ender cuffed Hyden's.

"What's going on?" I asked. "Who are you?"

I looked over at Hyden. They were emptying his pockets, pulling out his phone. He was sweating. I knew the touching was killing him, but he struggled not to reveal his weakness as one of the Enders patted him down.

"No weapons," the military Ender reported.

"Check her as well," the leopard tattoo said. "Never let it be said I don't treat women equally."

The military Ender patted me down and nodded. "Clean, sir."

"You can't detain us. We're claimed minors." I realized after I said it that Hyden probably wasn't technically claimed since he didn't live with his father.

The leopard man stepped up. "If that were true, you wouldn't be chasing this girl all over town." He pointed at Emma. "You'd be in your warm home, with your loving grandparents, watching insipid talent shows on the airscreen. But you're here because you're Metals."

Surprised, I looked at Hyden, but he kept his eyes forward. He acted like he'd been imprisoned and interrogated before. Maybe with his father, he had.

"You led us into a trap." I glared at Emma.

She stood stone-faced. The leopard man was about to respond when someone banged on the door. The leopard man nodded for them to lower the lights. One of the Enders opened the door partway, standing behind it. I gasped when I saw who stood on the other side.

Michael.

He was squinting, trying to see in the dark. Someone put a light on me.

"Callie!" Michael smiled with recognition.

"Michael, no, run!"

But it was too late. He stepped inside like an unsuspecting fawn stumbling into a hunter's trap. The lights came on and one of the Enders snapped cuffs on his wrists. Poor Michael stared wide-eyed at the scene in front of him.

⊗ ⊗ ⊗

Hyden and I sat on hard metal chairs, our hands still cuffed behind our backs. The uniformed Enders kept guard over us, but the leopard man and Emma had taken Michael through a door to the left. Large airscreens were projected on the wall, monitoring the "café" that was empty now. The charade was all for us. The sad customer and the bored barista both entered, sporting their black uniforms and no longer sad or bored.

Why did they take Michael away?

"What're they doing with him?" I asked Hyden.

A uniformed Ender nudged me with the nose of his rifle. "Quiet."

The cold metal against my skin made me flinch. Why, why, why? Why were we there? All I wanted was a normal life with my brother, and here I was, a prisoner again. Only this time it wasn't Institution 37.

It was a lot worse.

Besides the airscreens, there were special projections in the room that transformed the space. It cycled through different scenes accompanied by scents and soft sounds that matched the scene. Right now it was a bamboo forest rustling in the wind and a grassy perfume. I didn't know if this was their idea of decorating the warehouse space or if it was some special technique to keep us disoriented. If it was the latter, it was working really well.

Hyden glanced over at me. His eyes communicated sadness. He sighed and closed them a moment. I knew it was a "sorry" gesture.

If I had been allowed to speak, I would have told him it wasn't his fault. I was the one who had insisted we follow Emma. If I hadn't done that, we wouldn't be handcuffed here, and Michael wouldn't be off in some room possibly being tortured.

My eyes blurred. I knew what that meant. Another memory of Helena's was coming on. My sight soon sharpened to show me a vision as clear as an Xperience. I was in Helena's bed with the canopy, in the moonlight. I turned on the table lamp and slipped out of bed to the open closet. The carpet was pulled back, exposing the hidden compartment in the floor. I lifted the lid to the case and saw the gun inside.

I picked it up and held it against my cheek, feeling the power it contained. The metal was icy cold.

The memory ended abruptly—like I'd woken from a dream. I was freezing. I shivered but couldn't shake the memory. Her memories seem to come on most during times of stress. Sometimes they helped me. But I couldn't see any meaning in this one. Just one more sign that my brain really didn't belong to me.

I was very much awake and aware, here in the bamboo forest environment.

Hyden's head was forward and his eyes were closed. Asleep? I couldn't tell.

The door to the side room opened, and the leopard man came out. Alone.

"Bring the girl," he said.

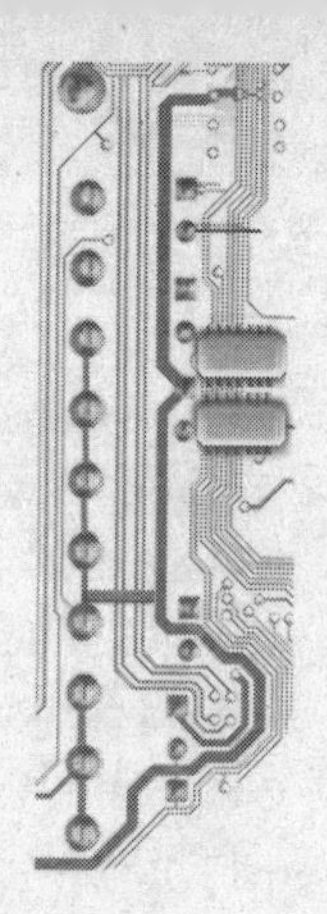

CHAPTER FIFTEEN

Hyden's eyes opened as one of the military Enders came over and yanked me to my feet.

"What about him?" the Ender asked the other guard.

"Just the girl," the first one said.

"No, take me!" Hyden shouted. "I'll go instead!"

"You'll get your turn," his guard said as he kicked him in the shins.

My guard pulled me harder, through the door on the left, and then shoved me into a small room. It had the projection illusion of being inside a rock cave. He pushed me into a metal chair.

"You can go," a voice said to the guard. It was the leopard man.

The guard hesitated, as if I were some kind of dangerous assassin he didn't dare leave with his boss.

The leopard man stood with his hands on his hips.

"Yes, sir," the guard said, and left.

Leopard Man wore a black long-sleeved knit shirt and

black jeans. He kept his white hair as long as a mane. In fact, when he walked around my chair, I was reminded of a lion on the prowl, stalking his prey. He examined my face from every angle. Then he went to the back of my chair and pushed my head forward. He parted my hair, exposing my chip insertion scar. I felt his cautious fingers probing it.

"What are you doing?" I said.

He ignored me. After a moment of examination, he moved away, and I raised my head.

"You have no right to keep us here. I want a lawyer."

A sharp laugh blew from his lips. "You think we care about rights? Lawyers?" He bent so we were eye to eye. "You're mine. Like a doll. I'll do what I want, when I want."

I detected a slight accent, but it was too subtle to place. His eyes were gray-blue and lined with fine wrinkles. His face might have been called handsome once, but now it was just cruel. His hands were rough, with large knuckles and calluses. I had no doubt he was capable of any level of torture.

My eyes scanned the room. Two doors. Nothing that could be used as a weapon. I looked up at the ceiling. Through the cave illusion, I noticed panels in the ceiling. It might be possible to hide up there.

He came around and sat on the table. He stared into my eyes. I wasn't sure what he was doing. Was he examining me for something in particular? Or was he just doing it to intimidate me? I refused to look away. Finally, he straightened and walked to the other door.

He opened it, and a female Ender guard with cropped white hair stepped in.

"Take her," he said.

The wiry guard lifted me roughly by the arm. As she dragged me past the leopard man, I didn't take my eyes off his. I wanted to show him I would stand up to him, even if it meant dying.

Then I thought of Tyler, and my bravado melted. He would have Eugenia and a good life but zero family if he lost me. I had to find out what they wanted, find out if there was some way to negotiate for my safety. And for Michael's and Hyden's too.

The guard marched me down a hallway that had a projection of a rushing river and took me into a room that looked like a high-tech doctor's office. A pine forest was projected on one wall, with birds flying through the trees. The guard sat me on an examining table and raised it with a foot pedal. The motor buzzed as I was elevated to the perfect height to be scrutinized.

A doctor entered. A short, plump Ender, he nodded solemnly to me.

"I'm just going to examine you." He said it as if he needed my consent.

"And what if I say no?"

"I'm afraid that is not an option," he said. "So can we proceed?"

"No. I refuse. I'm here because I'm being held prisoner." I jiggled my cuffs. "You can see I'm handcuffed. But I've done nothing wrong."

The doctor's arms hung at his sides.

My voice softened to a plea. He might be the last reasonable person I encountered.

"Please do what's right," I said quietly. "Let me go."

He exchanged a look with the guard. My words must have reached him. He had to see how wrong this was, holding me this way. He went over to her and whispered something. I hoped he'd asked her to undo my cuffs. They were so tight, and my arms ached from being forced in this position for so long.

Then they turned to me. The looks on their faces, those stone-cold expressions, were not ones of sympathy.

The guard held me down with all her strength.

"What're you doing to me?" I screamed, struggling on the cold table.

The doctor had his back to me, but I could see that he was preparing an injection. He came over with a hypodermic syringe. The guard dug her bony fingers into my skin as the doctor stabbed my arm with the needle.

⊗ ⊗ ⊗

I dreamed of being back in my family home, the nice middle-class ranch house where my brother and I grew up. Tyler and I were in the living room, playing a silly card game on the floor, on a Saturday afternoon. It didn't make sense, because he looked his present age. Then my father came into the room.

"Daddy?" I asked, surprised to see him.

"What, Cal Girl?" he said.

For some reason, he was wearing a black suit. Then my mother came in the room wearing a floaty evening gown and put her arm around his waist.

"Mom?" I said.

She cocked her head. "What, dear?"

"I thought you were both gone," I said.

"No," she said. "We've always been here."

⊗ ⊗ ⊗

I awoke in a cramped room atop a thickly padded hospital bed. It reminded me of a baby's crib. But instead of bars, I was encased on all sides with clear plexi walls.

Above me, stars twinkled. Projections. An illusion to calm? Or to confuse?

"She's awake," someone whispered.

I turned my head to the sound. A female guard was outside the room, her face bisected by the door.

An Ender wearing a tight, light-colored jumpsuit entered. In her hands, she held a small machine with a cord that she drew out and touched to my forehead, then my wrist, then my heart. It was then that I realized my wrists were bound to the bed with hospital restraints.

She checked her machine and seemed satisfied. She left without ever having met my gaze.

I turned my wrists and pulled on the cuffs to see if I could get out of them. Impossible. Panic crept in like water under a door. I twisted harder, but it just made my wrists raw.

Someone opened the door. This time it was Emma. The Ender guard remained in the hall as Emma entered and then shut the door.

She carried a shopping bag.

"Hi, Callie," she said, all smiles and cheekbones.

"What do you want?" I didn't trust her, but it wasn't like I could get up and leave.

"I brought you a smoothie. Thought you'd like it." She pulled it out of her bag. "Strawberry-banana."

"I can't hold it. If you untie me—"

"I'll hold it for you."

She came over to the bed and held the straw to my mouth. I wanted to refuse it, but I was so thirsty. And hungry. It flowed cold and sweet down my throat.

"Easy," she said. "Not too much at once or you'll choke."

Emma looked a lot like her grandmother, up close. Helena must have looked like this when she was younger. That stately face, high cheekbones. Of course, Emma's nose had been reduced at Prime.

She pulled back the smoothie cup while I swallowed.

"Why did you do it?" I asked.

"What?"

"Act as the bait. You were the lure . . . for them."

She looked down at the cup and fiddled with the straw. "I didn't have a choice," she said in a lowered voice. "They made me."

"How?" I kept my voice low as well.

I wondered if she was being jacked right now. Could I trust what she said?

"They said they would hurt my grandmother if I didn't do what they said," she whispered.

"Your grandmother? Helena?"

"That's right." She winced, as if she couldn't bear to think of Helena being hurt.

She pulled up a chair and sat with her legs crossed. I noticed she was wearing a large anklet, the latest style, her name in gold script around her ankle:

Emma.

"That's pretty," I said, pointing to the anklet.

"Thank you. It was a gift from Grandma."

I took a deep breath. Emma didn't seem to know anything about me. She had no idea that her grandmother rented me to assassinate the senator. And when that didn't work, her grandmother had come up with another plan: to find out what happened to her granddaughter. This seemed like a lot to unload on Emma. But she had to know the bottom line about Helena, especially since she was operating on the misconception that she could still save her.

This was, of course, if she was telling the truth.

"That must be your favorite piece of jewelry, that anklet," I said. "What other kind of jewelry do you like?"

"Other jewelry?"

"Yeah, what do you wear, collect?"

"Lots of stuff. Pins. Things my mother gave me. Things my grandmother gave me. A charm bracelet that Doris gave me."

I nodded. She wasn't being jacked. This was the real Emma I was talking to. I'd seen the bracelet in her bedroom when I first went to Helena's house, when I was a donor.

"I had one just like it," I said. "From Doris too."

"It was pretty." A wistful look came over her face. "Wish I still had it."

Her expression and the way she spoke made me aware something was wrong. She seemed off, the way people do when they've been kept captive for a long time. I'd seen that look in some of the institution girls—even in my friend Sara. Emma was submissive and dreamy, not fully present.

"Emma, when did these men get to you?"

"When?"

"You did the body bank rental; then what happened?"

"I couldn't go home. Grandma would have been so angry. I couldn't lie. She would have seen my makeover."

"So you ran away?"

"With my friend Kevin."

My focus sharpened. Kevin. That was the name of Lauren's missing grandson.

"Did Kevin also go to Prime?

"Yes. He said he wanted the makeover, but I think he went there because I did. He liked me, but he wasn't my boyfriend. We pooled our money from Prime. We were going to get an apartment."

"But the man with the leopard tattoo found you?"

She nodded. "Dawson. He was the man who said he owned the apartment."

"I see."

"Kevin was supposed to meet me there, but he never showed up."

I wondered if Brockman's men found him. But she wasn't ready to hear any of that.

"How long have you been with these people?" I asked. "Dawson's people?"

"I don't know." She shook her head. "What day is it?"

She was really out of it. She could have been here a week or a month.

"Emma, these ties are so tight. They hurt," I whispered. "Could you just loosen them?"

The guard opened the door wider to let us know we weren't alone. Emma glanced in the woman's direction. She straightened.

"Callie, they need to perform some important tests on you." Her voice was louder now.

She sounded like she'd rehearsed a speech. I let her go on.

"They are required of all of us. I went through them," she said. "They're fine."

I could see in her eyes she was lying.

"Maybe for you," I said. "But I'm not doing them."

Her shoulders dropped. "Callie, please, listen to me. You have to; you really don't have a choice."

The leopard man—Dawson—came in the room.

"You can go, Emma," he said.

He spoke sternly and firmly as though to a child. She looked afraid but didn't move.

"Emma, go," he said.

She took the drink with her and left. Dawson leaned on the wall of my bed, his white hair falling down around his shoulders like some evil wizard's.

"So how do you feel?" he asked without a smile.

"How do you think I feel, tied up like this? Like an animal," I said.

"If you agree to cooperate, we can release you. No shackles whatsoever. But you have to agree."

"I want to be untied and set free. There's nothing else I'll agree to."

He sighed and pressed a button. The walls of my bed slid down to the floor with a heavy *thunk*. No safety codes here. He pulled a large knife out of his pocket, flicked it open. The long blade gleamed in the light as he turned it. I tried not to flinch as he brought it closer.

He slipped the blade under my restraints and sawed through them until I was free. He pulled them away, closed the knife, and slid it in back into his pocket. I rubbed my sore wrists.

I got out of bed. I was still in my clothes.

"Where are my shoes?" I asked.

He grabbed me by the upper arm and pulled me out of the room. Barefoot.

The guard followed us down the hallway. We came to a turn and he went right, dragging me roughly along the tiled floor. "You're hurting me," I said.

"Really? So sorry, Your Majesty."

Muffled screams reached us as we approached the end of the hall.

I recognized the voice. Hyden.

Terror shot through me. "What are you doing to him?" I yelled, struggling to pull myself from Dawson's grasp.

He gripped me harder and shoved me in front of a large window, pressing my face against the glass. Inside a room sat an enormous tube-shaped machine. A projection of a tranquil forest on the wall was in direct contrast to the violent scene being played out in front of it. Two Enders held on to Hyden's arms as he tugged and twisted, trying to get away. A third Ender stood against the wall, watching. He had an amused look on his face, which disappeared as soon as he spotted Dawson.

This would have hurt anyone, but for Hyden, who felt pain just from touching, it must have been torture.

Dawson nodded curtly to the men. Instead of being more gentle with Hyden, they began to push him back and forth between them, as if they were tossing a ball. Hyden struggled to stay on his feet.

"Stop it! Stop them!" I pounded my palms on the glass. My insides were being twisted.

Sweat beaded on Hyden's face, and his skin had never looked so pale. Dark circles ringed his eyes. Had he been beaten?

"You don't understand. This could kill him," I said.

"Only you can stop it," Dawson said. "You know what I want to hear."

Hyden fell, but the Enders caught him as he slumped and pulled him back up on his feet. They dragged him over to the window, right in front of me, and pressed his face flat against the glass.

"Hyden." My heart felt like it was going to crack in half.

"I'll do it," I said to Dawson. "I'll do your tests."

Dawson smirked and nodded to the Enders behind the glass. They let go of Hyden. But he stayed against the glass, his hand moving up to match my palm.

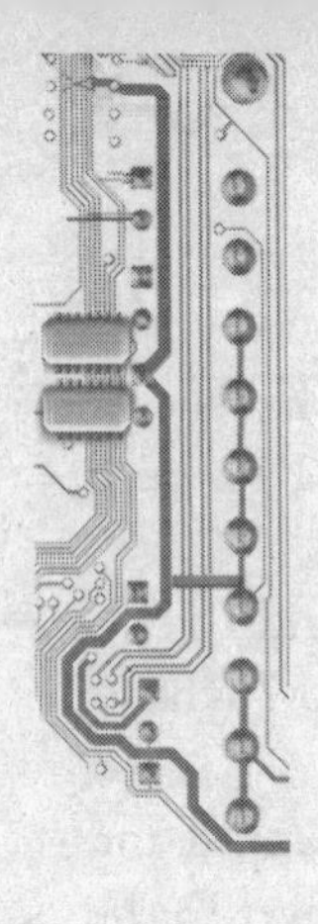

CHAPTER SIXTEEN

"What about Michael?" I asked as Dawson escorted me back down the hall. I was still barefoot, but for the first time since I'd arrived I was walking on my own instead of being dragged. They knew my weakness and how to get to me. But I couldn't help it; I had to stop them. Now I was even more determined to find a way to get us all out of here.

"What about him?" Dawson said.

He opened a door, and we entered a lab where a female Ender was putting on white rubber gloves.

"Where is he?" I asked Dawson.

"Resting," he said before walking out.

I wondered if Michael was really all right. Or whether "resting" really meant some Ender was now jacking him.

The female Ender wore white rubber clothing, pants, boots, and an apron over a nylon shirt. She made me strip and then stand on a rubber platform that drained to the floor while water sprayed at me from different directions. She put on goggles and rubbed me with a rough cloth. It reminded me of the body bank, only not as fancy. Whatever this place was, their budget was a lot smaller.

After I dried off, she handed me a surgical gown.

"What is this for?" I asked her. "What's going to happen to me?"

She didn't even make eye contact. It was like I had no voice. She took my arm before I could put on the gown. I held it to my front while she pulled me into another room. A different Ender waited for me there.

I hurried into the gown while this new woman, short and pasty, watched. She had me lie down on a platform. They put a helmetlike cage over my head and locked it down so I couldn't move at all. I hated it. It was so restrictive, I could feel my pulse speeding up in the blood vessels in my head. Pound, pound, pound. I wanted to scream.

"Just relax," she said. "You're not going anywhere, anyway. Don't move."

She pressed another button and a coffin-like cage device encased my body.

"What is this?" I screamed.

With a buzzing sound that made me think of a saw, the platform slid back into the tube-shaped machine. There was no opening at the back. At the front, where I had entered, a panel slid down, shutting off any glimpse of the space outside.

Air started blowing, but it didn't make me feel any better. I felt like every nerve in my body was on fire. I wanted to crawl out of my own skin, and I thought my heart was going to explode out of my chest. The Ender's voice came through a speaker near my ear.

"Hold your breath until I tell you to breathe again."

"Starting when?" I asked.

"Now."

I inhaled and held it for what seemed like a very long time. The machine made loud clanking noises, as if someone was working on the outside with a jackhammer. Just when I was about to burst, she spoke.

"Okay. Breathe."

This went on for an eternity. Once, she claimed I took a breath too soon and I had to do it all over again. Eventually, the panel opened and she removed the restraints.

I rubbed my neck. I felt completely drained but so relieved to be out of there.

The next test involved one Ender holding a scanner near my head while another Ender monitored a computer to see the results. Of course they grabbed my chip ID number: they did that first thing. But what they were looking for after that, I had no idea.

"Why are you doing this?" I asked. "What are you trying to see?" They weren't answering any of my questions. I was their lab rat.

⊗ ⊗ ⊗

I endured many more tests that examined my physical abilities, my eyesight, my ability to identify smells, tastes, tactile properties. Finally, they finished, or at least I thought so, because they gave me fresh clothes—a T-shirt and olive-colored pants—and gave me back my shoes.

I had to drink a glass of red liquid, and the next thing I knew, I was asleep.

I woke up on the floor of a room with gray padded rubber walls. A foam cushion sat in the corner, a cube that could be used as a stool. And in the opposite corner was a hole in the floor that made a constant vacuuming sound. The toilet.

This was my cell, outfitted so I could not hurt myself.

No projections in here. Or my shoes.

I spotted a security camera in the ceiling and one in the corner, up high. I yelled at it. "I've done all your tests. I want to see my friends!"

The camera lens just stared back at me.

There I was, locked up again. I pounded the walls with my fists but only made dull thumps. I screamed. No one answered.

I was far away from the outside world, far away from Tyler. He had to be worried about me. This was all supposed to be over with when the body bank came down. We were supposed to have a normal life, one where he would attend school and play games and fish in the lake. We were going to be a makeshift family, Michael and me and Tyler with Eugenia, a sort of substitute grandmother.

Eugenia. What could she be thinking, with Michael and me gone for so long? Was she calling the authorities? Would she try to comfort Tyler, making up a lie, assuring him we were fine? He'd see right through that.

I missed my little brother. I missed his rabbit-brown eyes, his soft hair, his shy smile. It was so good to see him healthy again, but I hardly had time to enjoy that because suddenly we had to leave the mansion, to run and hide. Had anything changed? It seemed like we were always running and hiding. Only now we ran from bigger and better houses.

What would happen to him if I never came back? Could Eugenia take care of him? Lauren was his legal guardian, but would she actually want to raise him?

I thought about the last time I was locked in a cell. Institution 37. No good had come of that.

How long had I been lying there unconscious? They must have drugged me.

Then I heard a man's voice in my head.

Callie.

I sat perfectly still, waiting to hear it again.

Can you hear me?

It sounded like Dawson, but I wasn't positive.

"Who is this?" I asked.

Who do you think it is?

"No games. I have too much time on my hands, so I'll win."

It doesn't matter who I am. What matters is that you can hear me.

It was Dawson, I was sure.

How are you feeling?

I remembered he had asked me that before—in that same clinical tone that contained no hint of actual concern.

"Tired. Tired of being in here."

Would you like to leave the room?

Was he really asking me that? "Yes."

The door opened. Was that a trick? Whatever, I'd be a fool not to try to leave. I got up and walked out. The Ender guard was nowhere in sight.

We don't need the guard if we can watch you.

I gasped slightly.

Don't worry, I cannot hear your thoughts. Those are yours. Private.

"It's the only thing left that's private around here."

I walked to the end of the hall and went through the door. Another hallway. I followed it and turned right.

It's quite a maze, this place.

"So where's the exit?"

He laughed. I hated having him laughing in my head. I had a horrible desire to knock him out with something hard and heavy. Lot of good that would do me.

The hallway ended at another door. I opened it and saw a child's playroom. Tables heaped with colorful wooden blocks and puzzles lined the room. But there were no children in sight. And it was too clean, too set-up.

You're in the fun room, I see. Why don't you have a seat?

I went to the door opposite the one I entered and tried to turn the knob. It was locked. I went back to the door I had entered through, and it was locked from the other side.

Yes, you really should sit down.

I pulled up a chair and sat. I was clearly stuck in this room with locked doors and no windows.

You see before you several colored blocks of wood in various shapes. Can you pick up the red circle?

I picked it up and held it in front of my face so he could easily see it.

Perfect. Now place it on the tray in front of you.

I did what he asked.

Now lay your hands on the table, straight out in front of you. Keep them relaxed.

I had no idea what he was testing. This seemed too easy.

"If I do this, will you let me—"

One thing at a time. Just stay there, like that, until I give you another instruction.

I waited for a few moments. Then something horrible happened.

My right thumb moved. Only I wasn't making it move.

A chill ran up my neck.

"What are you doing?" I asked.

Just relax. Don't speak.

My right hand vibrated uncontrollably, shaking back and forth. Then it rose an inch off the table and moved toward the red circle block. It hovered over it, shaking, while I could do nothing but watch.

The hairs on my arm raised.

Just relax, let go. His voice sounded smooth and even, as if he were trying to lull me into a trance.

Then my hand fell on the red block like a claw in an old-time arcade machine, and my fingers clumsily clutched it. My hand rose and brought it back in front of me. And dropped the block there, on the table. My hand then collapsed on top of it.

"What did you do?" I asked.

I controlled you. He couldn't contain the glee in his voice.

I hated this. I focused with all my will to kick him out of my head. I didn't know how to do this, I just knew that I wanted it, I was willing it. I concentrated on picturing him gone, blown away by an invisible tornado, until my mind was clean, clear, and all my own.

I don't know if he left on his own or if I'd actually succeeded, but suddenly all was quiet.

⊗ ⊗ ⊗

I sat there in silence for fifteen or twenty minutes, until an Ender guard arrived. He brought me to another room—a large indoor shooting range.

"Proceed to the last stall," a female Ender's voice boomed over the loudspeaker.

I looked around. She stood behind a glass wall, in a viewing area off a control room on a second level. She wore the black military uniform but was tall and elegant, with her white hair worn upswept.

A rifle waited for me at the last stall. I picked it up. I wondered—if I shot the glass wall, would it be bulletproof? Of course it would.

The rifle was heavy for my weight. I heard the creaking of a target moving into place with a mechanical sound. It was a special holo of an Ender man, dressed in what looked like terrorist gear. A mask covered his face, and he held his own gun pointed at me.

"On the count of three," the Ender woman said over the mike. "One."

I put the rifle to my cheek and aimed.

"Two."

I breathed in.

"Three."

I took one shot at the target, aiming for the heart. The rifle kicked back, but I held my ground.

"Hold your fire," she said.

The target was moved forward so I could examine it. The holo had frozen and recorded the shot. The hole was right at the heart. I turned and stared up at the Ender. Her face was expressionless.

She had me repeat the test several times, and each time a red circle lit up for the spot I was to aim for. Each time I hit it. My father's lessons were not forgotten.

Then the target holo changed to an Ender woman wearing a floral dress and carrying a cane.

"Shoot," she said.

"At an innocent civilian?" I asked.

"Shoot."

"No."

She turned away so I couldn't see her face. I could vaguely

make out that she was conferring with another Ender in the control room.

My scalp started to tingle. I sensed someone inside me.

Callie?

Dawson. Oh, I hated having him under my skin!

Don't worry, little Starter. You don't have to do anything. Just relax.

Oh. He was going to try to control me again. I tried to resist. I gripped the rifle.

But my arms raised slowly. This was horrible. They rose into a shooting position. I tried to fight, tried to push them down.

He had control of me.

My head lowered so my cheek was up against the rifle, and my eye lined up the shot. It pointed toward her heart.

Sweat beaded on my forehead. I tried to make my hands stiff, so they wouldn't be able to move. But my finger slowly bent and pulled the trigger.

BANG.

I glanced up at the control room. The Ender at the glass-enclosed viewing area spoke to someone inside.

The target rolled closer. That poor old Ender lady had been killed by a fatal wound to the heart by my gun.

Excellent.

I felt my fingers loosen their grip on the rifle. Dawson had given me back control. It must have taken extreme concentration on his part to maintain a connection, and now he had to recharge.

"This is disgusting," I said. "You're a horrible, sick person."

Sometimes we have to do things that aren't pretty. For the greater good.

The Ender target moved away with a sad electronic buzz of the motor, and a new target moved into the original position.

Let's try this one.

It was a holo of a Starter. At this distance, I guessed he was about my age, in typical street Starter wear: rags and a water bottle, handlite. Dirty, scraggly.

It was an image of Michael.

I felt my stomach lurch. I was going to put the rifle down, but I couldn't.

"No . . ."

My hands brought the rifle into position, and my eye focused on the target.

"Stop this!" I screamed.

My mind raced. Was there anything I could do to stop his control? If relaxing helped, then would panic break the connection?

"You can't make me do this!"

But in painfully slow motion my finger pulled the trigger. Nothing I could do would stop my finger from moving. Everything was happening in spite of myself.

The rifle fired with a bang.

The Enders in the control room pressed buttons that made the target move forward so I could see the results.

A wound was outlined in red, showing that my bullet had gone clean through the holo image of Michael's forehead.

If it were really him, he would be dead.

My stomach tightened into a knot. I felt my arms get lighter. I had control again.

I gripped the rifle and sprinted down the walkway to the door. The female Ender shrilled over the microphone.

"Callie Woodland, return to the stall. Stop now!"

Callie!

I tried not to listen to Dawson but held on fast to my anger. It seemed to be fueling me. I burst through the door. The Ender guard on the other side came at me. I aimed for his leg and pulled the trigger.

It wouldn't move. The trigger froze.

Do you think we can't control those? They don't work outside the shooting range, little Starter.

"Stop calling me that!"

I raised the rifle and used the butt to slam into the Ender's stomach. He doubled over. But what I couldn't see was the Ender who came up from behind me and pressed something hard against my spine that zapped my nerves to jelly. My knees buckled, and everything turned black.

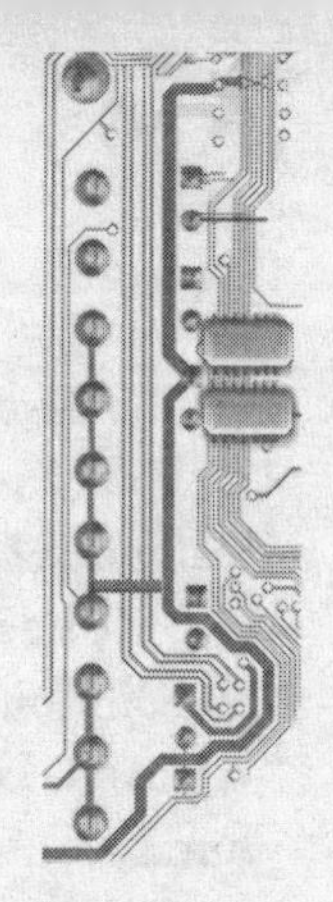

CHAPTER SEVENTEEN

I woke up in the padded room with a killer headache and a mouth that felt stuffed full of cotton. The door opened, and a female Ender guard let someone enter the room. Emma. She closed the door behind her.

I looked at her. "No smoothie?"

She sat on the floor next to me. "I heard they locked you up."

"What else did you hear?"

"That you were an expert shooter. But you attacked a guard."

"I refused to shoot my best friend. What did they think?"

"It's just a holo. Maybe they wanted to see if you could follow orders."

I shook my head. "They knew I wouldn't do it. That's why they set up that situation."

She bent her knees and rested her arms on them. I noticed her large name anklet again.

"So Michael, is he like your boyfriend?"

"No. He's my friend." Why was she asking this? Did she really care? "How is he?"

"He's doing fine. *He* did all the tests." She emphasized "he" to point out what a good Starter does.

"And Hyden." She played with her hair. "What about him?"

"What about him? Is he all right?"

"He's okay. Is *he* your boyfriend?"

I didn't like this inquisition. The less I revealed, the better. Plus, I figured cameras were filming us.

"No," I said. "He's also a friend. Where is he now?"

"In another room. He refused to finish his tests too."

I imagined Hyden being told to shoot a holo of me. It made me feel good to know he wouldn't do that. But Michael had finished his tests. Did he have to shoot me?

She ran her hand through her hair. "It just makes everything go longer when you guys won't cooperate."

"What do you mean? Have you had other Metals in here before?"

She nodded.

"Where are they now?"

"I'm not supposed to talk about that." She twirled her hair around her finger. "I wanted to ask you something. They said you knew my grandma."

"They told you that?"

"Yes. That she rented you. Is it true?" She seemed sharper than earlier when she had been so spacey.

"How do I know you're really Emma?"

"I thought I proved it to you, last time we talked. The bracelet, remember?"

"Maybe you were listening when Emma and I were talking," I said.

"My grandma always kept a gun in her bedroom."

"Lots of Enders do."

"In the floor of their closet, under the rug, under the floor panel, in a wooden box? A Glock eighty-five?"

That stopped me. "Okay."

"She said it was better to be prepared than to be afraid. I think the war did that to her."

"The war changed a lot of us."

"The one thing I hated was she wouldn't let me get any surgery. I wanted my nose fixed. My mother would have let me do it if she were alive. I told Grandma that. She cried. I don't know if it was because she missed her so much, or because I'd hurt her. If I do get to go back someday, I'll tell her I'm sorry. I think about that a lot."

I couldn't tell Emma the truth now. She wasn't ready to hear it.

"Even though she should have let me get the surgery," she went on. "I had such a beak."

"Emma, I saw your pictures, from before. You had your grandma's nose. It was strong, and it looked good on both of you. I know it sounds lame, but it's true—what's on the outside isn't as important as what's on the inside."

"Oh, easy for you to say." She looked me over.

"Sure, I got the makeover like you did, but it didn't really change me. Someday, we'll both be Enders, and even with green laser surgery, eventually we'll be old and wrinkled. Like everybody. But we'll look a lot better if we're happy inside. If we used our brains and our talents instead of stressing over what someone else defines as 'pretty.'"

Emma frowned. "You don't know what it's like. You were probably never ugly."

"Neither were you. It's not that we shouldn't be the best we can be. But surgery at sixteen? Or thirteen or twelve? I'll bet you knew some mean girls who looked like holo-stars."

"Oh yeah."

"But let me guess: no one decent wanted to be around them because they were stupid bullies?"

She was silent.

"I'm telling you, if there's one thing I learned from this whole body bank mess, it's that looks are overrated. Beauty isn't about meeting some holo-star standard, it's about being you. Because looks come and go. But nobody else can be you."

She stared at me as if I were crazy.

"You're never going to change my mind," she said. "If I hadn't already done it, I'd get this doctor who's here to do it. He can do anything."

"What doctor?" I said.

"He's a surgeon and a tech expert." Her eyes were on fire.

A female Ender's voice came over an invisible speaker. "Emma, you are wanted in the front office."

She pouted. "I gotta go." She got up and left.

I felt like an idiot wasting my energy trying to convince her to appreciate herself. Did she listen? No. Meanwhile, Dawson was probably cooking up some new torture for me. After attacking his guard, I hated to think what would be in store for me.

Callie?

Someone was in my head. And it wasn't Dawson.

"Hyden?" I stood. "Is that you?"

Yeah, it's me.

"How is this happening?"

I stared at the gray padded walls.

Dawson and his people made me hook up. They're here.

"I see." So Dawson had some new test.

I'm sorry. . . .

"About what?" Without intending to, I was moving toward the door. The door opened. The Ender guard stepped back to let me out. I walked out into the hallway. Everything felt floaty and dreamlike.

Keep going. You don't have to do anything. Just don't resist me.

It was a strange sensation. Sort of like ice-skating down the hallway without any skates. I wasn't trying to walk, wasn't trying to resist. But I was moving.

I didn't know where I was going. Not just the final destination, but whether I was going to open a door, or turn, or go to the end of the hall. I just put one foot in front of the other.

Surprisingly, it wasn't alarming. It was almost calming. Maybe it was because I knew it was Hyden controlling me, even if Dawson was giving the orders.

Just stay with me.

I wasn't stupid; I knew they were making him do this. Dawson probably had a rifle aimed on him. So something was going to happen. I could hear concern in his voice.

I recognized where he was making me walk. The shooting range.

The new Ender guard there was taller and bigger than the one I'd attacked. This one opened the door for me, and I entered.

I looked up and saw the same elegant female Ender from before watching me from the glassed-in viewing area off the control room.

I thought I was going to the last stall again, but I stopped midway. I turned, and instead of a rifle, I saw a gun, a Glock 85. It was the same kind of gun that Helena had had me use. Did they know that?

I didn't see a target. I didn't want to touch the gun, but it wasn't my decision. Hyden did it for me.

My hand moved down and wrapped around the cold metal of the gun. It raised.

The Ender woman behind the glass spoke to someone in the control room. I heard a rustling on the range and turned my attention there. This time, instead of a target, an Ender man wearing a black bulletproof bodysuit and a helmet walked out. He faced me, a living version of the target image I'd shot at before.

"That's a bulletproof suit, right?"

They tell me yes.

Hyden raised my arm and aimed, using my eyes. My finger pulled the trigger. The Ender stumbled back from the impact but remained on his feet.

The Ender behind glass spoke through her microphone. "Would the target please move forward?"

The man walked toward me until he was ten feet away. I could see where the bullet had torn a hole in his suit, at the heart. It was easy to see because of a red powder that had been released where the fibers were torn.

"Good job," the Ender said through his protective helmet. His eyes narrowed in a look of approval.

"Target. You are dismissed," said the Ender behind the glass.

He left. I wondered what that proved to them. Probably that if I trusted someone, that person could control my body more easily. So now . . .

Oh, they wouldn't.

But yes, they did.

Michael entered the range. He appeared to be wearing the same kind of bulletproof bodysuit and helmet.

But was he?

He tried to leave, but I could see that they had locked down his boots magnetically. He struggled but couldn't lift his feet. He was forced to stand there.

It was a horrible test. This wasn't just a nameless, able-bodied Ender; this was someone I knew and loved like a brother. What if his suit wasn't bulletproof?

They're telling me to tell you to relax.

"Don't do this, Hyden."

They say he won't get hurt.

My arm holding the gun raised.

Michael flinched.

"Make it stop," I said. "Refuse!"

It'll be just like the last one.

"Don't make me. Please, Hyden."

I could see Michael's eyes through the helmet. He closed them.

"I won't do this!" I shouted at Hyden.

I fought as hard as I could. My insides were torn to shreds. I could not gain control of my hands.

"I'm so sorry," I said to Michael.

My finger pulled the trigger, the gun went off with a loud pop, and Michael fell backward to the floor.

Instantly, I had my control back. I dropped the gun and ran to him. I pulled off his helmet.

"Michael, can you hear me?"

His eyes fluttered open. "Callie?"

I looked at his chest. Same hole, circled with red, just like the Ender.

A look of surprise came over Michael's face. "You shot me."

⊗ ⊗ ⊗

Ender guards came and took me away, to another one of their rooms with a projection of a beach. A few chairs were placed around a plain, school-issue table. A moment later, they brought in Hyden and left us alone.

"What were you thinking?" I said.

He held out his arms. "I didn't have a choice."

"Making me shoot Michael? I can't believe you did that."

"They made me. They threatened to torture you if I didn't cooperate." His eyes pleaded. "They said the bullets were fake."

"He could have been killed. People can die from blanks, from the impact if they're too close."

"We can't all be shooting experts like you."

He ran his hand through his hair. He looked awful, with bags under his eyes.

"Have they hurt you?" I asked.

"They've been treating me like a prince."

I glanced around the room. I assumed cameras and listening devices spied on us everywhere.

"Who are these people?" I whispered.

He rubbed his forehead. "I'm not sure." He kept his voice low. "They want the chip, my chip. They've figured out how to use it. So they're competitors."

He covered his mouth with both hands so a camera could not read his lips, and whispered, "The question is, are they my father's men?"

I hadn't even thought of that possibility. That would explain why they had mastered the transpositions.

I remembered what Hyden's father said to me. *Trust no one but yourself, and then question that.*

⊗ ⊗ ⊗

Not long after our conversation, they finally brought in some food and water. It was just bread and a thin soup, but we were starving.

"Where's Michael?" I asked the Ender guard who brought the food.

He ignored me.

"What could they be doing to him?" I asked Hyden.

"It could just be tactics. Keeping us separate. Who knows? Maybe he's getting a cheeseburger and fries?"

He smiled a little, to try to cheer me up. It didn't work. My mind went to the worst places, worrying about Michael. I didn't know why they'd want to interrogate him. Of the three of us, Hyden had the most to reveal. Was it possible they didn't know who he really was?

I looked at him.

"What?" he asked quietly.

"Nothing." I didn't want to risk even whispering it.

After we finished, the same Ender guard who had brought the food returned. "Hold on," Hyden said. "Be strong."

I gave him a half smile. He nodded.

The guard escorted me down the hall to a small, stark room with a table and two chairs. A female Ender entered, wearing a white turtleneck and pants. She nodded to dismiss the guard.

"Hello, Callie. Please sit down."

She sat in the chair opposite me. She turned on her palm airscreen so it could transcribe our conversation. I could see the letters, backward, as she spoke.

"So, Callie, how long ago was your chip implanted?"

"Three months, two weeks, and five days."

"Do you have any physical problems that you can attribute to it?"

"Headaches."

"Is that all?"

I thought about not telling her. But I could see something else on the airscreen—a moving meter that looked like a graph. It was a lie sensor, and it now wavered just because I was thinking of a lie.

"I have memory episodes."

She leaned in. "What are those?"

"Times when I relive a memory from my renter, when she was in my body. When I was unaware. They come back to me, out of the blue."

"How does it manifest itself?" Her words flashed across the airscreen.

"It's like watching a holo," I said. "A short holo. It only lasts a minute." I shrugged to try to make light of it. But she was far too interested to buy that.

"And you say it is a memory from your renter's experience? How do you know that?"

"Because . . ."

I hesitated and the graph spiked.

"Just tell the truth," she said.

"I knew who she was. I recognized the places in the memory, her room."

"And is there some emotion that comes with this?" Her brows raised. She licked her lips and drew closer.

"Yes. It's like I'm reliving her experience at that time. But I don't know why. It's not like it answers any questions. Or like I can explain why it comes on. There's no revelation, just this stupid holo in my head, and then it's over."

I saw my words form on the screen. It was strange.

"So who is this surgeon you have here?" I asked.

She looked up at me. She didn't deny his existence; she didn't answer. She just kept on quizzing me.

"And what do you know about Hyden?" she asked.

My muscles tensed. I heard her device make a high-pitched sound like a bird.

"Relax, please," she said.

"I think you should ask him that," I said. I relaxed my muscles and the sound subsided.

"But I'm asking you."

"And I'm saying you should ask him."

Her machine went silent. So did she. She wrapped up her palm airscreen and stood. Without another word, she left the room.

Dawson entered. I hadn't seen him face to face for a while. But having him in my head was a creepy experience. It felt almost embarrassing to see him in person again.

"You are a feisty little Starter," he said.

I stared back at him. He pulled out a chair and sat.

"I would like to know more about Hyden," he said.

"As I told the last Ender, I think you should ask him."

"Wouldn't you rather we not do it that way?" He squinted, as if contemplating some unsavory task.

"I don't know much about him."

"Is it true he invented the chip that you have in your head?"

"He would have to be pretty smart at his age, to do that."

"He is pretty smart." He leaned forward on the table and grabbed my wrist. "You, Callie Woodland, were the one we wanted. You're the only one with an altered chip that allows you to kill. You're the only one who is an M.A.D."

I tried to pull away, but he held on.

"Multiple Access Donor. You're the only one who can have someone in your head without totally transposing you. You are still aware. You can hear them. And that means that you can also have another person inside. This is something no one has been able to re-create in any other Metal."

His nails were digging into my skin. "You're hurting me. Do you really want to hurt the only M.A.D. Metal?"

He looked down at my wrist and let go. I put it behind my back. I didn't want him to see me rubbing it.

I remembered what Hyden had said. So these guys were his father's competition? Maybe they were going to sell the chip off to some terrorist group or enemy country. Or maybe they were a terrorist group themselves.

"So you've been doing all this research about chip technology . . ."

"Yes," Dawson said. "We have."

"With these experts . . ."

"We have some of the best."

"But you can't re-create the chip yourselves."

"It is the keystone, and it eludes us."

"We don't want these chips in our heads anymore," I said. "You can have them. I believe you have an expert here who can remove them."

"You know it is very difficult. Very precise work. The skill required is a cross between a demolitions expert and a brain surgeon."

"Yes. But you have the person to do it, don't you?"

He stared at me with piercing eyes. I could tell he was considering it, as if it could be the answer to all his problems.

"Remember, you asked for this," he said.

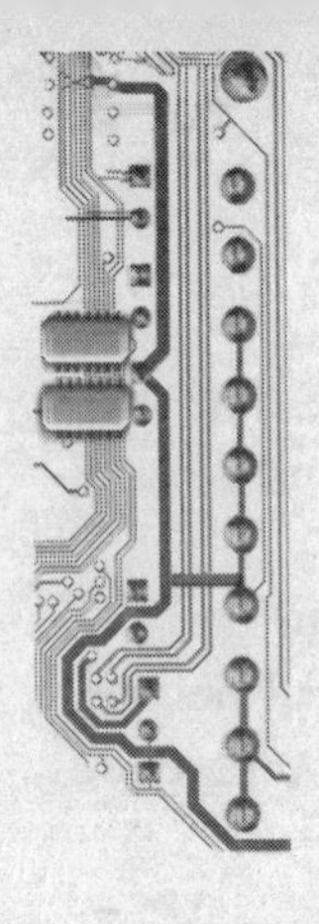

CHAPTER EIGHTEEN

Dawson gathered all of us in the large room where we'd first entered. Hyden, Emma, me, and Michael. The projection now was of the snowy Himalayas.

I rushed over to Michael, wanting to know how he was, what they'd done to him, but Dawson stopped me. He'd brought in an Ender he referred to only as "the Doctor" to talk to us. He had an accent, Swedish or Norwegian.

"Removal of the chip is a risky process," the Doctor said. "We know from the scans that it is attached with a weblike pattern."

"It's quite ingenious. The chip itself creates the web," Dawson said.

"Due to variations from human to human, it makes it trickier to determine how to unhook it," the Doctor said. He motioned with his fingers, curling them like hooks. "But finally we have the inventor of the chip here with us to ask."

Hyden glared at him. "You need to ask my father. I had

the concept and the initial designs. He created the physical chip and figured out how it would be implanted."

The Doctor's smile melted.

Dawson pulled out a chair and sat. "Have you ever watched an implantation surgery?"

"Lots of times," Hyden said. "But never a removal."

"But it can be done?" Dawson asked.

"Theoretically. But practically, I wouldn't touch it." Hyden folded his arms. "And neither should you."

"Why is that?" the Doctor asked.

"Because it's a big risk."

"Any surgery is a risk," the Doctor said. "But we do them."

People started talking at once, arguing the pros and cons of chip surgery until no one could be heard.

Emma stepped forward. "I want mine out."

Everyone stopped talking and turned toward her.

"Take it out," she said. "You can have it."

With a surprised expression, the Doctor turned to Dawson. "We have a volunteer."

She held up her hand. "Yes. Use me."

"Emma, are you sure?" I asked.

"Why, you want to go ahead of me?" she said. "You can't. I asked first."

"Do you know the risk you're taking?" Hyden asked her, shaking his head almost imperceptibly.

"Don't you try to talk me out of this. I hate this thing in my head. Worst decision ever," she said. "I don't want men tracking me, chasing, hunting me down." She pointed at me. "You know, you all do, that this is what it's going to be like for the rest of our lives. We will always be hunted for what we can do, for the chip itself. Let's just get it over with now and go back to living our lives. I want to go back to my grandma. Finish school. Go to parties again. The war is over, but I'm still living it, every day. I'm so sick of it. Take the stupid thing out of my head. Please."

An icy silence fell. Dawson cleared his throat.

"All right," he said. "Let's do it."

Emma smiled. I went over and took her arm.

"We know chips can explode," I said. "I saw it happen, at the mall. Someone set it off."

"That's different." She pulled her arm away. "No one's going to be setting mine off. They're going to remove it."

She had a point.

Hyden came over. "It's proof there's an explosive component in there." He gestured to her head. "The webbing of my design is entwined with the explosive."

"So you do know something about removing the chip after all," Dawson said.

"It's like a hundred random cords in a junk drawer," Hyden said. "I can't tell you how to untangle them."

Dawson stared at Hyden a moment. Then he shouted to the Doctor. "Get Emma prepped for surgery!"

Before Emma left, she leaned over to me and whispered, "You should get yours done too. What if they don't want to take out everyone's? Better get in while you have the chance."

She looked the happiest I'd ever seen her as she strolled out of the room with the Doctor, Dawson, and a guard.

Michael came up to me. "Are they really going to do this?"

Hyden shook his head. "It's insane."

But I understood everything Emma said. I felt the same way. I wanted more than anything to be normal again. And she was right: we'd never be safe until we were rid of the chips. Someone would always be jacking us or trying to kidnap us to get the chip. And I'd rather be opened by this expert surgeon than some thief.

Still, Hyden, who should have known better than anyone, looked pale at the thought of Emma going under the knife.

"I'd heard maybe the chip would be disabled if someone tried to remove it. To protect the technology, it would self-destruct," I said to Hyden. "And maybe explode."

"It was my father's idea. I found out too late he'd put the explosive in my design."

He looked distracted. Upset. Michael held my hand to comfort me. Hyden noticed and his eyes reflected pain. I wanted to do something, anything to connect the three of us in this moment, while we waited to hear the fate of one of our own.

I reached out my hand to him.

He looked surprised. Then he walked away.

I knew he couldn't touch me. But I had to try.

⊗ ⊗ ⊗

An Ender brought out hot chocolate and sandwiches for us. Hot chocolate? I felt so confused. Were we prisoners or experiments? Were we going to get what we wanted most, to get the chips removed? But then they wouldn't need us anymore. Maybe we were stupid to hope they would let us go.

All we could do was wait and see how well it worked with Emma. We pulled a table and chairs over into the corner of this huge space, far away from the doors and walls, to feel like we had a little privacy from any hidden cameras. We ate in silence, inhaling the food due to our hunger. Like all the furniture here, the table was totally utilitarian: folding legs, metal. Maybe they'd rented it. This whole place seemed like they'd moved in no more than a couple of months ago.

I sat between Hyden and Michael. When we finished, Michael pulled his chair over to my side. Hyden looked at us with a question on his face.

Michael put his arm around the back of my chair. Hyden got up and walked to the other side of this huge space, far beyond hearing range. I felt sorry for him, because it wasn't his fault he couldn't handle touching; it was his curse.

"Hey," Michael said to me.

He tugged on my hair. He had that look on his face, that caring look that told me he understood how I felt. I was scared for Emma and scared for us. If they were able to get the chip out of her, what would happen next?

I leaned in to whisper to Michael, hoping the room was large enough that any cameras and mikes wouldn't pick up our conversation. "So if they can get the chip out of Emma, they won't need her anymore."

He squinted, as if he was unable to imagine that. "What're you saying?"

"What will they do with her? She could talk. She knows about this place. She knows about them," I said.

I stared at the table. It had paint splatters on it. Red. I looked away.

"Don't even think about that," he said.

"What would they need with us, if they took the chips out?"

"Nothing," he said. "So they'd let us go."

"They'd want to keep Hyden because he invented the chip," I said.

"You don't think they bought that story that his dad invented it?"

"I don't know," I said. "You didn't, did you?"

Michael leaned his head on my shoulder for a moment. "Nope." He sat back in his chair.

"And my chip is different. I don't know if that means they'd want to remove it or if they'd want to preserve it in me." I touched the back of my head. "Who knows if it would make the next donor act the way I did?"

"You mean giving that person the ability to kill?"

"No, I mean the way I can stay aware while someone is jacking me. I can hear them talking to me. They see out of my eyes, but I'm still there, conscious."

"That had to be scary when you watched yourself shoot me. It sure was for me."

I swung my legs over the side of my chair so I sat facing him.

"I don't ever want anyone jacking me again. Emma's right. Our best hope is to get the chips out."

"You sound like the next volunteer."

If I died, Tyler had no family left. If I made it through, then I was free.

"I could be a normal girl again. It would be a nice life, in the mansion, Tyler and you. Emma could come back and live there too."

He let out a soft laugh. "Seeing as she owns half of everything, I think she might."

"What about you? Are you going to volunteer?" I asked.

"Somehow, I don't think it's going to be up to us," he said. "But yeah, if given the choice, I will. Otherwise, we'll be running for the rest of our lives. The war may be over, but it will never be over for us."

I looked into his eyes. I hadn't realized it, but at some point his hand had traveled down from my shoulder to my hand. It felt so warm and comforting to have human contact again beyond being shoved around by guards. This was how people were supposed to treat each other.

Tears sprang to my eyes, but I forced them back. This wasn't the place or the time to get emotional. Soft. Too much was at stake.

I let go of his hand and stood.

"Shouldn't they be done soon?" I said. "How long is this going to take?"

Hyden was at the far side of the room, pacing like a caged animal. I walked over to him and tugged on the collar of his shirt. "How much longer do you think it's going to be?" I said.

"Dunno." He shook his head.

"Will you volunteer?" I asked.

He looked at me like I was crazy. "Are you kidding? It'd be suicide. Of course not. And you better not."

"It's my only way out of a lifetime of being someone else's puppet. *If* they'll remove it from me."

"I don't know who these people are, but they're not as bright as you think to risk this. We have to find a way out of here."

"How can we get out? They have guns. Guards."

"Did you ever escape from someplace before?"

"Yeah. Institution thirty-seven."

"That's rough. But you got out."

An Ender guard stood against the far wall, staring at us with an icy face.

"This place seems a lot harder," I said.

"I know." He looked around and then lowered his voice. "The guards were talking about my father and the summit meeting."

"What did they say?" I whispered back.

"Just confirming what you heard when they raided my lab. Some of our enemies—some countries, some shady groups, are gathering at my father's lab. He's going to sell the technology to the highest bidder, along with the Metals he's collected."

I put my hand on my stomach. "That's horrible. Not just for the Metals, but for the country."

"It's just like my father."

I was going to ask him more about his father and what he'd do, but a loud sound interrupted us.

An explosion.

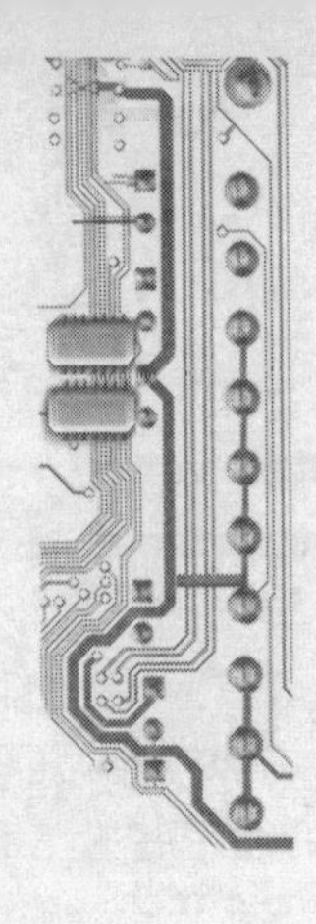

CHAPTER NINETEEN

Hyden, Michael, and I ran toward the sound, down a hallway past peaceful waterfall projections. Guards spilled out of rooms along the corridor and followed us. As we approached, we heard agonizing screams.

A group of Enders bunched up in a doorway at the end of the hall. Frantic voices, confusion, and a bitter odor in the air—a chemical, burnt smell—assaulted me.

I heard a man screaming in pain, but I couldn't see him over the tall Ender guards. I hunched low and caught a glimpse of an Ender sitting on the floor. It was the surgeon. He clutched one arm, which shook violently. His hand was burnt, his arm black up to the elbow. His cries subsided to a horrible moan, but then they started up again, just not as loud or as constant. The hairs on my arms rose. The pain must have been unbearable.

Someone shouted, "Get a doctor!"

"He *is* the doctor," an Ender guard said.

A few of the Enders in front of me left and I straightened

to get a better view. A shield meant to separate patient and surgeon was blackened and shattered but might have saved the doctor's life. Next to it, Emma's body lay on the operating table. Someone had covered her upper body and head with a sheet. All that was visible were her feet and her anklet that spelled out

Emma.

Dawson went to the Doctor and got down on one knee. "What happened?" he asked.

The Doctor struggled to push the words out through his pain. "It . . . blew up."

My chest tightened. By "it" he meant Emma.

"When you touched it?"

He gritted his teeth. "I had almost thirty percent done and then I made one cut exposing it, and—" He shook his head. "Boom."

His face contorted in pain. Then his eyes rolled back, and he slumped over. Just before his head hit the floor, Dawson grabbed him by the shoulders.

"Someone take him."

"Is he . . . ?" a guard asked.

"He's just out," Dawson said, disgusted. Two guards wheeled in a gurney.

Emma was gone.

I'd never really gotten to know her. I thought we'd have time for that once she moved back into the house with us.

"Everyone get out of here." Dawson swept his arm over the room. Then he looked at me and pointed. "Except you. And your friends."

I swallowed hard. It sounded like we were going to be blamed and punished for this horrible outcome.

Enders filed out. The guards came and stood by Michael, Hyden, and me. We traded nervous looks as the room emptied, and it was just us, the guards, and Dawson.

And poor Emma.

Dawson grabbed Hyden's arm. The pain was obvious. Everything that would just hurt anyone else was excruciating to him.

"Let go of me," Hyden said.

"You knew this would happen!" Dawson shouted.

"I told you it was risky. That there was an explosive. You didn't listen," Hyden said. He motioned to Emma's body. "*She* wouldn't listen."

"Come on, let him go," Michael said to Dawson.

"You let it happen to Emma," I said to Dawson. "It's your fault more than his. You call the shots around here."

Dawson released Hyden and came up to me, his face inches from mine. I didn't step back or look away, just held his gaze as coolly as I could.

"You think I wanted to waste a Metal?" Dawson said. "There are only so many of you. And most of them are kept by one man. His father." He pointed at Hyden.

I must have made a small involuntary gasp, because Dawson turned to me. "Oh, we know," Dawson said. "We know everything."

He stormed out the room and we followed, a guard at our backs. I tried not to give anything away. How much did he really know?

"And we know about *your* father, Callie," Dawson called over his shoulder.

"My father?" I said. My heart beat faster.

Dawson stopped and crossed his arms. "Your father also worked in neurochip technology."

"My father invented the handlite," I said slowly, not sure where this was going.

"And what did he do after that?" Dawson prompted.

"He didn't talk about work. The most he'd say was 'research.' And then he died, like my mother."

"He was trying to do what he"—Dawson pointed at Hyden—"and his father were able to do. Create the neurochip for transposition. He specialized in trying to create chips that can communicate with other chips."

The thought that my father was involved in this chip tech made me dizzy. And Dawson seemed so sure. But Hyden and Michael stared at me like I had kept some huge secret from them all this time.

"And now the two of you are together." Dawson gestured to Hyden. "Coincidence?" He shook his head. "What exactly are you working on?"

"We're not working on anything!" I exclaimed. "I didn't even know about my father."

Hyden kept quiet. I realized that was probably what I should have been doing. Too late now.

"I just wanted to get the chips out of all of us," I said.

"Well, after what just happened to Emma, you don't anymore, do you?" Dawson said. "Kaboom."

I swallowed hard. I was exhausted. Everything in my body hurt. I hated this. I had no idea who to believe. Who was Dawson really? Maybe he was making all this up to cause some rift between the three of us. Wouldn't I have known that was what my father did?

I crossed my arms. "My father never said anything to me about this. I was just a kid."

Dawson stared at me. "You expect me to buy that? You're no ordinary kid."

I let out a small laugh. "How do I know you're not just making this up?"

"You don't." Hyden got in Dawson's face. "We know what your agenda is. You just want the secrets. You'll say anything to get it."

"Now you know," I said, "you can't take the chips out of us. We've told you everything, you've tested us backward and forward, so let us go."

Dawson stared at us with his deep-set eyes. His hair gleamed under the bare lightbulb hanging from the ceiling in the hallway.

"No." His eyes shifted between us. "He knows too much," he said, nodding at Hyden. He turned to the guard. "Lock them up."

⊗ ⊗ ⊗

They put us all in the same padded cell this time. We figured the room was bugged and they hoped to learn something from our conversations. Any smart person would have kept their mouth shut, but we were exhausted to the core and didn't care anymore. It seemed like they knew more than we did, anyway.

Michael, Hyden, and I sat on the floor. We kept our voices down. If they were listening, we weren't going to make it easy for them.

"I can't believe she's gone," I said. "We didn't even get to say goodbye. "

"This is going to sound pretty insensitive, but . . . did anyone really like her?" Hyden asked.

"There wasn't much time to get to know her," Michael said.

"And what're you supposed to say, anyway?" I asked, fighting a rising tide of hysteria inside me. "'I'll say my goodbyes now, in case something horrible happens to you'?"

Michael sighed. I put my head in my hands.

"So you really didn't know your father was working on transposition?" Michael asked.

"No, of course not. I would have told you."

Hyden leaned his head against the wall. "They'll want to learn whatever they can from what's left of Emma's chip."

"Are they going to be able to duplicate the chip now?" Michael stretched out so he was lying on his back.

Hyden shook his head. "There won't be enough left to go that far."

"And you can't make more neurochips?" Michael asked Hyden.

"Not without my father. His strength was the hardware."

"And he can't make them without you?" Michael asked.

"No. That's why he's collecting all the Metals." Hyden looked around at the padded walls. "I don't think they'll be content to keep us locked up in here."

"What do you think they'll do?" I asked.

"Whatever they can."

We fell into a hushed silence. I lay back on the floor, hoping to get some sleep, but thoughts kept rushing through my mind. What happened to Emma could have happened to any one of us. Being Metals, we were vulnerable.

My father, working in neurochip technology? I remembered that argument between my parents about the vaccine. My mother had been angry that some adults were getting the vaccine either through the black market or because the government decided some key players in government and research should have it. Plenty of Enders and Starters didn't get the vaccine. Some parents were terrified of it, paranoid of claims that it could cause paralysis or worse. Many just refused to get it. But she thought my father could get it. She must have known what he was working on and how important he was.

My mother wasn't a bad person. She'd just fought to keep her family together. Alive.

⊗ ⊗ ⊗

I dreamt that I heard my father talking to me. He called my name, over and over and over.

My eyes opened. I could still hear him.

Callie?

My heart leapt. "Dad?" I whispered.

Michael lay on one side of me, sound asleep with his back toward me. On the other side, Hyden slept on his back, one leg bent at a right angle underneath the other. The vacuuming sound of the toilet helped cover the sound of my voice. Maybe I had imagined hearing my father. Or just dreamt it?

"Daddy?"

Can you hear me?

It was him! His voice.

"I hear you, Daddy, I hear you."

Cal Girl.

"Tell me it's you," I said, my voice cracking.

I've been trying so hard to get through.

The warmth in his voice. I wanted to run into his arms, have him sweep me into a bear hug and protect me.

"They said you worked with the neurochip. How did you know I had one?"

Please listen, Cal. There's little time. I left a z-drive at a place called Club Rune.

"I know. I have it, but it was encrypted."

It's valuable.

"Tell me where you are."

I don't want you to try to come. It isn't safe.

"What city? Daddy, tell me how to find you."

No, it's too far, all the way in the desert. And this man is dangerous.

Garbled sounds followed.

"Daddy? Daddy." My voice woke the guys, and they began to stir.

"Who are you talking to?" Michael asked, his voice groggy.

I put my fingers in my ears, willing my father to return. To talk to me again, help me get to him. Help me get out of this place. But it was as if someone just disrupted his transmission. My chest tightened.

Michael scooted closer. We kept our voices low. "What's up?"

"I just heard my father."

"What are you talking about?"

Hyden sat up. "What's going on?" he asked quietly.

"My father just talked to me in my head," I said.

"How do you know it's not my father messing with you again?" Hyden said.

"He knew about the z-drive."

Hyden straightened. "What else did he say?"

"That he's being held prisoner."

"Did he say where?" he asked.

I shook my head. "No. Just that it was the desert."

When he heard that word, Hyden sat back. I could see from his expression that he finally believed me.

"Then he's with my father."

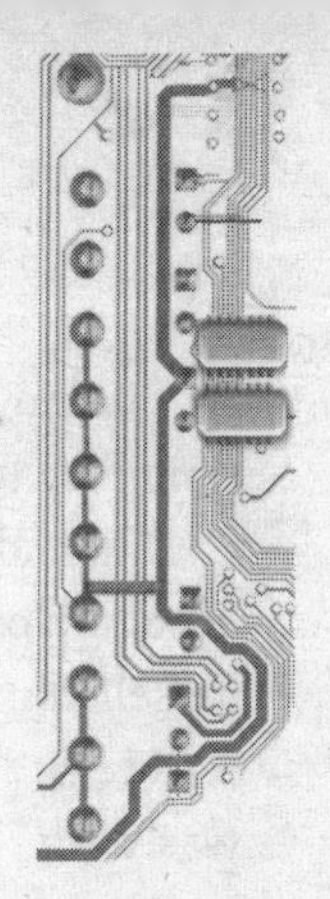

CHAPTER TWENTY

"My father loves the desert. Because only the tough survive there," Hyden went on.

We leaned in close so we could keep our voices down. If Hyden's father had kidnapped my father, he would have faked those death records. He might have held my father captive for an entire year.

For a split second, I allowed myself to dream about a reunion. "I hope we both live long enough to see each other. Wait till Tyler finds out."

"If it helps," Hyden said, "my father would want desperately to keep your father alive. He'd want to know everything he knows."

"After a year, don't you think he'd know?" I asked. My stomach tightened. "We have to find him. Don't you have a single clue where his lab is? An educated guess? Anything?"

We heard a noise at the door. We all stopped and stared at it. It opened a crack. And then stayed like that.

Hyden went to the door and looked out. Then he motioned to us to follow.

The hallway was empty—no guard in sight. We followed Hyden alongside a projection of the rain forest, and I braced myself for someone to leap out at us at any moment.

He peered in the window cut into the door of a room. It was dark, but the dim light of an airscreen chip scanner in save mode glowed like a candle flame. Hyden nodded to us, and we went inside.

Hyden waved his hand in the air, and the screen intensified to full brightness. We left the lights off in the room—this glow was all we needed. A projection of a glacier played against one wall. Otherwise, the room was bare-bones: a table holding the airscreen, another table with a few office supplies, some folding chairs.

Hyden's chip ID number popped up on the airscreen. Then two other chips showed up.

Hyden pointed to each of three numbers. "That's mine, that one's yours"—he pointed to me—"and that one's yours." He pointed to Michael.

Hyden pointed to his chip number and tapped the screen twice. It connected with his chip.

"I'm in," he whispered.

"It sees your chip," I whispered.

We watched in awe as his eyes turned to slits, and he used his mind, not his fingers, to move through files. He searched for "Brockman" but came up empty.

"They don't know where he is," Hyden said.

Then Hyden moved to a different area and located a new file area: "Security." With his mind—and the chip—he fanned through files at top speed. He found the alarm system and found a way to shut it off.

"Wow," Michael whispered.

We smiled. But then someone opened the door.

An Ender woman stood in the doorway wearing a black jumpsuit. She was slender, with beautiful bone structure and white hair she left long and flowing, just past her shoulders.

She came in and closed the door behind her.

"It's all right," she said. "Don't be afraid."

I recognized her voice. "You're the one in the office at the shooting range."

She was the Ender who had observed and relayed instructions to the team inside.

She kept her voice low. "I've seen what they've put you through, and it's shameful."

"Why would you help us?" Hyden asked.

"I'm a grandmother. I was. I lost not only my children but also my grandchild in the war. She refused to get the vaccine because she didn't trust the government."

I noticed that Hyden had changed the screen so it was just a pattern.

"If you stay, what they will do to you is horrendous. That's why I'm risking my job to get you out of here."

The three of us exchanged worried glances.

"You must get away now," she said.

"You're the one who unlocked our cell door," I said.

"Yes. I was going to lead you out, but a guard came by. I had to distract him." She reached into her pocket and pulled out our car keys. "Here. I saw you disable the alarm," she said to Hyden. "Go now." She tossed the keys to Hyden.

We turned and ran in the direction she pointed, through a series of doors that opened into a short hallway with a projection of a field. The last door was the door to the outside. It opened with no sounds, no alarms.

We walked out into the brisk, sweet night air. We were outside. Free.

"Where's the car?" I asked.

Michael pointed toward the far corner of the building, out at the end of the parking lot, toward the street. "That way."

We ran, crossing the street and making our way to the next block. We tried to stay behind cars and in shadows as much as possible. Finally, we reached the car, and I unlocked it so we could climb in.

Hyden started the engine. The sound broke through the quiet night.

"Hurry," I said.

Hyden drove down the empty street. Michael reached over to give me a high five.

"Don't celebrate so fast," Hyden said. "I want some distance between us and that place."

I looked past Michael to the airscreen in the back. It was still closed, but a faint glow peeked out from under the cover.

"My dad's z-drive," I said. "Maybe it finished processing."

We needed a quiet, safe place to view what my father had left. Hyden knew of a place that would be open—an underground hydroponic co-op garden.

"What's that?" I asked him.

"A place where we can also get some fresh food," he said.

"Let me guess. It's belowground because they want to avoid spore dust?"

"It's the new 'organic,'" Michael said.

"That," Hyden said, "and some of the people stay low as much as they can. The Enders come right after work. They're that afraid of a future attack."

We got out of our car. A Starter immediately wiped it down like at the flea market. The air here was humid and warm and smelled earthy. We didn't care; we were so glad to be free from Dawson.

We had to step into shallow troughs filled with a murky liquid before we were allowed to enter the green market. They had several set up.

"So we don't track in spore dust?" I asked Hyden as I swished my shoes in the trough.

"It's got a chemical agent in it." He stepped out of his trough. "We're lucky the head gardener isn't here today. She makes you put a paper gown over your clothes."

I looked to my right and saw Michael shaking his wet shoes like a cat coming in from the rain. Inside, there were tables of tomatoes, cucumbers, lettuce, all manned by Enders and Starters alike.

"They get the light from tubes leading to the outdoors," Hyden said. "And from lights run on portable batteries they charge in their cars."

The garden itself was behind the tables of produce. Large trays of vegetables were set in larger trays of a water bath. I looked at the range of gardeners spraying water on the plants.

"The people here . . . ," I started to say quickly.

"All kinds," Hyden said in a low voice. "They just don't trust the safety of food sold up there."

"Can't blame them," Michael said.

We picked up fresh tomatoes and cucumbers and juices. Having paid for the produce, we were able to stay in the parking spot to look at the airscreen. Hyden and I got in the backseat and popped up the airscreen while Michael stood outside, leaning in, munching on a cucumber. The drive had finished deciphering the encryption and was ready to play. Hyden started it and an image of my father appeared on the airscreen.

Dad looked worried. His hair was uncombed. There were dark circles under his eyes. He seemed to look directly at me when he spoke, as if he knew I would be here someday.

"This drive contains confidential proprietary material not intended for any other transmission. In the case of my death, I, Ray Woodland, declare that the research contained herein should benefit my two children, Callie and Tyler."

He was doing this for me. My heart ached.

"Callie, if you are watching this, the work I leave behind may provide for you and Tyler. I've been developing a process of transposition, a mind-body transfer. I know I am not alone, that others have succeeded and surpassed me, but my findings on reverse transposition have a particular function that I believe no one has been able to achieve to date. It will be of value for you to sell to provide for yourselves."

"Reverse transposition?" I asked.

Hyden froze the image in the air with a tap of his fingers. "That's when a donor body, like you, gets back into the body of the renter and controls it. It's something no one has done yet."

Me? Control my jacker? What a concept.

"Going into my jacker's body? Seeing through his eyes? Making him move? That would be incredible."

"It's still just theory," he said.

Hyden touched the airscreen and it resumed playing. My father continued speaking. I'd never seen him so serious.

"I may not be alive by the time this is played, I know that," he said.

It hurt to hear those words. But he'd just been in my head. He had to be alive. Unless...

"During the past month, I've been followed and confronted and harassed because I refused to work for a man whose vision for the technology did not match mine. I've documented my key research on this drive in the event that something happens to me. Protect it and use it wisely."

His image cut to black and then a series of numbers and formulas flashed at a rapid pace. Hyden watched the screen with fascination. Suddenly, it went blank. Just like that, gone.

"What happened?" I asked.

"It's okay, it's all there," Hyden said. "Don't worry. I'll examine it later."

The video "visit" with my father was painfully short. I longed to play it again and again.

"Those numbers you saw flying across the screen?" Hyden said. "Well, now I can use his program and upgrade your chip. This opens the path for you to reverse the transposition."

"Then if Brockman jacks me, I can see through his eyes," I said slowly. "Make him do what I want."

I was sure my father never could have imagined that I'd be the one to use his discovery. We had to make it work.

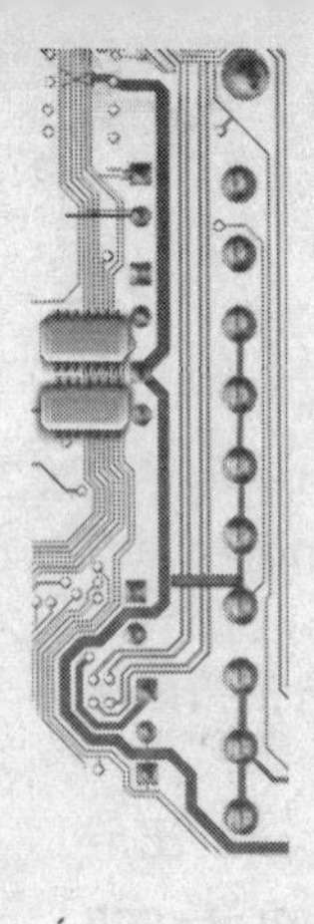

CHAPTER TWENTY-ONE

Hyden believed the transmission would be easier outside. With time closing in on us, he wanted to increase our chances of success, so we parked outside, near a shut-down miniature golf course. The barbed wire at the top of the fence made me sad and afraid. It was late and dark, but I could see that the windmill inside was broken, with only two blades left. It reminded me of the last time I was at a place like that, with my mother. It was the day the spores fell.

"You coming, Callie?" Michael poked my arm with his finger.

I got out as Hyden opened the back of his vehicle and started up the airscreen.

He used my father's program to try to wirelessly upgrade my chip. "Stand over there," he said to me, pointing to a small tree about ten feet away. "No guarantees it worked. We're going to have to test it."

Michael stood behind Hyden and looked over his shoulder. "What're you doing now?"

"Setting her chip ID," he said. "There. Got it."

Hyden then climbed into the lounge-seat and closed his eyes.

In a few seconds, I could hear Hyden inside my head.

Can you hear me?

"Loud and clear," I said.

It was strange having Hyden inside my head again. The last time had been when Dawson was forcing me to shoot Michael at the range. But now we were the ones pulling the strings.

Okay, don't move, don't do anything. I'm going to establish control.

I stood there and waited, my arms at my sides. Then my right arm rose slowly, until it was over my head.

Good. So now see if you can resist. I'll keep your arm up there and you try to bring it down.

It was sort of like arm wrestling with an invisible opponent. Hyden was strong, mentally, and I was not making any headway. I focused, even gritted my teeth, but my arm stayed up.

"I can't," I said.

It's because you're not scared. You know this is safe. Okay, I'll lower your arm.

My arm came down. I felt like a failure.

Let's try the reversal. Just work on getting inside me.

"How?"

I found something in your father's notes on the drive. He suggests focusing on imagining a string between us. A taut cord. Visualize a blue light around it running from me to you. Now picture a gold light going from you to me. Take the blue light and turn it gold. See the flow from you to me.

I tried to see what he wanted me to. I understood it

intellectually, but making it real was something else. I worked at it for several long minutes, but I never was able to get inside his head and see what he was seeing. I was still in my own body.

Now I really felt like a failure.

"It's not working," I said.

Hyden got out of the special seat. He looked at the airscreen, examining the program. And then he climbed out of the car and joined me.

"I looked at the program. I did it right. It should work."

Michael came over and put his arm around my shoulders. Hyden looked back at the car.

"Let's try another location," Hyden said.

"Isn't all this exposure dangerous?" Michael asked.

"If he jacks her, then we'll really have a test," Hyden said.

We all got back in the car, and Hyden drove.

I realized we were missing something important. "We have no phones."

"They're all back at Dawson's." Hyden motioned with his head. "Wanna go back?" He grinned.

I grabbed a bottle of water from the car's cooler and handed one to Michael. Behind him, I saw a looming shape following us on the lonely road. A massive SUV.

Its headlights were off.

"We're not alone," I said.

Michael turned around to look. The hulking SUV drew closer.

Hyden squinted in his rearview mirror. "How long has he been behind us?"

"Just saw him," I said.

"It could just be a guy who forgot to turn his lights on," Michael said.

"I don't think so," Hyden said.

"One of Brockman's?" I asked.

Hyden nodded. "I shouldn't have done the test outside. He scanned us." He slapped the wheel. "Hold on. I'm going to lose him."

He sped up and did a fast turn down a small street in this mixed industrial area. A cat darted out in front of our car.

"Watch out!" I said.

"I see it," Hyden said.

He swerved and hit a trash can, knocking it into the street. The SUV behind us just plowed through it, sending garbage flying.

I turned around. "Michael, is that a Starter driving?"

He looked. "Sure is. A guy."

I squinted. "And he looks jacked. Do you know where you're going?"

"No! I'm just trying to lose him," Hyden said as he held on to the wheel.

I pulled up the airscreen nav and saw a dead end ahead.

"This road is blocked," I said. "There's no way out."

"Good," Hyden said.

"Good?" Michael shouted.

Hyden went faster. The jacked Starter was right on our tail. I could see a tall concrete wall at the end of the street.

"We're heading for that wall!" I shouted.

"I know." Hyden gripped the wheel. "We're not going to hit it." The wall was coming up fast. "We're going to hit *him*. Get ready." He slammed on his brakes and jammed into reverse.

The SUV rammed into our vehicle with a horrible, earsplitting metallic crunch. Our airbags deployed, cushioning us from all angles.

We all caught our breath.

"You two all right?" Hyden pressed a button; our airbags deflated and seat belts released.

"I guess," I said. My body was shaking from the impact. "Michael?"

"I'm a lot better than that guy." Michael stared at the SUV behind us.

Hyden grabbed a gun—so did I—and got out of the car. "You stay," he said to Michael.

Hyden's vehicle was essentially a tank, but I hadn't expected we'd come out of that without a dent. The front of the other guy's SUV had accordioned against our rear, a mess of metal, but Hyden's ride was as solid as ever.

We approached slowly. Hyden aimed his gun, looked in the driver's side, then opened the door.

The Metal fell out.

"No seat belt," Hyden said. "He's dead."

He was bleeding from the head and his eyes were open in a frozen last stare.

Hyden checked his pockets and came up empty. I checked the SUV to make sure no one else was inside. I opened the passenger's-side door and looked around. There were no papers to tell us where he was from.

Hyden stepped over the body and reached in the driver's seat, calling up information from the nav airscreen. "I want to find out the last place this thing has been."

A moment later, he found it.

"Joshua Tree," he said. "Used to be a national park in the desert."

Brockman's place.

⊗ ⊗ ⊗

Two hours later, we roared through the desert in the darkness of night, the moon backlighting the cacti. The wind howled outside our SUV, blowing the scent of sweet desert grass through our vents, making me shiver with fear and anticipation. The desert frightened me. A harsh climate that would freeze you to death at night and burn you to a crisp in the day, with no shelter or water for miles.

It wasn't my kind of place, but one that I could appreciate, the way I liked seeing scary holos on Halloween. It was the middle of the night, but I wasn't tired. I felt exhilarated.

"What are we going to do once we get there?" Michael asked.

Hyden glanced at me and then back to the road. "Guess we'll storm the place," he said with a half smile.

"Maybe we should wait until morning. Get an Ender like Lauren to alert the marshals or something," Michael said.

Hyden turned to me. "Do you want to wait?"

All I could see was my father's weary face in that video. "No. We're so close now. What if they run and we lose them?"

"Let's scope it out," Hyden said.

Michael sat back in his seat. I'm sure he thought we were crazy and reckless. I didn't blame him, but it wasn't his father in there.

⊗ ⊗ ⊗

The navigator alerted us that we were approaching our destination. A wind kicked up, sending a tumbleweed rolling across our path. Up ahead, I spotted a low building in the shadow of the moon. As we drew closer, I could see that it was actually a compound of several concrete buildings surrounded by desert land.

I stared, looking at it through the bug-pocked windshield. "That's it?" I asked.

Hyden nodded. "Somewhere in there is my father."

"And hopefully mine."

Hyden looked at me. We were bonded in that instant.

"How do we know that Brockman hasn't faked your father's voice the whole time?" Michael said.

"We had the video of my father. I saw him," I said.

"And you created a fake broadcast of the Old Man to get the renters to return to Prime. You know just because you see it doesn't make it true." Michael thumped the back of my headrest. "We could be walking into a trap."

"What do you suggest we do?" I snapped. "Give up? Go sit like moles in some underground parking lot? I've gone this whole year believing my father was dead. I won't know for sure until I see him in person. I want to try."

"If you want, you can stay with the car. Be a quick getaway for us," Hyden said.

Michael blew a puff of air out of his mouth. Meanwhile, we were a quarter mile from the building. Hyden slowed down the SUV and brought it to a stop. I looked at him with raised brows.

"We shouldn't drive up there," Hyden said. "Too noisy."

"But our chips will be on their radar," I said.

"They've got a whole bunch of chip heads in there, so maybe they won't notice ours." He turned to look back at Michael. "So what's it going to be, Michael? Stay or go?"

"I'll come. You're going to need all the help you can get in there."

Hyden pulled down the weapons attached to the inside walls of the SUV and handed one to me.

"It's loaded," he said. "Michael, you know how to shoot?"

"No, he doesn't," I said before Michael could answer.

"Yeah, I do, Cal," he said. "I went to target practice with my dad."

I made a face. "You never told me."

"There was no reason to. We didn't have a gun, did we?"

Hyden gave him a handgun. "Now you do. It's loaded. Safety's on." He also passed out strap-on holsters, knives, and plexi-cuffs.

"It's a lot of stuff," Michael said uneasily. "Maybe we should alert the marshals ourselves."

"And how often do they come when you call them?" Hyden asked. "And just what are you going to tell them? We have these guns so we can *avoid* a shoot-out. If the marshals did come, and they won't, that's what we'd have."

A slight breeze carried the sweet scent of juniper. Moonlight cast blue shadows on the cacti that watched us as we passed.

A small creature—a scorpion—crossed my path, scurrying to get out of our way.

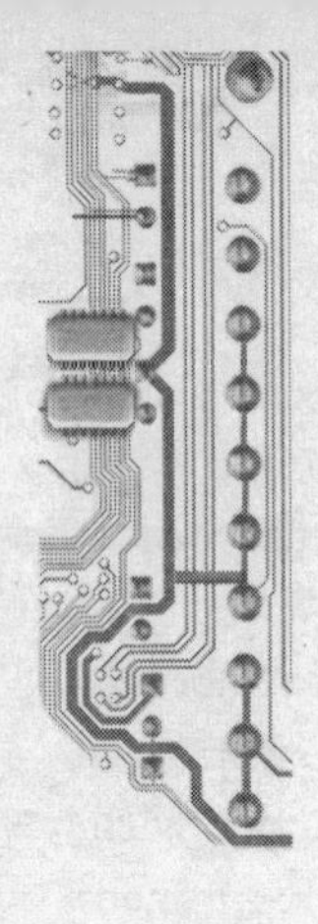

CHAPTER TWENTY-TWO

We walked in silence on the hard sand, weaving between the Joshua trees and shrubs to make a stealthy approach. I thought about everything I wanted. How I might see my father. Maybe get my chip out. Maybe Brockman could be forced to tell us how to remove it. Then I might get to be a Starter again, instead of a Metal.

My eyes scanned the sand for any creatures to avoid stepping on. That was probably why I didn't notice a covered jeep driving off-road, heading our way, until it was a hundred yards ahead.

The headlights were off. The last time we'd seen this, it hadn't been good. And now we were too far from our vehicle to run back to it.

We were caught, out there in the desert night.

"Spread out. Get behind something!" Hyden shouted. "Shrub or rocks."

Michael and I scrambled to find the biggest source of protection.

"Get your guns out," Hyden said.

I got down on the hard sand behind a cluster of shrubs, my gun aimed. The guys did the same so that we formed a large triangle.

The jeep stopped before it reached us. The driver turned off the engine and opened his door.

My heart pounded, a thump-thump in my ears.

The driver had long white hair and thick black-rimmed glasses. He was tall and wore jeans and a long-sleeved shirt.

"Easy, guys. I come in peace," he said, his arms raised.

I recognized his voice. The Ender geek from Prime. "Trax?" I said.

"Yeah, it's me. Callie?"

Hyden stood, his gun still aimed. "Why are you here, Trax?"

"Hyden," he said. "You mean you can't guess?"

Michael remained crouched behind his shrub, slightly behind Trax. I suspected Trax hadn't seen him.

"I have to know something, Trax," I said. "Did you kill Helena?"

I lowered my gun, but it was still in my hands.

"Why would I do that?"

"Because you worked for my father," Hyden said.

"I worked for the Old Man," Trax said. "The Old Man. And for old time's sake, I came out here on my own—Brockman has no idea—to warn you."

"Warn us about what?" I asked.

Trax came closer to me, his hands still raised, but lower. "Warn you that it's dangerous in there."

With one swift move he pulled a gun out of his pants, hooked his arm around my shoulders, locking my arms, and pointed the gun at Hyden.

"Drop yours," Trax said.

Hyden knelt and put his gun on the ground.

"Get your hands up," Trax said to Hyden. "Where's the other Metal?"

"Never mind him, what about you?" Hyden said. "You killed Helena, didn't you?"

"Tinnenbaum ordered me to. Because your father ordered him to." Trax tilted his head toward Hyden. "She was going to bring big trouble."

Trax started pulling me backward. Toward his jeep. I couldn't aim my gun anywhere but down. Could I aim for his foot? Or would I just shoot mine?

"She would have jeopardized everything," Trax said. "He couldn't have that."

I twisted my torso, trying to get free. "So the Old Man ordered her killed?" I asked.

Trax stopped. "The Old Man?" He looked at me. "You don't know who the Old Man really is, do you?"

"Brockman," I said. I figured the more I could keep Trax talking, the better.

Trax laughed. "No, but you're close. Brockman is the Old Man's father."

I squinted. What was he talking about?

"Brockman is a Middle," I said. "He can't be the Old Man's father. He *is* the Old Man."

I looked to Hyden, expecting him to chime in, but he just stood there, quiet. Silence hung in the night air.

"Why would you say that?" I asked Trax.

"Hyden knows what I'm talking about," Trax said. "Tell her who the Old Man is." He nodded to Hyden. "Just who is that masked man?"

None of this was registering with me.

"Spell it out for her," Trax said. "Or I will."

The expression on Hyden's face was like nothing I'd ever seen before. It was as if he just realized he'd swallowed poison, but it hadn't yet hit his stomach. His lips started to move, but no sound came out.

"She can't hear you," Trax said in a singsong voice.

"It's me," Hyden said in a low voice, looking straight at me. "I'm the Old Man."

A half laugh came out of my mouth. "You can't be. You're a Starter."

"It was me," Hyden said softly.

For a moment, my heart stopped. My brain stopped. And my ears must have quit as well because everything seemed muffled. I was not hearing this.

"What are you talking about?" I asked.

"She needs proof." Trax pulled something out of his bag and threw it at Hyden.

It landed on the sand. I couldn't tell what it was.

"Pick it up," Trax commanded.

Hyden bent down and took it. When he held it in his hands, I recognized it. The Old Man's mask.

"Put it on," Trax said, still pointing his gun.

Hyden didn't move. He stared at the mask in a way that reminded me of Hamlet and the skull.

Hyden, the Old Man? Couldn't be. This was some trick that Trax had cooked up.

"He won't put it on because it'll prove what I'm saying. The mask is only biocompatible to his skin. He's the only one who can activate it." Trax pushed me closer to Hyden. "Put it on him," he said to me.

I had to see. I took the mask out of Hyden's hands. It didn't look like Hyden. He held still while I slipped the strap over his head. The mold fit his features perfectly.

I held my breath for a moment.

"Just wait. It'll glow all pretty-like," Trax said.

The mask lit up. That chilling blue light. An image of a face formed pixel by pixel. Then it changed to form another face.

"And there's the magic. The mask of a hundred thousand faces," Trax said.

Hyden pushed a button in the front, in the bottom of the mask, near his neck.

That awful metallic voice came from Hyden—the Old Man's voice. "I'm sorry, Callie. I wanted to tell you."

"Oh, the creepy voice," Trax said. "I really missed that."

My skin felt like tiny bugs were crawling up my arms, my legs. "No," I said, fighting the horror inside me. "You're not him. He was taller. Bigger."

"Use a little imagination, dear," Trax said. "He had a full costume with special tricks. The coat, the gloves, lifts in his shoes . . . and with a wig and hat, he made a very believable Ender. I believed him until Brockman told me."

This was insane. It had been Hyden all along. Not his father. Him.

"You never should have left me out to dry when Prime got busted, boss," Trax said to Hyden. "I'd be stuck in jail like Tinnenbaum if your dad hadn't gotten me out."

"I found out you two were spying on me and reporting to him," Hyden said, still with that electronic voice. "Why should I save a traitor?"

The mask glowed that eerie blue light as different faces

cycled in random order. I reached out and ripped the mask off his face, breaking the strap. The mask tore at the edge.

I threw it on the ground. It still played a face from the residue of Hyden's energy, but now flickering and dying like a confused chameleon. Finally, the face disappeared and only the blue pixels glowed.

"You lied to me," I screamed. "The whole time!"

"Would you have listened to me if you knew the truth?" he asked. "Would you have let me protect you?"

I punched Hyden across the jaw so hard my fist throbbed. He didn't even try to defend himself. I started to go at him, but Trax yanked me by the arms.

"How many lies have you got in you, Hyden? How could you?"

Trax pulled me back to the jeep. I was so focused on Hyden, I didn't put up much of a fight. But before Trax could open the door, Michael leapt out from behind the jeep, surprising Trax by grabbing him from behind. Michael pulled us both backward, and Trax had to loosen his grip on me to fight off Michael, giving me my chance to get loose.

I twisted out of Trax's hold and ran forward. I turned to see Michael holding Trax's gun arm, and Trax resisting, aiming it wildly in the air, then at Hyden, even me. Hyden rushed to help, knocking away Trax's gun with his own. It fell and spun on the ground. Trax tried to go for it, but Michael held him back.

Then Hyden pulled out his plexi-cuffs and Michael cuffed Trax's wrists and ankles.

I watched and rubbed my arm, sore from Trax's grip.

"Is it true Brockman didn't know you came out here?" I asked.

Trax nodded.

"So you knew we were coming," I said.

"I saw you on the grid," he said. "That's part of my job."

"Why didn't you tell anyone?" Michael asked.

"Because he had his own agenda," Hyden said. "Revenge."

Trax's long white hair hung over his face. He shook it off. "I got what I wanted. Humiliated you in front of your girlfriend."

"I'm not . . ." I couldn't even repeat the word.

"He's never cared about anyone the way he cares about you." Trax looked to see if he'd gotten a reaction out of Hyden.

I kept my eyes on Trax during the awkward silence when no one wanted to speak.

"What do we do with him?" Michael asked.

"Leave him here." Hyden patted down Trax, taking something metal from his pocket.

Michael pulled me aside, away from Hyden.

"What do we do now?" he asked in a low voice.

I rubbed my temples. The desert was playing tricks on me. The cacti seemed to be moving, vibrating.

"My father's so close."

"But can we trust Hyden?" Michael said. "Talk about a trap."

Doubts crowded my brain. But I needed to make this work.

"You can trust me!" Hyden shouted.

I turned back and took a few steps closer. "Why?"

"Because one thing Trax said was true. About me and you."

"It's a trick." Michael took my arm and pulled me away from Hyden. "You can't listen to him."

My stomach ached. What Michael said made sense. But we needed Hyden.

"If Hyden was leading us into a trap, I don't think Trax would have come out the way he did. Trying to separate us. And Hyden never helped Trax, he fought against him." I shook my head. "I don't know. I can barely wrap my mind around this."

I looked back at Hyden, standing there in the desert moonlight.

"All this time," said Michael, "he was the one behind the mask. Think about that."

I thought about all the things I'd done with the Old Man while he was in Blake's body. How much I liked that guy—not Blake. And how it had horrified me to learn it was really the Old Man. I didn't know how I could live with that. Now it turned out he wasn't a creepy Ender after all, but a Starter. A Starter I thought I knew.

But who was he really? And could I trust him?

No matter what, there was one thing I knew. One thing I wanted. And it was true in spite of Hyden and his lie.

"We have to save my father," I said. "So let's go."

"With him? Shouldn't we cuff him?"

I thought about it for a second. "What good would he be to us then? We need all the help we can get against Brockman. I believe he hates his father. He'll want to take him down as much as we do."

⊗ ⊗ ⊗

We left Trax, still cuffed, lying on the backseat of his jeep. Before we took off on foot, I looked back at the mask lying on the desert floor. Random pixels were still pulsing, doing their sad dance for no one but the cacti and the stars.

The three of us still had a long walk to go across the hardened sandy soil to Brockman's compound.

"Callie, talk to me," Hyden said. "I know you must have a million questions."

"I don't talk to liars, you lying liar."

"Come on, ask me anything," he said. "I'm serious. I'll tell you anything you want to know."

"Where do I begin?" I shrugged. "How about what the heck was going through your mind? Why?"

"It isn't what you think," Hyden said. "I was trying to save the unclaimed Starters."

"By turning them into permanent rental bodies?" I asked. "Putting them to sleep forever?"

"I was never going to do that. I just wanted the Enders to believe that. I was in complete control. I never would have let anyone hurt the Metals."

I stopped to take this in. "But you used us. You sold our bodies for profit."

"I had to establish the business to attract the rich Enders. And to get them used to switching bodies. Revolution isn't cheap."

"So you were going to kill the Enders?"

"Keep them in a deep sleep. Somebody had to do something," he said. "I was going to set their alarm clocks for one minute after I made the world a better place."

I tried to let this sink in, but it was the opposite of everything I had believed about the Old Man.

"I was going to find out where they kept their money so I could drain their bank accounts," Hyden said.

"So you're a thief," I said.

"To use the money to finance change. To get the Starters

out of the institutions and then disband that system altogether."

"But you had nothing to do with Helena?"

"I was suspicious of her. I followed her and that's when I met you. At Club Rune."

"And you kept track of me so you could keep track of her."

"Partly."

"And you wanted to see what my altered chip could do."

"Partly."

"You wanted to see if I could kill. And I almost did."

"But I also came to help you. To help save you."

I glanced at Michael. He was walking with his hands in his pockets, just listening.

"What do you think, Michael? Would you trust him?"

"Are you kidding?" He pointed at Hyden. "He kidnapped your little brother and put a chip in his head!"

"I would never. That was Tinnenbaum, Trax, and a doctor under my father's thumb."

"How did you even get yourself in that position?" I asked. "Running Prime."

"When my father wanted to sell off the research to the wrong people, I had to create an Ender identity to front Prime. And it worked. People believed I was an Ender. I was already wearing some protective gear. . . ."

"Because you were scared of being touched?" I asked.

He nodded. "I added more and created a disguise. But the whole reason Prime existed was to end the slavery of Starters."

He stared off at the moon over the desert landscape. "But when you broke apart Prime, there went my plan."

"How do I know you're not working with your father

now? He admitted that he was using the Old Man's electronic voice."

Hyden nodded. "That was him at the mall in your head. And ever since Prime came down."

"Why would he do that?" Michael asked.

"To test it. He wanted to gain access to her chip, to map it. Once Prime fell, Trax gave him as much tech as he could get."

"Testing," I said.

"And messing with your head. Power plays," Hyden said. "Because that's what he does."

"So what else is a lie? What else should I know?"

"The rest is true. My father is evil. He's got an auction planned for the richest Enders in the world, and he'll sell the Metals and the technology to the highest bidder. And odds are, they'll use it against us. Against our country."

"All that stuff you just said." I pointed at him. "How he was messing with my head, that he likes the power—it was really about you."

"No," he said.

"Because you're a lot like your father after all. That's how come you understand him so well."

My words had the effect I wanted—he looked pained.

I stopped walking and faced Hyden.

"We need you. So we have to work together. But it doesn't mean I forgive you or even trust you, after what you've done."

"I don't blame you," Hyden said. "Just give me a chance to win back your trust."

I wasn't about to grant him anything at that point.

⊗ ⊗ ⊗

Brockman's facility was in the middle of the desert, and yet it seemed oddly unprotected.

"There's no fence," Michael said. "How come?"

"It's pretty isolated out here," I said.

"It would draw more attention. And there are more dangerous barriers than fences," Hyden said. "It's like saying to the world, my security's better than some puny fence."

We walked around, past the side of the building. There was no landscaping, just some small cacti around the edge. Windows dotted the upper part of the building, too high to do anything but let light in during the day.

Hyden went to a set of tall double doors that formed the back entrance. I looked at the back parking lot, which was huge. There must have been room for over a hundred cars. At this late hour, I counted only seven. That was consistent with what Trax had said. It gave me some hope that we weren't facing overwhelming odds.

Hyden pulled out a passkey from his pocket that he waved over a metal panel to the right of the doors. We heard a click. Then one of the large doors silently swung open.

"Thank you, Trax," Hyden whispered. He motioned for us to follow him inside.

We were in some sort of lobby. An illusion of green bamboo stalks was projected onto a glass floor. I spotted two doors to the right labeled *Employee Lockers*. One was for women, one for men. We all had the same idea at once. Michael and Hyden ducked into the men's room, and I slipped into the women's locker room.

Inside, it looked like what I'd seen in the holos as a luxury spa. More illusion floors, teakwood cabinets, giant bamboo plants and orchids, even a waterfall. I imagined that during the day they probably played peaceful flute music.

I opened a locker and found their version of a lab coat—

a short white kimono. I put it on over my clothing and tied it at the waist. I put on a white surgical hair cap. When I came out, both the guys had their kimono lab coats and caps on as well.

"Now what?" I said quietly.

"Let's go to work," Hyden said.

Hyden opened the door leading to the main part of his father's facility. I looked over his shoulder and saw only a dark expanse of hallway.

While we held back, Hyden started down the hallway, which blossomed with gently glowing lights as he made his way. Hyden had decided that he would go first and look for a computer while I split off to look for my father. He turned a corner and disappeared. Michael was set to go last and be on the lookout for our Metal friends.

I made my way down the sterile hallway, moving between shadows and pools of light. I cradled the holstered gun underneath the kimono, hoping I would not have to use it.

I opened a door at the end of the hallway and stood there a moment, stunned at what I'd found. The room stretched on forever and contained a wild profusion of plants and small trees with low-hanging branches. I entered the lush space. The air felt warm and smelled rich and earthy. It seemed like they'd modeled it after a rain forest—a total contrast to the desert outside.

I spotted Hyden in one of the side rooms, working on an airscreen. He looked up and motioned for me to join him. I popped in.

"I'm in, so take this." He gave me Trax's passkey and I slipped it into my pants pocket.

I went to the back of the jungle room and exited through

another door. It opened to a hallway that had a wall fountain halfway through. The sound of the bubbling water filled the space. I walked on, peeking in what appeared to be offices or meeting rooms. They'd decorated the spaces in the style of various countries—India, Russia, Japan. I recognized them from my school studies before the war. School. Would I ever have a chance to return? Not to a Zype School, to a real one.

At the halfway point, near the fountain, all the rest of the rooms had closed doors.

I loosened my kimono for faster access to my gun and went to the first closed room. Even with my ear to the door, I couldn't hear any sound inside. I held up Trax's passkey to the metal plate to the right of the door. *Click.* Slowly, I opened the door.

My eyes quickly adjusted to the dim lighting. In sharp contrast to the spa atmosphere of the rest of the place, this was clinical. No plants or pictures here. The large room was crammed with metal platforms that served as beds. Night-lights dotted the walls, illuminating the bodies. One perfect body after another, all with flawless faces, all asleep. The Metals were bound to their beds with restraints around their wrists.

My heart sank. So Brockman was as bad as Hyden had said—and worse.

One thing I didn't understand at all—the Metals had tubes in their noses that led to small plastic pouches strapped across their chests. Why?

As I glanced around, I recognized some of the faces: Briona. Lee. Raj. I'd spent time with those bodies, but not those people. I knew them only as donor bodies occupied by Doris, Tinnenbaum, and Rodney, the horrible Enders at Prime

Destinations. They'd spied on me. At least, I'd thought so at the time. Now I knew differently. Doris and Rodney had been keeping an eye on me for Hyden. To make sure I didn't kill the senator. And then maybe to protect me.

Tinnenbaum had been keeping an eye on me for Brockman.

I stepped on a squeaky floorboard and the nearest Metal, Lee, stirred. I took another step and he opened his eyes.

The real Lee was the Asian guy with incredibly good looks. He squinted at me a moment in the dim light. "Who're you?" he asked in a groggy voice.

Briona, nearby, was awakened by his voice. She turned her head to examine me. "She's new," she said slowly.

She was as beautiful as ever, with her buttery bronze skin, but now she had desperate, haunted eyes.

"How come you're dressed like that?

"I'm here to help," I whispered, hoping she'd keep her voice down.

"And they let you walk around?" she asked.

The nearest Metals began to wake. Raj was one, the third member of their trio. No one was able to sit up; they were all tied to their beds. I examined Lee's restraints. They had small metal pads on them. I pulled out Trax's key and pressed it to Lee's right arm restraint. It unlocked, but he didn't move.

"What're you doing?" he said. "I'll get in trouble."

"What have they done to you?" I asked. "What's that tube?"

"It's how they feed us if we're not working," Lee said. "It keeps our weight steady."

"And makes us dependent on them," Raj said in his lilting Indian accent.

"Please undo me," Briona said. "I have nightmares. Things they made me do . . . I relive them."

More Metals started to wake up.

Raj stared at Briona. "Shut up, Briona," he said. "She can't help you. She's stuck here like us now."

He hadn't seen what I could do. I unlocked Briona's restraints. She sat up and rubbed her wrists.

"Says you. Look at me. I'm free," Briona said.

"Do me!" a blond girl shouted.

"Shhh," I said, my voice lowered. "I'll unlock all of you. We can't get you off the compound right away," I said. "But we will. For now, tell me what you know about this place."

Lee found the courage to sit up. I moved on to unlock the rest. There must have been twenty Metals in this one room. One of them looked familiar.

Blake.

He looked so pitiful and strange with a tube coming out of his nose.

He was groggy. He struggled, as if trying to sit up, but his bindings kept him down.

"Blake, it's me, Callie." I unlocked him.

"Callie?"

"How long have you been here?" I asked.

"Too long," Blake said. "But not as long as some. Some have been here for months. Did they catch you too?"

"No, I'm here to get you out," I said. "Are there more of you?"

He nodded.

"How many?"

"Another three dorm rooms," Lee said.

Maybe as many as one hundred Starters here, kept captive.

"Have any of you ever seen a man, a Middle, named Ray Woodland? He has dark brown hair, tall, good-looking? He has one scar on his cheek, here." I pointed to my face.

They shook their heads.

I refused to believe my father wasn't there. Brockman was keeping him hidden, I was sure of it.

"Where are the guards?" I asked.

"Don't know. Asleep? It's late," Briona said.

"No, someone's awake." Raj came up and joined us. "There's always someone at night."

I was hoping that was Trax.

"Are you guys healthy enough to fight?" I asked.

"Absolutely," Lee said.

I asked them all my questions and they answered them. I promised that my two friends and I would help them escape. But first, I had to find my father. Then I heard a voice in my head.

Callie Woodland?

"Who is this?"

"Who's she talking to?" Briona asked the others.

I walked away from them, toward the door, so I could listen.

I'm disappointed. You seemed like such a smart girl.

Of course I knew who it was. But I was so hoping he'd be asleep right now and never know I'd crashed his facility.

"So do I call you Brockman or just Hyden's dad?"

He chuckled. *I am so happy you finally came. As I'd hoped.*

"You hoped?"

I opened the door and motioned for the Starters to come

with me. Briona, Lee, Raj, and several others followed. I averted my eyes from them so Brockman wouldn't see them.

I couldn't get my latest young Starter to bring you in.

"That driver."

Yes. Shame to lose a valuable commodity like that.

I slipped the key to Briona behind my back and closed my eyes. I let the Starters move down the hallway without me. When I opened them, they had disappeared in another room, probably one with more sleeping Starters.

But I needed both of you, and Hyden isn't good about keeping in touch.

"You didn't really expect that Metal to get us. You just wanted him to lead us to you."

It worked, didn't it? He paused. *What are you looking for here?*

"My father. Where is he?"

Would you like to see him?

"Of course."

I can arrange that. But first, why don't we take this opportunity to meet each other?

All of a sudden, I came to a halt. I stood rooted, growing slowly aware of someone gaining control of my body. It felt like I had heavy mercury rushing up through my spine. From my feet to my legs, my hips, my abs, my chest, my arms. Even my throat felt constricted. One female Metal came out of a room. With what was left of my voice, I shouted, "Run. Run and hide!" It was raspy and not as loud as I'd hoped.

Fear clouded her face. She hesitated, then ran off, notifying the others.

The sensation continued up my neck and finally reached my head. I felt like I'd turned to stone.

My right foot moved forward, then my left. I was jerky at

first, almost robotic. After a moment, I walked in a smooth movement that would have fooled an onlooker into thinking I was doing exactly as I wanted.

I bet you're wondering where you're going.

I would have answered, but unlike previous times when I'd been controlled, I could not speak.

He made me walk to the end of the hall and turn right. It was so strange moving this way. When Hyden had controlled me at Dawson's lab, it felt like when you stepped on your daddy's shoes and let him move your feet to dance. This was like being invaded, possessed but aware of every awful moment of it.

I tried to hide my torment as I watched my arm shoot forward to open a door at the end of the hallway. Then I remembered—the reversal. It hadn't worked before, but I could try again.

I concentrated on pulling my arm back before it could open the door. But my fingers wrapped around the handle.

No, I told myself, don't. Let go of the handle.

But I had no control. Brockman overpowered me. My hand opened the door.

I entered the lobby of a building. It had an open configuration, with a second story, all surrounded by glass. Several guards approached me.

I handed them all my weapons. My own hands patted me down to make sure nothing was left.

The guards took the weapons away, leaving me alone. Then I felt my body return to me. It started from the tip of my head, a tingling sensation that vibrated down through my face, my neck, my chest, my belly, my hips, my legs, and finally my feet. It felt like shaking the pins and needles from your foot after it's fallen asleep.

I looked around, trying to decide where to run. I started to go across to the other end, but I heard a noise up above, on the second story.

"Where are you running to, Starter? Or would you prefer to be called a Metal?" I looked up and saw a Middle standing there above me. He leaned casually against thick, bulletproof glass, grinning down at me like the Cheshire Cat in his tree.

He looked to be in his forties, fit and stylish in an illusion suit that changed colors as he shifted his weight. His handsome features, his chiseled bone structure, even his posture looked exactly like Hyden's.

So this was Brockman. Hyden's father.

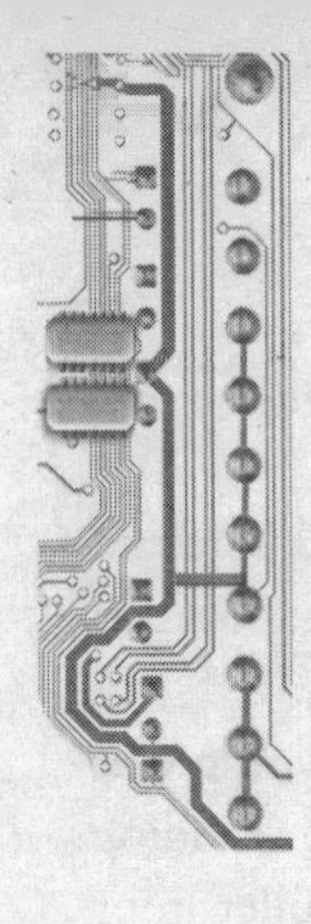

CHAPTER TWENTY-THREE

Brockman stared down at me, arms folded like a pompous dictator. Now that I had control of my body again, I moved toward the open stairway. A guard stepped out of the shadow, blocking the way.

A microphone in Brockman's room amplified his voice. "So, it turns out you are very easy to control."

"Where's my father?"

"You'll get to see him very soon," he said with a smile. "In fact, I'm dying to have you see him. But first, let's talk a little. You are a very special girl, Callie Woodland. And of course you are the only M.A.D. Oh, if only we had more of you."

"But you don't," I said. "And you don't really have me."

"Oh, that's where you're wrong." He looked past me. "And you know who else we have?"

He nodded to someone behind him, there in his office, someone I couldn't see. Two guards stepped forward, wrestling another person between them. Michael. His hands were cuffed behind his back. He pulled away from them and lunged toward the glass.

"Don't hurt him," I told Brockman.

"I don't think there will be any need to," Brockman said. "Because you'll be doing exactly what we want you to do."

He motioned for the guards to pull Michael away, out of sight.

"What do you want from me?" I asked.

"I have several prominent guests staying here from various countries. Now that you have arrived, we're going to hold a special demonstration of the technology. And then we'll have a little auction."

My pulse raced.

"You're going to sell us like slaves?" I asked.

"No one is going to hurt you. They'll want to take very good care of their investment."

"So you're all about the money? You're not even doing this because you believe in something?"

"People will do anything for money." He examined his fingernails. "Don't you know that by now?"

I hated him. He was as cruel as Hyden had said. It killed me to see so much of Hyden—his facial features, voice, even little mannerisms—in this despicable excuse for a human being. Why did the good people like my mother die and scum like him survive?

"My son is obviously infatuated with you, and I can see why. You have everything—brains, looks, courage, and the only killer neurochip."

He turned and walked down the open stairway until he was on my level. He came closer.

"Yes, you are exquisite. The bidders will be excited to see you. They have been notified of your arrival and are getting ready."

A guard whispered in Brockman's ear.

"Wonderful. Bring him in."

Another guard escorted Hyden into the atrium. Brockman looked at Hyden from head to toe. "You're looking fit. Good to see you without that silly disguise. Now that you're here, I can demonstrate this to both of you."

Brockman pressed a spot behind his ear while staring at me. I felt that awful sensation come over me, from my toes on up to the top of my head. I couldn't speak, couldn't make an expression, no way to let Hyden know what was going on.

But I'm sure he guessed, because his face reddened.

"Stop this," he said to his father. "Leave her alone."

I saw my body turn toward Hyden, my arm lift, and my hand slap him hard across the face. Brockman broke out in a huge grin.

"I just love controlling Metals," he said. "And it's even better with you, Callie, because you're aware of it. Such an intimate, sharing experience. Makes me tingle all over."

Hyden glared at his father and leapt toward him, punching him hard in the jaw. Brockman was caught by surprise, and Hyden grabbed his shoulders and took him to the floor, attacking him. Rage, it appeared, was the cure for his condition. The guards jumped in and pulled him off his father.

I regained my control the moment Hyden hit him.

"Hyden!" I shouted.

Hyden was on the floor with one guard holding him down. Brockman grabbed the ZipTaser from the other guard and turned it on Hyden. The blue light arched to Hyden's body. Hyden shook and let out one piercing scream.

"Stop!" I said.

Brockman shut off the ZipTaser. It had done its job. Hyden was unable to move, on the floor in extreme agony. Then he went completely silent. Was he all right?

I knelt by Hyden. "Hyden." Without thinking, I unbuttoned the top of his shirt and slipped my hand in to feel his heart.

It was beating.

Then I stared down at my hand, realizing my mistake. Hyden opened his eyes, his lids heavy from the trauma of the ZipTaser, and looked at my hand. He gave me an almost imperceptible smile.

He could tolerate my touch? Or maybe he was just numb from the ZipTaser.

Brockman did not notice. He was busy addressing the room.

"You see? My son makes bad decisions. That's why I will be the one to handle the sale of the technology."

I removed my hand as the guard came over. He yanked Hyden to his feet, gripping him by the arm. I stood with him.

"You killed Reece." Hyden lunged at his father. The guard held him back. "And Helena."

"She was about to kill a senator," Brockman said to his son. Then he spoke to the guard. "Put them in room fourteen until it's showtime."

⊗ ⊗ ⊗

The walls and floor of the small windowless chamber were made of steel. The door was also made of thick metal, affording no method of escape.

"They didn't even bother to cuff us," I said.

Hyden sighed. "That's because there's no way out of here."

"Is that why he put us in here together?"

"We are his most valuable commodities. So we have to share the escape-proof room."

I looked up at the flickering light from fluorescent tubes embedded in the high ceiling. "What kind of man needs a room like this?"

"A man who has more enemies than friends," Hyden said.

We sat on the floor with our backs against the wall.

"None of the Metals had seen my father," I said.

Hyden lowered his voice. "Don't talk about them. In case . . ."

"You think he's listening?" I whispered.

He shrugged. "Unless he's too busy getting ready for the auction."

"It doesn't really matter now what we say. We're headed out of here. Probably somewhere very far away, someplace where we don't speak the language," I said.

"We probably won't be together," he said.

I looked at him. "Were you really going to use the money to end the institutions?"

"Lobbyists to senators, I had it mapped out. Even had plans drawn up to convert the institutions to schools equipped with the latest airscreens and privatecasts."

"I'm sorry I got in the way," I said.

"No. No, don't ever say that. I learned a lot from how your chip was altered, and I used Blake to keep close to you so I could stay on top of the no-kill change, but more than anything, it was about you. I felt responsible for you. Everything in your life would have been different if I had never started Prime."

"So . . . you felt sorry for me?"

"No." His eyes met mine. "I fell in love in with you."

I froze. Time froze.

There might have been a cold metal floor beneath me, but I was not present in this cell. I was somewhere else, struggling to put it all together. I hadn't had a chance to process the discovery that Hyden was really the Old Man. It explained so many things. At least I knew now why I felt so connected to him. We'd shared so many special times together, when he was inside Blake.

A warmth radiated from my core. Hyden was waiting for my reaction, but I didn't know how to put it into words. I saw the burn mark on the back of his wrist. It was in the shape of a diamond.

I wondered if the touch before was a fluke. I reached out my hand. He didn't back away. With my forefinger, I touched his skin that encircled the ZipTaser mark.

"The ZipTaser," I said.

His eyes reflected some pain, but he let me touch him.

"Is this all right?"

"It's not easy." He swallowed. "But it's worth it."

"You had a breakthrough," I said, removing my hand.

"Getting zapped with that many volts will do it to you, I guess."

"Maybe. And all the manhandling you had here and at Dawson's."

"Desensitize or die," he said.

I guessed that confronting the monster who was the source of his pain was the real reason. But it didn't matter why.

I put up my hand, hoping he'd remember the time at Dawson's, when we were separated by glass.

He lifted his hand too. Our palms met and touched in the air. He tensed, but he held his palm there. He closed his eyes for a moment, and when he opened them he looked a little more relaxed. He nestled his fingers and wrapped them in mine, our palms still connecting. He pulled me closer as he leaned in and kissed me.

He kissed me. For the first time as himself. Not as Blake or Jeremy or anyone else.

It was never better.

But all too soon, the door opened.

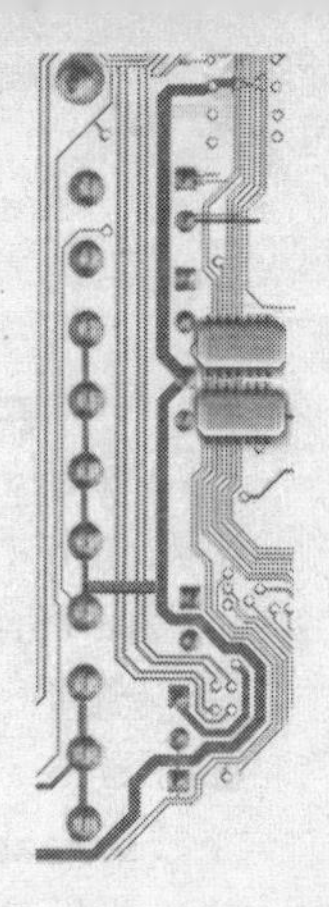

CHAPTER TWENTY-FOUR

Briona held Trax's passkey in her hand. "Come on," she said quietly as she gestured for us to get up.

"It's okay, that's Briona," I whispered to Hyden.

"I know," he said. "From Prime."

We followed her down the hall. Briona looked a lot better without her nose tube.

"Where are the others?" I asked.

"Hiding. Some are looking for food."

"No one's been caught?" Hyden asked.

"Can't say. None that I know of. But everyone's scattered."

"I don't like this," Hyden said.

"I know where your father is," she said to me. "Woodland, right?"

"Yes," I said. "Where?"

"I'm taking you to him. One of the Starters found a file. This way."

"Is he okay?" I asked. "Did you see him?"

"No time," she said. "I wanted to get you first."

My heart was racing. The thought that I was finally about to see my father, alive . . .

We turned a corner. The number on the door read 511.

"He's supposed to be in here," she said, pausing. She looked confused.

I was about to shove the door open when she grabbed my arm. "Wait. This room connects to the back of the theater."

"I don't care if it's the bathroom as long as my father's there," I said, pushing past her and opening the door.

As I stepped inside, I heard applause. Brockman stood on the opposite side of a round stage in this small theater, about twenty feet away.

"There is our star, ladies and gentlemen," said Brockman, using a microphone. He stepped onto the stage, turning his back to the audience to face me from across the room.

Hyden was right behind me. We were all still standing in the doorway.

"No, it's a trap!" Hyden said.

We turned to run, but three guards appeared in the hallway, blocking our path. They forced us to turn around and enter the theater.

One of the guards whispered in my ear, "You don't think we have monitors everywhere?"

Briona, who looked genuinely upset, was pulled over to the side. She'd been used. Maybe if I'd listened to her doubts at the door, we could have run. But they had probably been watching us all along.

The theater was in the round, with a small stage in the center and a sharp slope to the seats that surrounded it. The lights made it hard for me to see the audience, but I could make out about twenty Enders wearing tuxes or evening gowns or brightly colored traditional robes of their nations. It was like they were dressed for opening night at the opera. Huge jewels glittered on the women, and the sea of illusion fabrics made me almost dizzy.

Hyden was taken by a guard to stand out of the lights of the stage, off to my right. Another guard escorted me to Brockman's side, in the center of the stage. To my left was a small table and to my right was a larger table with various colorful objects on it.

"She's a little shy, ladies and gentlemen. This is Callie Woodland, the only transposer who is a true M.A.D., Multiple Access Donor, which means more than one person can inhabit her body at the same time. And they can communicate with each other. Sort of like riding tandem."

He laughed. I wanted to hit him the way Hyden had. But that wouldn't get me anywhere. I couldn't be stupid. I had to stay smart to survive and rescue my father.

"And that's not all. All of the other transposers have no-kill programming—except for this one. When she is being occupied, she is the only one who can be used as a weapon. And her muscle coordination skill set is phenomenal—she is a perfect marksman, able to use any weapon, to eliminate any opponent or terrorist or competitor. Imagine this. You could have a team inside her body—say, an intelligence expert, a hacker, a bomb specialist all at once. And when they've found their way into the hideout of that terrorist or that ex-employee who has stolen your trade secrets, you personally can enjoy the thrill of being behind her eyes when she takes him out. Could there be anything better?"

The glittery international crowd of Enders laughed and

applauded. I looked to my right, at Hyden. He was shaking his head, signaling me not to say or do anything.

"But let's see her in action," Brockman said.

Brockman turned his head away, and this time I could see he was wearing a small headset that almost blended in with his hair. There was a small disc attached to it that pressed against the base of his head. This must have functioned as a wireless remote so he didn't have to be hooked up to a computer.

"I'll need a volunteer for this. Who would like to come up?"

An Ender woman wearing a sleek evening gown with an upswept hairdo was assisted onstage by a guard and positioned behind the small table, which held a stack of large white cards.

"I could make her move like a puppet, but you would never know, if she was just doing as she was told. As proof that I am controlling her body, you are going to pick the objects that Callie will lift. Are you ready?"

Brockman stared into space for a second. Then I felt the heaviness, the sinking sensation of losing control again. Brockman inhabited me. I felt that awful, violated feeling of having him move my body as he made me turn so I could not see the woman or the cards she was about to pick.

"Now, if you'll be so kind as to choose one card and show it to the audience," Brockman said. "Good choice, thank you."

My arm jutted forward and waved over the objects. There were at least twenty. My hand lowered on an ugly pink stuffed bear. I lifted it high. The audience reacted with oohs and aahs and then applauded.

This continued for several more objects, and then he had the woman return to her seat.

"Now, who would like to make her move?" Brockman asked.

Half of them raised their hands. But one very old Ender with flowing silver hair and wearing green robes volunteered himself by coming up onstage. Brockman fitted him with the same almost-invisible headset that he wore.

"We'll just outfit you with this, and she's all yours," Brockman said. "Remember what I said earlier, and concentrate."

Brockman must have given them a little training session before I arrived. I felt Brockman release his control, but only for a moment. Too soon, this green-robed Ender began to work his way into my body. What was strange was that I could feel a difference. I couldn't explain it, but I sensed a different person inside.

The green-robed Ender made me look at the audience and wave my hand.

"Very good," Brockman said. "You got it right away. See how easy this is?"

He then made me walk across the stage as if it were a catwalk, making my hips jut out in that exaggerated way. I stopped, smiled at the audience, and turned around to sashay back. He had me stop with my back still to the audience. Now what? That creep had me wiggle my butt. Everyone laughed. It was awful.

He made me turn and face the audience. I felt my mouth open. He's not going to make me talk! But he did.

"I'm so pretty" came out of my lips.

The voice didn't sound exactly like me, but it didn't sound like him either.

"Excellent," Brockman said. "Look how fast you got the hang of it."

Now every male hand rose to volunteer. Some of them were shouting in their native language. One man in a tux leapt up onstage as the green-robed man removed his headset and handed it to Brockman. I felt my control come back, but it was getting blurrier now, this moving back and forth so quickly. I didn't feel completely in control, but more in a state of limbo.

I glanced at Hyden. His face was red: he was livid. A guard restrained him by the arms.

This new Ender volunteer had a tan, short white hair, and a huge diamond ring.

Brockman put the headset on him and he concentrated for a moment. Nothing was happening. The audience shifted in their seats. Someone coughed. Then I felt my hand raise and move to the top of my shirt.

It went to my top button. And undid it.

No. He wasn't going to . . . but he was. My hands unbuttoned my shirt; my hips swayed as if I were some cheap stripper. He closed my eyes and tossed back my head as if I were in ecstasy over this. My hands undid the last button, revealing my camisole underneath. I was grateful for this underlayer, but how far would he go?

I sensed everyone holding their breath, including me. He had me take off the shirt, twirl it over my head, and toss it at the audience. A man in African robes caught it and waved it triumphantly.

The jacker made me tease the audience by lifting up the bottom edge of my cami, pulling it out from side to side. Then he had me lift it up all the way, exposing my bra. My hands pulled the cami over my head and tossed that into the audience, to the delight of another creepy Ender.

The jacker then had me look at him, on the stage, and slowly walk toward him. What was he going to make me do? With every step, my imagination came up with worse scenarios.

"Stop this!" It was Hyden's voice.

I was able to look in his direction. My jacker had lost his concentration. Hyden was being held back by two guards.

"That's enough," Brockman said. "We have a spectacular demonstration for you now that will show the full power of this technology. It is something you will never see anywhere else, and something you'll never forget."

One of the guards handed me my shirt, and I quickly put it back on. I glared at the man with the diamond ring.

"You are a perv," I hissed.

"Let us begin," Brockman said.

One of the doors toward the right of the stage opened, and they rolled in a man standing up, strapped at his wrists and ankles to a board larger than a door. It was like a dangerous circus act. He had dark hair and a beard, a Middle.

As he was brought closer, onto the stage, I knew who he was.

A Middle I had not seen in over a year. A Middle I thought I'd never, ever see again because I was told he was dead. A Middle that I shared a lifetime of memories with. And our own special code.

My father. I ran to his side.

"Daddy!"

"Callie," my father said, his voice weak.

His eyes looked worse than in the video. He was gaunt and frail compared to the dad I knew.

"In case you didn't hear that, this is Callie's father," Brockman said into his mike.

"What have you done to him?" I whipped around and glared at Brockman.

"The question is, what are you going to do to him?" he said with a wicked grin.

I felt sick at the thought of what was to come.

My body felt flushed as Brockman took control. He made me walk away from my father, about ten feet. A guard came to me, holding a tray with a gun on it.

"Ladies and gentlemen, this girl is about to shoot her own father, in a final demonstration of how powerful this process is," Brockman said. "If we can make her do this, the person who walks away with this package I offer tonight will be able to use her to assassinate anyone."

My body broke out in a damp sweat. He couldn't really mean what he was saying. My father had expertise Brockman could use.

No, no, he can't, he can't want to really do this.

As the audience buzzed with anticipation, only one Ender, a woman, got up and left. Brockman turned off his mike and leaned over to me.

"All we needed was his research. Thank you for delivering the z-drive. We've started the decryption process. In a few hours, we'll have your father's technology."

They'd found Hyden's car. Now they had everything they needed from my father. And we had brought it to them.

Brockman switched his mike back on. "Watch carefully," he said to the audience.

My hand picked up the gun.

My father looked at me.

There was so much I wanted to say to him, how I'd been mother and father to Tyler, how I tried to do everything he'd taught me to protect my brother. How I did my best but it ended up making everything worse. I just wanted to be his little girl again and curl up on his lap and be told everything would be all right.

Then the worst thing possible happened. My arm began to tingle. It rose—not of my doing—until the gun in my hand aimed directly at my father's head.

My father hadn't seen me in a year, had probably thought he'd never see me again. And now here I was, pointing a gun at him. It was the last thing on earth he'd ever see.

I'm inside. Controlling you. And it feels so good.

Hearing Brockman's voice inside my head, I wanted to crawl out of my own body. I tried to force myself to take control again, tried to move my arms or legs—anything—to drop the gun, to not do this horrible thing.

But the only thing I was responsible for were the tears streaming down my face.

Please don't make me shoot my father.

Brockman's voice came into my head.

A perfect test. And ironic, since he's the one who taught you to shoot so well.

"It's all right, Callie. It's not your fault," my father said. His sad eyes were still soft and kind. "No matter what, I love you," he said. "I know this isn't you. It's not your fault."

I heard Hyden shout out, "Callie, fight back now!"

In the trauma, I had forgotten. I had to try. I remembered what Hyden tried to teach me, my father's method. Picture the cord with a light. . . . What color was it? Blue. A blue light running from Brockman to me. Then a gold light going from me to him. Make the blue light turn to gold.

I'm still in control, Callie. Brockman's voice boomed in my head.

My poor father stood rigid, the agonizing threat looming, my gun still pointed at him. I tried to focus my mind, visualizing the cord, blue to gold, then pushing Brockman out. I pictured him as I saw him last, standing there, so smug, and I saw myself, with my arms pushing him away as far as I could push him.

My gun hand began to tremble.

It was the hardest thing I'd ever done in my life. I had to maintain complete control. If I faltered for a second, my hand steadied. I had to forget about the gun, forget about my father, forget about everything but the cord. I kept at it even though it was like holding your breath forever, longer than is humanly possible, and my hand shook wildly.

Callie . . . Brockman's voice in my head now sounded desperate. That gave me strength.

I visualized myself pushing so hard that Brockman fell backward, until he got smaller and smaller.

My hand came back to my control. I was able to drop the gun, and it fell to the floor. The audience gasped. Brockman glared at me.

I wanted to run to my father, but I had to maintain focus. I still had the connection to Brockman; I only had to reverse it, to see myself in his body. I felt myself going into Brockman. It felt cold, as if ice water were running through my veins. But I was in his body.

I made him walk to the gun. I felt his resistance.

No sense fighting me, I communicated to him.

You can't do this.

"Just watch yourself," I said.

I made his body bend down and pick up the gun. He tried to resist me, but it was a losing battle.

"How does it feel now?" I said.

I swung him around and made him point the gun at the guards at the back of the stage. I make Brockman speak.

"Lay down your weapons," I made Brockman say.

The guards hesitated, their faces taut with confusion.

"Do it now!" I made Brockman command. "And throw down your cuffs."

The guards obeyed, placing their guns and cuffs on the floor.

"Keep your hands in the air," Brockman said.

The audience murmured, obviously confused. Some seemed unclear whether this was part of the show.

"It's part of the act," the perv with the diamond ring said, laughing.

A few laughed nervously along with him. I made Brockman point the gun at the perv and he stopped laughing.

"The show is over," I made Brockman say.

I aimed Brockman's gun high, pointing at the empty back row, over the heads of the audience, who were all seated in the lower seats. I fired off some shots.

The crowd leapt out of their seats and dashed for the exits, tripping over their gowns and each other.

I swung Brockman around to check the guards. They were scattering, not to be trampled by the crowd scrambling for the exits. I shot a few rounds in the wall behind them, and the last guards also ran out the doors.

My father and Hyden were left, but I couldn't think about them. I was still seeing the room through Brockman's eyes, still in control of his body. I made him walk to the cuffs on the floor left by the guards. I had him set his gun on the floor and pick up a pair of cuffs. I moved his hands so he clamped the cuffs around his ankles. Then I picked up another set and clamped those around his wrists.

Done. Time to leave this creepy body. I let go and was soon seeing the room through my own eyes.

Brockman started screaming at the top of his lungs.

I rushed to my father's side.

"Daddy!"

"Cal Girl."

I threw my arms around him, kissing his cheek, until Hyden came over to untie his restraints. My dad rose on wobbly legs and held me tightly.

"Callie, baby." He held my head with one hand against his chest.

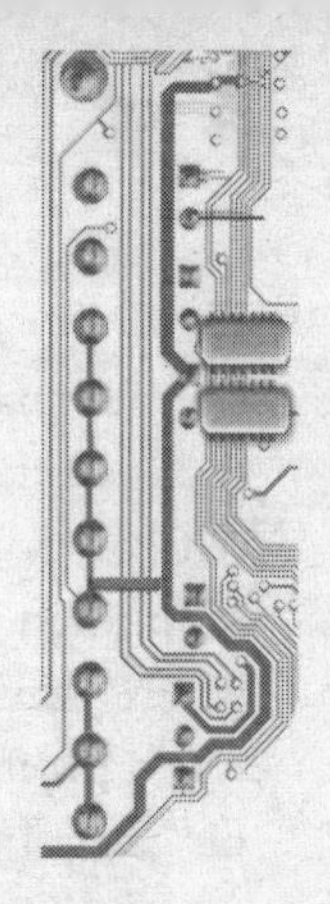

CHAPTER TWENTY-FIVE

Some three dozen marshals came to arrest Brockman, the guards, and any of the billionaires who hadn't escaped by helis. They confiscated the airscreens and led the hundred-plus Metals to sit at the back of the auditorium to begin debriefing. I saw all the Metals who had been taken from our lab, including Savannah, Avery, Lily, and Jeremy. I was glad to see nobody was hurt. And I was thrilled when I spotted Kevin, Lauren's missing grandson. She was going to be ecstatic.

We gathered in the large atrium downstairs, my father and I sitting in the lobby seating just below where Brockman had stood when I first saw him.

The marshals brought one more Metal into the room—Michael. He was all right. I ran over to give him a hug.

"What happened to you?" I asked.

"The guards caught me, but I managed to escape and join the other Starters."

We sat next to my father, who put his arm around my shoulder. He felt so bony. He was about thirty pounds thinner than when I'd last seen him, and the year in captivity showed in his eyes. But he was alive. I couldn't stop smiling when I looked at him.

Hyden entered from a door at the far end of the room, where the head investigator was standing. Following Hyden was a group of Enders dressed mostly in black. Dawson and his gang. I tensed and looked at Michael. At the same instant, we got up and went over to the head investigator.

"That man," I said, gesturing to Dawson, "kept us prisoner."

Dawson approached. I stepped back, my body tensing at the sight of him and his leopard tattoo. He flashed his air badge. A ray of color sparkled from a symbol I couldn't make out.

"Callie, I'm Matt Dawson, head of the Transposition Research Team."

"No way you're with the government," I said.

Hyden came closer and stood next to me. Michael was on the other side.

Dawson lowered his voice, conspiratorial. "We operate off-book, so officially we don't exist. We do things outside the rules because we have to."

Images of the horrendous treatment we suffered flashed through my mind. "What about Emma?"

"That was an unfortunate casualty," he said.

"Enders," I said under my breath, mostly for Michael and Hyden. "But the way you treated us . . . You were brutal," I said, not understanding. Was he really on our side?

"You've never been in the military," he said. "We were not authorized to divulge anything at that point. We didn't know how much we could trust you."

"What about all that testing?" Michael asked.

"We had to assess the threat to national security."

I started to put it together. "So you *wanted* us to come here?"

He nodded. "We couldn't raid the place. We knew that Brockman would destroy everything, the Starters, the scientists, your father."

"And the technology," Hyden said.

"And we had to catch him in the act of committing treason, as well as round up these dangerous people who would buy and use the technology. Timing was crucial."

"You used us as bait," Michael said.

"You didn't care if we survived or not," Callie said.

"But you did. The three of you. And you came through golden," Dawson said. "And that's why we want to recruit you as our first enrollees in our special academy. Whoever passes will join our team."

I looked at the guys. We had to all be thinking the same thing—why would we ever want to be part of a team under Dawson?

A woman came up and stood beside Dawson. I recognized her as the Ender who had pretended to feel sorry for us and slipped us the keys.

"No wonder we could escape your compound," I said.

She put her arm around his waist.

A smile lit his features. "My wife," he said.

Three days later, I stood at the gate to Institution 37. A male Ender guard scanned me with a body wand; then a female Ender patted me down with a rough hand.

"She's clean," the woman said.

The male guard pressed a button and the gate opened with a grating sound. It made me close my eyes a moment, taking me back to the day Sara died. The day I escaped because of her sacrifice.

With the guards flanking me, I marched to the administration building. Our shoes clacked and echoed in the heavy dark hallway with its musty odor and walnut sideboards with twisty legs. When we reached the headmaster's door, it opened before the guards could knock.

Beatty appeared in the doorway. I had heard her voice over the gate's intercom, consenting to my visit, so her face registered no surprise. She wore an expensive suit that her bulky, shapeless body couldn't do justice to. She'd probably always had a body for a uniform.

"Callie, what a delicious surprise."

The guards stepped forward to accompany me, but Beatty's raised hand stopped them.

"We'll be fine, thank you," she said. "You can go." When they hesitated, she asked, "Did you search her thoroughly? Both of you?"

"Of course, ma'am," the woman said.

"Then I can handle her." She pulled me inside by the wrist. "I always did."

She closed the door in their bewildered faces. I yanked my arm back out of her grasp and rubbed my wrist.

"I'll remind you I have my ZipTaser, Callie." She patted a bulge in her suit pocket.

"Of course you do." I thought about Sara.

Beatty's face was as mean and ugly as ever. But something was different, as if she looked the slightest bit less hideous.

"That's it," I said. "You got rid of your moles."

Her eyes widened.

"That's one way to blow your headmaster's salary."

"Still haven't learned your manners, I see."

She crossed to her desk. It was military-neat, with only her airscreen, the stiletto letter opener, and a set of crystal glasses and a bottle half-filled with an amber liquid. She poured two glasses one-quarter full.

"Let's toast to your visit." She held out a glass for me. I didn't take it. "Just a sip." She pushed the glass until it touched my hand.

"What is it?"

"Two-hundred-year-old scotch. Better than maple syrup."

"I'm a minor. I can't."

She smirked and put the glass on her desk. "Suit yourself." She sipped hers and savored it.

"So why are you here, Callie, all by yourself? I thought you were smarter than that. Something change in your life? Guardian changed her mind? Had enough of you?"

She obviously knew nothing of Brockman.

"I have news for you," I said. "The Old Man? He's really a teen boy."

I noticed her pupils enlarge. She'd had no clue.

"So?" she said.

She was trying to hide her surprise.

"He used you to release Starters from your institution," I said. "So they could run free."

She put down her drink and folded her arms. "What do I care? He paid me."

"Couldn't have been much. Because he was just a Starter."

"Ten thousand dollars. Per child. That's nothing to sneeze at."

"You sold them, knowing they were going to be used by Enders, maybe forever."

Her hand moved to her ZipTaser.

"You can hurt me, but you can't kill me with it," I said. "Not like Sara."

"Sara had an unfortunate condition."

"You knew about her weak heart. And you allowed your guards to use it on her anyway."

"Nobody escapes my institution." She narrowed her eyes and picked up her drink. "Not Sara. Not you."

She threw the scotch at me, drenching my face, my shirt. I wiped at my eyes and saw her grab an object off the desk. The letter opener. She gripped it like a dagger.

I took a step backward. She smiled and took a step toward me. I hadn't prepared for this. I had no weapons.

My heart quickened as she raised the letter opener. But instead of attacking me, she brought it down on her other arm and stabbed herself in the forearm. Her scream made my skin crawl.

"Don't!" she cried. "Don't hurt me!"

Blood trickled down her arm. She thrust the handle of the weapon in my palm. I dropped it, letting it fall to the carpet.

The door opened. I turned, expecting for a split second to see her guards. But of course it was Dawson, flanked by two marshals.

"She stabbed me." Beatty held out her wounded arm.

"Get her," Dawson said to the marshals.

As they approached us, Beatty slipped me a smirk that no one else saw. "Thank goodness my guards called you. She stuck me with that." She pointed to the letter opener on the floor.

Dawson looked down at the letter opener and shook his head. "No, she didn't."

"She did. That girl is dangerous," Beatty said.

"That's certainly true," Dawson said. "But she didn't touch you."

"Give it up, Beatty," I said. "He saw it all through my eyes. Heard it through my ears."

Beatty's jaw dropped as she looked from me to Dawson. "He was . . . in you?" She stood there, in shock, still as stone, like a troll caught in the sunlight.

Dawson nodded to the marshals. One pressed a handkerchief to her wound to stop the bleeding.

"Good job," Dawson said to me.

"Just holding up my end of the bargain."

"What bargain?" Beatty asked.

"I'd do what he wanted if he'd let me take you down," I said to her.

I nodded to the marshals and they cuffed her behind her back.

"No! You can't do this. I'm the headmaster. I have connections." Beatty's face contorted.

"Not anymore," Dawson said.

As they carted her off, I made sure that the last memory Beatty would have of me was a huge grin on my face.

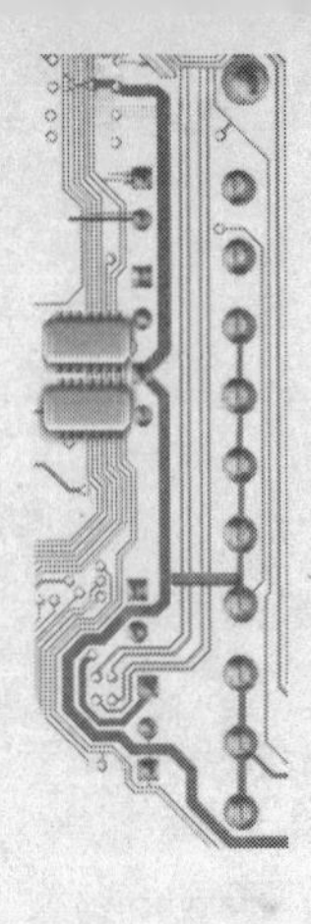

CHAPTER TWENTY-SIX

A week later, I stood outside a secret location in the middle of the desert and stared at a complex of imposing dark gray structures. A large seal with a logo was embedded over the entrance. This was Dawson's Transposition Research Center.

My father stood beside me, his arm around my shoulder. Michael was several yards away, keeping Tyler amused. Dawson's sales pitch played through my mind.

"Our enemies plan to take us over from within and without. We have to stop them."

"You want me to be a spy," I said.

"It isn't just for your country. The buyers who escaped will be after you and Tyler for your chips. They'll want your father for his expertise. Working with me is your family's best chance at survival."

I longed for a normal life with my father and brother, but with the chip in my head, I'd come to accept that my future was destined to be different. Brockman was in jail but was not cooperating. If he knew how to remove the chips, he wasn't talking. I couldn't live looking over my shoulder, always afraid, as if I were borrowing my own body.

I would be a trainee with the others, but only some of us would pass the tough three-month program and join the team. Many of the Metals I'd known would be here, but there was only one I was looking for.

I hadn't been in touch with Hyden since the day his father was arrested. He wasn't answering his phone. I couldn't imagine him joining, after all Dawson had put us through.

The transport vehicle that had brought us here waited behind us. Other vehicles pulled up and dropped off more Metal recruits.

Michael approached me at the drop-off location once the new prospects started to disembark. Savannah, the black belt with medical skills. Lily, the acrobat. Jeremy, the martial artist. Briona. Lee. Raj. Blake.

We exchanged greetings as they each continued into the Center. We waited as their empty transports drove away.

"Maybe he was here early," Michael said to me.

"He's never early," I said, swallowing hard. "He's not coming."

My dad patted my shoulder. "Time to say goodbye, Cal Girl."

I gave him a long hug. Then Tyler.

"You go make us safe," Tyler said.

I hugged Tyler tightly. "Be good."

They climbed back into their transport and were driven away. Tyler waved his hand for as long as I could see him. Then Michael and I turned and walked toward the building. We heard a vehicle in the distance and turned our heads at the same time to see dust kicking up across the desert.

One more transport was coming.

We stopped and watched. I squinted in the sun. I couldn't see who was inside.

The transport door opened.

It was Hyden.

He got out and walked forward to join us. He looked at me and gave a little smile. I saw in his eyes all the pain and anguish he must have gone through this week, coming to this decision. He looked at the Center.

"Some place," he said, shading his eyes.

The last time I had pinned all my hopes on a building, it hadn't turned out the way I'd imagined. Now, looking at the Center, I hoped we could work together, Starters and Enders, Metals and scientists. Eventually the Starters would become Middles and then Enders, and the newer generations wouldn't have the big hole that we had. Maybe then it won't matter so much if they're young or old, rich or poor, or what they looked like on the outside.

I took a deep breath. This day was far different from the day I had stood outside Prime Destinations.

This time, I wasn't going in alone. I was flanked by two guys who would die for me. And I'd do the same for them.

"Ready?" Michael asked.

"I was born ready," Hyden said.

I nodded. "Let's do this."

I took Michael's hand, then reached out for Hyden's. He hesitated a moment, then extended his hand and clasped mine. A slight flash of pain registered in his eyes, but he recovered and reassured me with a slight smile.

Hand in hand, together, we walked forward to face a future where we would shape our own destinies.

ACKNOWLEDGMENTS

Thanks to all the Starters, Middles, and Enders who helped me with *Enders*.

To Dean Koontz, the master of suspense: it meant the world to a debut author to receive your generous quote in praise of *Starters*. I will be forever grateful to you.

My wonderful agents, Barbara Poelle and Heather Baror, and my thoughtful editor, Wendy Loggia, thank you all so much for your help and support.

My talented writing group buddies, Derek Rogers and Liam Brian Perry, you guys will be next. My friend Dawn, writers S. L. Card, Suzanne Gates, Lorin Oberweger, and Gina Rosati, thank you all for your brilliant insights.

Kami Garcia, my sincere gratitude for generously giving us your great quote, and for your support.

Michael Messian, you have been a constant champion of this series. My husband, Dennis, thank you for always understanding how important the book was to me and for never once complaining about the missed concerts, films, and dinners.

To everyone else who helped me, from my wonderful publishers around the world to the reviewers, bloggers, booksellers, librarians and schoolteachers, thank you for believing in the series from the start.

And finally, to all the amazing readers across the globe: I'm deeply grateful for your patience and loyalty. You can always reach me at LissaPrice.com.

LISSA PRICE is an award-winning, internationally bestselling author whose debut ***STARTERS*** is published in over thirty countries. You can follow her on Twitter (@Lissa_Price), or visit her online at lissaprice.com. Lissa lives with her husband in Southern California.

It all began in . . .

First, Callie lost her parents.
Then she lost her home.
And, finally, she lost her body.
But she will stop at nothing
to get it back . . .